A PLEA FOR FREEDOM

A PLEA FOR FREEDOM

A NOVEL

RAYMOND HACKNEY

Vista, CA

ISBN: 978-1-61153-705-5 (paperback)

ISBN: 978-1-61153-706-2 (ebook)

ISBN: 978-1-61153-707-9 (large print)

Library of Congress Control Number: 2026904422

A Plea for Freedom is published by: Torchflame Books, an imprint of Top Reads Publishing, LLC, 1035 E. Vista Way, Suite 205, Vista, CA 92084, USA

Scripture quotations are taken from *The Holy Bible*, King James Version. 1611. Public Domain.

Song lyrics for "Joy to the World" by Isaac Watts. 1719. Public Domain.

Song lyrics for "And Can it Be that I Should Gain?" by Charles Wesley. 1738. Public Domain.

Cover design and interior layout: Jori Hanna

For Laura, Lela, and Laura Ellen,
who passed the story down to me.

CONTENTS

AUTHOR'S PREFACE

While this book is based upon true events in the life of an historical person, I have added fictional characters, conversations, and other details not known to have occurred. *A Plea for Freedom* is set in the colonial and the Revolutionary War period, with an attempt to convey the attitudes and language of that time. However, out of respect for Native Americans, I have omitted common words in that culture, such as "savages," "injuns," "squaws," and "braves," because of the racist implications of those words.

Daniel Asbury was my great, great, great, great grandfather. My grandmother and mother told me stories about Daniel Asbury's adventures as a teenager and young man. Daniel Asbury's story spurred my childhood daydreams and wonder as I placed myself in his shoes. In our family Bible there was a letter written to my great grandmother, Laura Asbury Finger, from her cousin, Sarah Asbury, in 1934. In this letter, Sarah said that Daniel Asbury's "journal" was sent to a printer in Charleston, SC. Unfortunately, a fire at the printer destroyed the "journal." Sarah wrote the word "journal" with quotation marks. I believe it was not a true journal with daily entries, but a recollection of his days in in the wilderness and his later life. I have written Daniel Asbury's story in first person as a surrogate for his lost journal. My goal and prayer are that his story will rise above the ashes of that Charleston fire to again inspire wonderment at the life of Daniel Asbury.

DANIEL ASBURY'S FAMILY

BEDFORD COUNTY, VIRGINIA AUGUST 1777

DANIEL ASBURY (AGE 15)

PARENTS:

Father – James "Thomas" Asbury (age 51)
Mother – "Martha" Jennings Asbury (age 50)

SIBLINGS:

Sisters – Elizabeth (age 24), Molly (age 19), Patsy (age 11), Genny (age 7), Sally (age 5), Nancy (age 3)
Brothers – George (age 21), James (age 9)

OTHER:

Charles McGlocklin – Daniel's future brother-in-law
Rex – farm dog

CHAPTER ONE

"LIBERTY FOREVER"

MID-AUGUST 1777

"There's goin' to be a hangin' at the big walnut tree!" Those were the words that launched a chain of events that forever changed my life, like a leaf that lands on the water and is carried by the current, cascading down perilous rapids, compelled by powers beyond its control.

"They're goin' to hang two Tory traitors," continued Ben Kelly, my friend of the same age as me with coal-black hair, as he raced past Ma and me on a street in New London, Virginia.

I placed my hand on Ma's arm and examined her face. Her eyes displayed no interest. She pressed her lips together, quenching her normal smile. Before she could speak, I said, "I've got to see this." I spun and sped away.

I sprinted down the street, past Meads Tavern, and soon jogged beside Ben. We hurried toward the big walnut tree and Judge Charles Lynch's house which sat on a small knoll. The walnut tree, famous for being the loftiest tree in town, beckoned the crowd to gather underneath its long branches and deep shade.

Judge Lynch, a man in his early forties with a neatly trimmed goatee and mustache, sat behind a table underneath the tree.

Three other prominent-looking men sat behind Lynch. I guessed they must be judges also. The two Tories on trial stood about ten feet from Lynch with their hands bound behind their backs. Two guards stood beside them.

Judge Lynch called out, "Will John Wyatt come forward as a witness." Wyatt, a muscular man but with a limp favoring his left leg, stepped forward from among the crowd and took a seat beside the judge. Lynch turned to Wyatt, looked him in the eyes, and said, "Please state your name."

"John Wyatt."

Lynch lifted a book from the table and thrust it toward Wyatt. "Now place your hand on this Holy Bible." Wyatt complied with the request. "Do you promise to tell the truth, the whole truth, before God?"

"I do."

Lynch returned the Bible to the table, then asked, "Do you know these two men standin' here?"

"Yes."

"State their names."

"Paul Huddleston and Samuel English."

"Please tell us how you know these men."

"Judge, ya know that I'm a patriot," Wyatt said. "With your knowledge, I joined a group of Tories as a spy for the patriot cause. I infiltrated their ranks posing as a British officer. I attended a meeting of Tories. They conspired to destroy the Chiswell's lead and saltpeter mines on the New River. They also planned to march on Richmond to free British prisoners."

"You may step away from the witness chair," Lynch instructed.

Wyatt rose from the chair, but instead of returning to his original place in the crowd, he walked toward Huddleston and English and spat at their feet. The two, still bound, lunged toward Wyatt with clenched fists and threatening sneers, muttered, "Traitor," and "Rat." Their guards pulled them back.

Paul Huddleston, a small, lean man in his thirties, with long brown hair, and Samuel English, a large, brawny, red-haired man of about forty, regained their calm.

"How do you plead to these charges?" Lynch asked. "Guilty or not guilty?"

Huddleston, "Guilty."

English, "Guilty and proud of it."

These two men were clearly proud of their allegiance to King George. I viewed them with distrust and dislike, and men I would prefer to avoid.

Lynch turned to the three men seated behind him. "How do you find these accused?"

"Guilty," Two of them said in turn.

Before the third judge pronounced his verdict my mother arrived and stood beside me. She grasped my elbow and motioned with her head and whispered, "Let's go."

I pulled my arm away. "I want to see what happens."

The third judge yelled louder than the other two. "Guilty. And may there be a swift punishment."

Judge Lynch pronounced their sentence: "You, Paul Huddleston, and you, Samuel English, have been found guilty of committin' crimes against the State of Virginia and the patriot cause. You shall each receive thirty-nine lashes on the naked back and be hung by your thumbs. If at any time you desire mercy, you must cry out so that all these witnesses can hear: 'Liberty Forever.' In return, you will be pardoned for the remainin' punishment. You will then join the Virginia militia for a period of eight months." Lynch then added, "String 'em up, one at a time. Paul Huddleston first."

Two guards seized Huddleston, untied the ropes that bound his hands, and ripped off his shirt. Huddleston offered no resistance and seemed to have accepted his punishment. He allowed the guards to secure small ropes around his thumbs and pull them tight. The guards brought Huddleston to the walnut tree and the ropes that hung over a branch. They hoisted his arms in the air, his feet still on the ground. The guard held a whip about three feet long, with multiple knotted tails, and stood ready to thrash at Lynch's command.

"Thirty-nine lashes," Lynch called out.

The guard glared at his target, moved his arms to give the maximum distance to strike the whip, tightened his muscles, and with all his power, slung the whip against Huddleston's back. Huddleston screamed. Several streams of blood ran down his back. I flinched when the whip struck his flesh. Ma stepped back, shook her grimacing head, but remained. That was one lash. What would thirty-nine lashes do to his back? Why not just put him in jail, without the whipping.

"One," Lynch hollered.

The guard proceeded to deliver the punishment. At number "five," I turned my eyes away, unable to witness another blow. At number "eight," those in front of me stepped back. At number "eleven," I felt a drop of blood hit my left cheek. Instinctively, I rubbed my cheek with my hand and examined the red on my finger. I lifted my head to see Huddleston's back was as bloody as a skinned pig. I turned my head down and focused my gaze on a small rock on the ground.

At lash number twenty, Huddleston hollered the words, "Liberty Forever." There was silence as the crowd exhaled.

"Paul Huddleston, not everyone heard you," Lynch said. "You must scream it so everyone can hear you."

Huddleston shouted his declaration once more.

"Paul Huddleston, you've just volunteered for the Virginia militia," Lynch declared. "You'll be escorted immediately to Captain Charles Gwatkins, who's enlistin' men in the Bedford County Kentucky Expedition. You'll remain in the custody of the Bedford County jail until Captain Gwatkins' militia marches out."

Huddleston's guards ushered him away.

"Samuel English, step forward for your punishment."

English remained where he stood. The guard gripped his arm. English resisted and jerked his arm away from the guard's grasp. The second guard joined the first, and they both seized English and escorted him to the ropes, where the guards hoisted his arms above his head.

"Thirty-nine lashes," Lynch shouted.

English received his blows without uttering a sound. His silence seemed to beg the guard for harsher whacks. The guard paused to push up his sleeves, tightened his muscles, set his jaw, and with a slight nod of his head struck the next blow. Still, English emitted no scream. I turned my head away.

I dared a glance at Ma. She peered back at me. Her face revealed a sour grimace as she shook her head slowly from side to side.

He received the full thirty-nine lashes. Blood covered English's back and splashed with every lash. Pools of blood formed on the ground below his feet.

"I'm leaving," Ma whispered as she leaned toward me. "This is too brutal."

"Ma, I gotta see this."

"I'll meet you at our wagon.," she said as she walked away.

Ben Kelly leaned over and said, "I'm stayin' too."

"Bring the table for the hangin'," Lynch said. "I warn you, Samuel English, if you hang for more than ten minutes, your thumbs will disconnect from their joints, and you will lose use of your thumbs, perhaps your whole hand, for the rest of your life. And . . . with all the blood you have lost, you might even die."

At the mention of death, the muscles in my face and stomach tightened. I closed my eyes. Part of me wanted to slip away. Why had I been so eager to see this? Another part of me wanted to stay and witness this. I opened my eyes to view the spectacle.

English stepped on a chair and then the table. The guards

stretched the ropes tight, put their entire weight on the rope, then secured the ropes to the tree trunk.

"Remove the table."

English hung by his thumbs. His blood-drenched back glared at the spectators. His once silent voice screamed in agony. I directed my head away from English. While I opposed English's political views and his criminal actions, I did not agree with this torture.

Ten minutes passed. English cried out, "You filthy rebels. You are the ones that should be hangin' for betrayin' your king."

"Your king betrayed us. He should be hanged," someone yelled back.

English hung in silence for another minute, then muttered, "Liberty Forever."

"What's that English?" Lynch shouted. "I didn't hear you. I know the others didn't hear you."

"Liberty Forever," English shouted.

Murmurs emanated through the crowd. Although English uttered the words, "Liberty Forever," he lifted his head and gazed at the crowd as if he judged them. Did this torture deepen English's hatred of patriots?

Lynch conveyed to English, just as he had to Huddleston, that he had just volunteered for the Virginia militia.

Judge Lynch stood and faced the people. "You are witnesses today. These two men admitted to their guilt for crimes against the state of Virginia, the thirteen colonies, and our fight for independence from the tyrannical British government, that enslaves us. The question is: Can we accept that bondage? Or must we seek liberty? It is liberty that we need, and we must fight for it. We are now in the storm—the storm of our fight for independence. Every family residin' in Virginia must support the freedom effort and join in the fight. Now is the time to join with General George Washington in this fight. Now is the time to sign up with Captain Gwatkins for the Kentucky Expedition to join the cause in the west. I want everyone here to repeat after me:" Lynch thrust his right fist into the air. "Liberty Forever."

I thrust my fist into the air along with most of the crowd as we shouted in unison, "Liberty Forever." The judge's words reminded me of the British oppression the Tories represented and elicited a deeper desire for our country's liberation. This was our fight—our freedom. I knew that was what I wanted.

As the witnesses dispersed, Ben and I walked back to our wagons.

"Did you ever think English would holler out 'Liberty Forever'?" I said.

"No. He's a Tory, loyal to the King, and there ain't nothin' goin' to change him," replied Ben.

"Yeah, I guess Lynch's warning about losing his thumbs scared him enough to convert to the patriots. But I don't think he's really converted."

We reached our wagon where Ma waited and Ben continued to his wagon. Many concerns vied for my attention. I suppressed the memory of violent torture, and instead thought about the war for our freedom: how it would proceed, how we would win. I thought about the freedom I wanted for myself. I wanted to make my own decisions, not be under the direction of Ma and Pa. I wanted to explore what was beyond our farm and Bedford County. Judge Lynch's speech aroused my eagerness, my hunger, but images of English's bloody back and his screams kept pushing into my thoughts.

Ma and I met without words, her usual smile still absent. I climbed in. Ma picked up the reins, but I stopped her. "I want them. I like havin' the reins in my hands." She paused and gave me that look that said, "Ask politely." I repeated my request, "Ma, may I have the reins?" She passed them to me, still silent. I snapped the reins to prompt our horse Millie to begin the five-mile journey along the dusty road to our farm.

My name is Daniel Asbury. I was born on Sunday, February 18, 1762, in Fairfax, Virginia, second son of Thomas and Martha Asbury. We were a family of nine children which included my six sisters, Nancy, Sally, Genny, Patsy, Molly, and Elizabeth, ages three to twenty-four, my brother James, age nine, and my brother George, age twenty-one. We moved to Bedford County, Virginia, in 1767. New London was the Bedford County seat where farmers and craftsmen sold or traded their goods and services, and where westward travelers replenished their provisions. The town sits on a knoll that offers a view of the Blue Ridge Mountains rising above the western horizon. My father was a farmer. He did the bulk of the work on the farm, but the rest of the family helped.

Millie plodded along the dusty, bumpy road. No grass or weeds grew in the road due to the many horses, wagons, and travelers on foot headed west to Big Lick, salt springs on a branch of the Roanoke River. Big Lick is where the Great Valley Road down the Shenandoah Valley from Pennsylvania joined the Wilderness Road to Kentucky. My daydreams often took me down this road, to the mountains, and the wilderness beyond.

"I think I need to sign up for the militia," I blurted out. "Since George has about finished his term, Pa has to run the farm, I'm almost—"

"No, Daniel. And that's final," Ma said in the tone that meant *you won't change my mind.* I stopped talking. Perhaps Pa would be more receptive.

About a hundred yards from our farm, I spotted Rex, our four-year-old farm dog, lying under the towering oak tree in our yard. Rex sprang up and raced toward us, his long reddish-brown and white rough-coated fur streamed behind him. He leapt into my lap and I cradled his neck as he licked my face as if to say, "I missed you."

When I entered our two-room log house I was captivated by the marvelous aroma of chicken stew, my favorite of all Ma's cooking. Ma prepared it by boiling a whole chicken until the meat fell off the bones. Cut-up tomatoes, corn scraped off the cob, potatoes, and butter beans were added to the chicken and broth, along with all the proper seasoning. The stew cooked for hours, and its fragrance filled the house. Since Ma was in town, Elizabeth had prepared it that night. In the large room there was a fireplace, where Ma and Elizabeth cooked our meals, and a large table where we ate. Ma and Pa slept in the small room in the back of the house, while us kids climbed a spiral staircase to sleep in the rafters. James and I slept on the porch during the summer months.

We gathered around the dinner table. Elizabeth's beau, Charles McGlocklin, joined us. Charles had just returned from fighting under Capt. Gross Scruggs's Company, the 5th Regiment, with my brother George.

"Charles, how's George?" I asked.

"George is doing well. Fortunately, he was healthy last I saw him. You know George, always the prankster. He put a black snake in Patrick Callaway's bedroll. When Patrick got in to sleep, he screamed so loud he woke the whole camp. You should have seen Patrick scrambling, trying to get out of his bed. Patrick got latrine duty for a week for waking up the camp. He never did learn who put that snake in his bed." Charles paused as everyone laughed. "I expect George will be comin' home soon. He's served longer than me."

"Ma and I saw a trial and hangin' of two Tories this afternoon," I said. "They were plottin' to blow up some mines and set some British prisoners free. They strung 'em up by their thumbs until they yelled out, 'Liberty Forever' and joined the patriot cause."

Ma held up her hand and shook her head, as if that would stop the conversation. The pain on her face spoke to the whole family. She said, "It was a horrible display. We're supposed to be livin' in a civilized society, but there seems to be hatred, killin,' and savage treatment of one another. I don't think Governor Henry would approve of whippin' and hanging prisoners by their thumbs."

"Was there a jury at this trial, and did the defendants have a lawyer?" Pa asked.

"No," I replied.

"That doesn't sound like a legal trial," Pa said.

"I thought it must be legal, but maybe not," I said.

"I heard Governor Henry wanted the prisoners to be transported to Williamsburg," Elizabeth said.

"Yes, they should have been," Charles said. "But the problem is there are outlaws who hide along the road and attack the transportation parties and set the prisoners free, and capture the guards."

"Well, I think Judge Lynch, and the other judges, have taken matters into their own hands," Pa said.

"After the trial, Judge Lynch spoke to all the witnesses and said that every family must contribute soldiers for the cause," I said. "They're signin' men to go to Kentucky to fight out west. Charles, do you think I might . . . "

"Our family's already contributed," Ma interrupted. "George has been fightin' for the past year and a half. I pray every day the Lord will keep him safe and return him home to us in one piece."

"Well, if there was a safer place to fight, it might be out west," Pa said. "I hear the British aren't fightin' out there, just the Indians," Pa said.

"Well, I hear the British are givin' the Indians guns and ammunition to fight the settlers in Kentucky," Elizabeth said. "What difference does it make if you die from a rifle shot by the British, or shot by an Indian? You're still dead. Also, I hear the natives capture pioneers in the west and burn them at the stake or force them to live in the wilderness."

I did not relish this conversation about Indian captivity and being burned at the stake. I laid my fork on my plate with a clank and stared at the table.

"Yes, you know the story of Mary Ingles," Ma said. "Some Indians captured her and her sons right here in Virginia, and she was with child! Although she managed to escape, she had to leave her children behind." Ma paused with a sigh and gazed at her plate.

"Mary and the other woman trekked about 800 miles," Molly added. "They nearly starved before they finally reached their farm in Draper's Meadow."

I lifted my fork again but did not take a bite. My tight stomach was not hungry. I suppressed the thoughts of Indian captivity.

"Years later they were able to get their eldest, Thomas, back, but she never laid eyes on her other two children again," said Ma.

"I understand the Ingles lived here in Bedford County for several years after," Pa said. "Now they run the Ingles Ferry across the New River, not far from where they were captured. I can't imagine Mary going back there."

Pa paused to eat a spoonful of soup. "When I fought in the French and Indian, I knew many men who died, lost their legs, arms, even an eye. Some of my friends suffered in French prisons.

"But I hear Kentucky is a land with lush forests and rollin' hills, filled with deer, buffalo, bear, and other game so plentiful that you could feed and clothe the whole country. Someday, after the war, I reckon I might go to Kentucky and get some of that land."

"My Pa talked to a man who had seen Kentucky," Charles said. "He said Kentucky was the closest thing to paradise on this earth. Not only are the forests filled with game, but the rivers and streams are crystal clear and loaded with fish."

"Kentucky may look like paradise, but I know it's not!" Molly exclaimed. "It's wild and deadly, even without the war. Not only could you be shot or captured, you could be killed by wild animals—rattlesnakes, broader around than your arms and longer than a man is tall. And then there are panthers with four enormous fangs they can sink into your leg, or arm, or your neck." Molly lifted her hands to simulate fangs biting Genny's neck, which made her scream. "Or you could be attacked by wolves. Imagine that—some wild beast gnawing on your bones. I say, let others tame the wilderness first, then you can go out to Kentucky after things are a bit more civilized."

"You're right about that, Molly," Ma said with a nod.

Elizabeth elbowed Charles who then choked on a bit of stew, then cleared his throat, and said, "Anyway war is horrible. Men I fought beside died." Charles paused, his face became expressionless, and his voice dropped to just above a whisper. "My best friend, Sam Cook . . . he . . . he stood behind a tree, not ten feet from me, firing at the Redcoats. Just as I took aim, Sam collapsed to the ground, shot in the head. Could have been me."

There was silence, except for a fork that clanged against a plate. I did not want to hear of these dangers of war or the wilderness. I endeavored to suppress them and think about the beauty of Kentucky.

Ma broke the silence. "Kentucky may be beautiful, but Virginia's beautiful too, and a whole lot safer than fightin' the British, or Indians . . . or panthers. Daniel, you get those senseless ideas out of your head about goin' off to war."

I slammed my fist on the table and rose from my seat, my face hot. "I'm tired of takin' orders from you and Pa! I wanna make my own decisions, get off this farm, and see what's out there—beyond these wretched hills!"

Everyone was silent. I sprinted out the back door and bolted into the darkness. I sped down the road to Big Lick until I stumbled on a rut in the road and fell on my face. I rolled onto my side and lay on the road. I pushed the horrors of war out of my conscious thoughts. I drove the terrors of the wilderness and the nightmares of Indian captivity out of my mind. I focused my attention on Kentucky's beauty and my desire to go there and see it for myself. The stories of untouched wilderness enticed me, fueled my desire to leave home to see what lay beyond the mountains, and get out from under Ma and Pa's strict control.

Saturday morning, I awoke to the scream of the rooster, perched about twenty feet from our bed on the porch. Rex, who slept at my feet, licked my hand and face. I had to milk the cows and take them out to pasture. Rex followed me to the barn where I milked the cows. I enjoyed milking the cows and being close to the animals. They were like part of the family. That cup of milk at breakfast was sweeter, knowing it was the result of my labor. After milking it was Rex's turn to go to work. His job was to herd the cows to pasture. I opened the gate to the pasture and Rex followed the cows, pacing back and forth to keep them moving toward the pasture.

Rex and I strolled back to the house, the sun now well above the horizon. Ma rocked in her chair on the back porch, reading her Bible. She started the habit of daily Bible reading and prayer a few years ago. I do not know what she hoped to gain from it. She said she prayed for George's safe return from the war, but I do not know what else.

As I stepped onto the porch Pa came out carrying two rifles. Pa and I often hunted on Saturdays. We hunted deer, bear, wild turkey, and occasionally buffalo. That morning, we mounted our horses, Millie and Henry, and headed toward Tomison's Creek.

After following a trail to a steep ravine with a delightful stream at the bottom, we dismounted and tied off our horses.

Pa knelt to examine a deer track. He motioned for me to follow. Pa knew the woods and how to follow tracks. He knew animals and where you could find them—what they ate, where they slept, and where they made their nests or dens. He knew how to move through the woods in silence. Pa could quickly aim and fire his rifle, rarely missing his target, and he could reload in one motion, then fire the next shot. I admired his patience, how he could sit down beside a tree in the woods and wait for long periods of time. He was always optimistic that our next meal would soon walk by. And it (almost) always did.

"Let's stop here by this rock," Pa whispered. "And let's see who'll come for a drink in this stream. Be as quiet as a panther stalkin' his prey."

I loaded my rifle and left it half-cocked. We sat on a rock beside an eight-foot-wide chestnut tree. Only the forest talked. The August breeze ruffled the treetops as birds sang their songs, accompanied by the hammering of a nearby woodpecker and the babbling of the water in the stream. As I constantly scanned the forest floor for game, I momentarily forgot my arguments with Ma and my desire to be on my own in the world. The forest was a peaceful place for me. After a while, Pa motioned that he would move to another rock to get a better view of downstream.

The leaves rustled behind me. I turned to view two bear cubs, about thirty feet from me. Then, the growl of a mama bear twirled my head back around. She hustled toward me; I was between her and her cubs. I swung my rifle around and shot. The lead ball only grazed her side and did nothing to slow her. No time to reload. I ran. The bear was ten feet from me when the second shot split the air. She fell two feet from my feet, blood gushing from her head. I stopped and turned my head toward Pa. He held his rifle to his shoulder. Smoke trailed from the barrel.

My hands trembled. I battled to hold back tears. I rushed to Pa and hugged him. "Thank you. Thank you. I thought I was going to die. I don't want to die."

Pa wrapped his arms around me. I stayed in his embrace and closed my eyes. I could not speak.

"I was scared too," Pa said, finally. "You're safe. She's no threat to us now. She's dead." Pa smiled. "We're havin' bear steaks tonight. Let's git to workin' on her and load her onto Millie."

Just then the two cubs rustled some leaves near us.

"What about the cubs?" I asked.

"Those cubs are old enough to make it on their own."

We never wasted any part of the animals we shot. We extracted the brain, then dressed and quartered her. We separated the fat to render into oil back at home, where we would tan the fur and hide to a supple, soft feel that would keep one warm and snug on an icy winter night.

Pa and I secured our prize onto Millie and started the journey home, with both of us on the back of Henry as I held Millie's reins. As Henry labored under his added burden, my chin dropped to my chest, and I muttered to myself all the way home, *"How could I have been so clumsy to miss my shot?"*

We arrived home and dismounted. "You can only improve your response to episodes like you had today by practice," Pa said, with a half-smile. "Tomorrow's Sunday. Why don't you take some time to practice. Practice loadin' your rifle, again and again and again until you can do it blindfolded. Take some practice shots. Next time . . . I may need you to save my life."

On Sunday morning, the family had breakfast together, and then we all scrambled into the wagon to go to the church gathering place, about four miles away. Rex took his usual place beside me. Pa stayed home. He was not interested in religion at all and did not attend the meetings. A noticeable change in Ma occurred about five years earlier. Ma had a religious experience at a Methodist meeting. After that experience, she started every day in prayer on the back porch, rarely missed going to church, and made sure all her children attended with her.

We arrived at a farm closer to town, to a gathering of about twenty people. We met outside in the yard between the barn and house.

Henry Miller, who owned the farm where we met, raised his hands, and hollered, "Everyone find a seat. We're ready to begin."

Everyone took their places in the grass, some on blankets, some on bearskins, and some just sat on the ground. We sang songs to the accompaniment of a fiddler. During the sermon, I pulled at the grass while daydreaming. I glanced at Ma, seated two people down from me, beside Elizabeth. Her eyes focused on the preacher. Two small boys in front of her picked at one another and laughed. She was oblivious to the distraction. During songs, she raised her arms and lifted her face toward the sky as she sang.

I continued to wonder about Ma's interest in church. What captivates her so about religion? I failed to see the use of it. As to whether God existed, I had no idea and did not see how one could know. I guessed He probably did since the world had to come from somewhere, but it seemed to have little to do with me.

That afternoon, I found a one-foot log, drew a circle on it with a piece of coal, and set it on its end twenty paces away. Loading my rifle, I measured the powder and poured it down the barrel. I placed the ball on the patch and pushed it down the barrel with the ramrod, and then poured powder into the pan and closed the frizzen. I aimed at the circle and fired my shot. I missed. I did it again, this time imagining the bear charging toward me. I missed. The third time I hit the circle. I practiced reloading then shooting, as fast as I could, again and again, all while I imagined that bear charging me. After a couple of hours of practice, I could see improvement, but the bear was often swifter than the shot.

We began a new week with farm chores and schooling for the children. In the afternoon someone knocked five times on our door, followed by a deep booming voice saying, "Thomas Asbury." I rose from our table, left my times table to open the door for Jim Talbot, Bedford County Justice of the Peace.

"Hey, Mr. Talbot," I said. "Come in. What brings you around?"

Jim stepped inside and removed his hat. "I need to talk with your Pa. Can you fetch him?"

"He's out in the far field. It'll take me a while to fetch him."

"Go fetch him, and I'll wait right here."

I ran past Ma out the back of the house. With haste, I saddled Millie, galloped to the far cornfield where Pa was picking corn.

"Pa! Jim Talbot from the county office is here to speak to ya."

"What about?"

"Didn't say. He just said to come fetch ya."

Pa mounted Millie behind me and we rode back to the house.

When we arrived at the house, Ma and Jim were engaged in conversation. There was a grimace, and pain in Ma's face. She greeted Pa with a tender touch on his arm but said nothing. Pa grasped her hand and gave her a nod. Ma gathered the younger children and left the house. I slipped into a seat by the window so I could hear the conversation.

Pa greeted Mr. Talbot with a handshake and a smile. "Hello, Jim. What brings you out here?"

"Tom, I'll git right to it. I have a letter here from Bedford County and the state of Virginia draftin' you to serve in the Virginia Militia, Bedford County." Jim handed Pa the letter. "You will serve under Captain Charles Gwatkins. You must go, or find an able-bodied man to go in your stead, or pay a tax of twenty pounds within twenty-four hours."

CHAPTER TWO

THE KENTUCKY EXPEDITION

END OF AUGUST 1777

"I hate for you to have to leave your family," Jim Talbot said. "Many families send their teenage sons. I also know Daniel will be sixteen soon. My two sons fight in Pennsylvania. The patriot cause needs men to fight and whip the Redcoats. Daniel could join the Kentucky Expedition in your place. It's much safer than on the coast."

"Yes, I heard about Captain Gwatkin's Kentucky Expedition," Pa replied. "When does this Kentucky Expedition head out?"

"One week from today, September 1st. You have until tomorrow to provide a soldier and sign up."

"We'll need to talk about this. We'll let you know."

Jim placed his hat back on his head and, without another word, left to go deliver the next letter.

My mind raced with fantasies of a battle against the British and a trek into the beautiful Kentucky wilderness.

"Pa what are you going to do?" I asked.

"Ma and I are going to talk. You're going to get back to your schoolwork."

There was not much talking during dinner that night. Ma

and Pa were quiet. Word had passed among us children about Pa's letter from Jim Talbot, but no one said anything.

"Pa, what did you decide?" I blurted.

"After dinner, Daniel." Pa answered.

As soon as we rose from the table, Pa stopped me, "Your Ma and I need to talk to you about Jim's letter. Let's sit on the back porch."

The three of us sat on the porch and talked as the August sun crept downward toward the distant trees. Patsy and Genny played a game of hoop and stick in the yard, throwing and catching a hoop from stick to stick.

"Daniel, you heard what Jim said this afternoon about Virginia requirin' me or someone else serve in the militia," Pa said. "We don't have twenty pounds to pay them. You and I are the only ones able to fight. Though you're still too young, they will take you. There are many teenage boys fightin' in the war. There's a heap of work to be done on the farm and the need to take care of Ma and your brother and sisters. We think it best that I not leave the family right now. I'm willing to let you go fight. I know you've been wanting to go, but how do you feel now that it is a possibility. Are you willin' to go?"

"Daniel, you know that I don't want you to go," Ma said before I could answer. "You're too young and it's so dangerous." Pausing, she looked into my eyes, as a tear formed in her right eye. She placed her hand on my arm. "But we don't see any alternative. The state of Virginia's requirin' our family send somebody. If your father went, it could endanger the whole family. So . . . " Ma hesitated to finish her sentence. Then, after another long pause, she continued. "I consent to your goin'."

I never imagined a day when my mother would discuss my going to war, not to mention allow it. My heart pounded with the weight of the decision before me.

"Well, three days ago, I would've said yes," I said. "Now, I am not so sure."

Pa moved closer, faced me, placed his hand on my shoulder. "Daniel, there are a lot of dangers. Your family'll be far away, and you'll find people out there that are ornery and cruel. I know you're brave and strong. I know you'll come back to us."

As Pa spoke my stomach tightened and a tear formed in my eye. Then, the tears erupted and flowed. I reached out to Ma and embraced her. Then I turned to Pa and wept in his arms.

"We're all cryin'," Ma said through her tears. "We're all scared for you. We'll miss you greatly. We want you to finish your year of service and come right back to us."

"Daniel, don't decide right now," Pa said. "Wait until tomorrow. Think about whether this is the right thing to do."

This seemed like a good idea. These newly discovered fears surprised me, like the bear that suddenly appeared on our hunt. I pondered this question all night and into the next day. I thought about staying here and taking Pa's place in the family. I did not think I would do a very good job of it—he had taught me a lot, but I was still green. All the things I did not know, or did not know well enough, rose in front of me as I imagined my siblings going hungry, or Ma being in danger. Soldiering seemed easier, somehow. But the dangers . . . I went back and forth. Finally, my awareness that my parents thought this was the best choice, coupled with my desire to see the world, see the wilderness, and be on my own, were too great for me to say no. I had to go.

That next day, at breakfast, I made the announcement. "Looks like I'll be leavin' to join the militia, to fight in Kentucky. I'm going into town this afternoon to sign up."

Elizabeth nodded in silence as a tear formed on her cheek. James leaned forward to hear more. Molly shook her head and stared at the table.

"Well, there seems to be no other solution to our quandary," Ma said, rubbing the tears off her cheek. "And I know it's what you've wanted to do."

"I'm scared, though," I said. "I know you could die in a war. I know there are dangers in the wilderness. I'll be careful and I'll be back."

"This afternoon we'll hitch up Millie and ride into town," Pa said.

"It's important for Daniel to look good when he goes into town." Elizabeth said. "Daniel, I'll give you your monthly haircut right after breakfast."

"Oh, thank you." I responded. "It's time for my haircut."

After breakfast I sat on a chair on the back porch with a sheet around my neck and over my clothes.

"Daniel, you have the easiest hair to cut," Elizabeth said. "It's just the right thickness, not too oily or too dry. It lays exactly where you want it and parts so easily. I love the color of your hair. It's too brown to be blond and too blond to be brown. Some people would call it blond, and some would call it brown. It's beautiful, or should I say handsome?"

"Handsome," I replied.

"You never want to cut it too short," Elizabeth said. "Who'd recognize you without those handsome locks?"

Elizabeth was silent as she slowly moved her hands through my hair. "Oh, Daniel," she burst out, "I don't want you to go, and I don't want Pa to go either! This war is a terrible thing. I hope it'll end soon, one way or the other."

"Oh, it'll end soon," I replied. "We're gonna whup those Redcoats."

That afternoon, Pa and I rode into town. At the county office, we found Jim Talbot, who sat at his desk and conversed with two other men, apparently there to sign up for the militia.

Finished with his conversation, Jim turned to Pa. "Well, Tom, what'd ya decide?"

"Daniel's gonna join," Pa replied. "Show us the paperwork."

Jim handed me a document. "This document states that you'll serve in place of your father, Thomas. Sit at that table against the wall, put your name, county, your father's name, and sign your name to the line at the bottom."

I signed as directed.

"Now you must sign the Oath of Allegiance," Jim said. "Place your right hand on this Bible and read it out loud."

I placed my hand on the Bible and read:

"I, Daniel Asbury, renounce all allegiance or obedience to George the Third, King of Great Britain; and I swear that I will, to the utmost of my power, support and defend the commonwealth of Virginia, against King George the Third, his heirs, his successors, and his assistants and will serve the United States in the office of private which I now hold, with fidelity, according to the best of my skill and understanding. I will report to appropriate authorities all acts of treason against Virginia or any of the United States of America."

I signed my name to the oath.

"This makes it official," said Jim. "The second page is a list of supplies you will need to bring with you. These include an approved rifle—that means a Pennsylvania rifle. You will need a shot pouch, a powder horn, blanket, knapsack, and proper clothing. Your clothing will include a hunting shirt, dyed brown, that extends to the knees, a belt—either skin or woven—a jacket, breeches, and buckskin moccasins. You will also need a hat with a round brim imported from England. Johnson's Store should have all these items. The Kentucky Expedition, under the command of Captain Gwatkins, will leave next Monday, September 1st, from right here at the county office."

"Also, all militia soldiers must participate in training," Jim stated. "Training starts tomorrow. Meet at the field across the street at noon to meet Captain Gwatkins and the others who have signed up."

"Noon tomorrow. Right. I'll be there," I responded.

Pa and I journeyed over to Johnson's Store. As we found each of the items on the list, Pa loaded my arms with the knapsack, blanket, and clothes. I already had the shot pouch and powder horn at home. When we came to the rifles, Pa placed his hand on the Pennsylvania rifle and lifted it from its place on the shelf. He examined its long barrel and beautiful maple stock.

Pa explained his admiration. "I see why they require you to have one of these. This long barrel increases its range and accuracy. And you see how the barrel is smaller? That makes it a lot lighter, but it also means it'll take longer to load. You'll need to practice loadin' and shootin' it tonight after supper. Feel how light it is," handing me the rifle.

I placed my supplies for purchase aside and received the rifle. I raised it up and took aim at an imaginary redcoat and pretended to pull the trigger—pow. "Yeah. Much lighter. And I like the patch box in the stock."

"Yes, that's a dandy patch box," Pa replied. "Also, these small barrels get fouled sooner. So, you'll have to clean it frequently. When you're in the thick of the battle, ya don't want your gun to foul. Now, let's git back to the farm. We don't wanna make the others wait for supper."

Just as we exited through the door Ben Kelly and his dad came into the store.

"Hey Ben. What brings you into town?"

"I just signed up for the Kentucky Expedition. Pappa was drafted, but I'm going in his place. I came here to buy supplies."

"Me too. Hey, we got training tomorrow. I'll saddle up Millie and come by your place and we can ride into town together."

"Great. I'll see you tomorrow."

The wide brim hat shaded the hot August noonday sun as Ben and I marched to the county office to report for training. I wore my new clothes and carried my new rifle, powder horn, and shot pouch. Ben had just turned sixteen a month earlier. Our mothers were friends and often visited at one or the others' house while Ben and I roamed and explored in the nearby woods.

That afternoon fifty of us gathered at the field across the street from the county office. I knew about half of the men.

"Hello, Daniel, aren't you too young to join the militia?" Richard Wade asked.

"Yeah, but they took me anyway."

Richard Wade was twenty-five-years-old. We respected the wisdom he displayed in challenging circumstances. He became an unofficial leader among us.

"Hello, I'm William Humphries," said a tall thin fellow to Ben and me. "I'm from the southern part of the county."

"William Humphries!" I said. "You're famous. You won the Buffalo Creek race three years in a row. I am very glad to meet you." Humphries was thirty-three and had a wife and two boys.

Captain Charles Gwatkins, a barrel-chested man in his forties, stood in the middle of the field as his long wavy dark red hair and beard flitted in the stiff breeze. He had a black eye patch over his left eye. He lost his eye as a young man when he was thrown from a horse and landed on some farm equipment. He wore a round dark green felt hat curled on one side, decorated with a white buck tail.

"Congratulations," Gwatkins began. His deep voice commanded attention. "You are now a member of the Bedford County Militia. Our mission is to support the settlers in Boonesborough, Kentucky. The Indians in that region constantly harass them. Their lives are in constant danger. Their supplies are low. We will bring them a supply of essentials, such as salt and ammunition. There are fifty of us in total. That includes the two captured Tories who agreed to serve in the militia. However, we won't be puttin' a gun in their hands right away. They must prove they are worthy to carry a weapon. So, they won't participate in the trainin' this week.

"You soldiers will start your trainin' this afternoon with target practice. If ya can't hit the head of a nail from fifty paces, then you aren't worth much to us. Our lives all depend upon each of us hittin' our marks, a rapid re-load, and then hittin' the next mark.

"Arabia Brown and John Brown, please step forward. Show us how it's done."

Arabia stepped forward. Picked up a loaf of bread that was beside Gwatkins, and then stepped off fifty paces farther into the field. John, who had the reputation of possessing the surest shot in Bedford County, took his Pennsylvania rifle, pouch, and powder horn. Arabia attached a piece of paper to the loaf of bread and placed it between his knees. Without any prop for the rifle, John took aim and waited for the captain's signal.

Was John really going to shoot a loaf of bread between his brother's knees?

Humphries murmured, almost to himself, "Don't do it, John."

Captain Gwatkins hollered, "Fire."

John fired. A hole appeared in the paper attached to the bread. The speed of his reload was even more impressive than the accuracy of his shot. It was almost in one motion. He proceeded to fire seven times. Arabia, who remained calm and confident throughout the whole episode, stepped forward and waved the mangled paper above his head.

We all clapped and cheered in recognition of the feat. Many yelled, "Brilliant shootin' John!" "Excellent!"

"Now, who's next? Any volunteers?" Captain Gwatkins said.

"I'll do the shootin', but not the holdin'," Ben yelled out.

We all laughed in agreement.

"Before this week is out, you will all do both the shootin' and the holdin'," Gwatkins continued. "You will perform more impressive feats than that. This is why we required you to have Pennsylvania rifles. Their long barrels and small shots deliver outstanding accuracy. The British muskets can't compete with our rifles. This afternoon, I want you to pair up and take target practice. Set up targets fifty paces away. Nail a piece of paper to a board with one nail in the center. Each of you take twenty shots at the nail in the center. Nineteen of those shots should be within an inch of the nail. If you are more than an inch away, you missed. You're workin' in pairs so you can learn that your partner can shoot straight, and you can trust him to shoot that loaf of bread between your legs. One more thing. Those twenty shots must be in rapid succession. Thirty seconds between shots."

As everyone started to pair off, I turned to Ben and said, "Let's go shoot some Redcoats."

"Yeah. Let's go bombard those Tory swine."

We practiced shooting and loading the rest of the afternoon. My first shot hit the board but not the paper, several inches from the nail. I struggled to rapidly load and fire, hitting the paper twice in twenty shots, neither within an inch of the nail. Ben hit the paper five times, one right beside the nail. We went several rounds of rapid firing, reloading, and shooting again. By the time we finished, I could see some clear improvement in both accuracy and speed, but I was not ready to shoot a loaf of bread between someone's legs.

When we arrived the next day, Captain Gwatkins had painted life-sized outlines of British soldiers on nearby large trees. "Today we are goin' to practice throwin' hatchets," Gwatkins began. "Look at those redcoats painted on those trees. I want you to take your hatchets, run toward the enemy and throw those hatchets. Hit them between the eyes."

My hatchet throwing did not hit the target most of the time

although my last throw would have parted the redcoat's hair if we had live targets.

After hatchet training, Captain Gwatkins gathered us back together. "Now let's practice shootin' and reloadin'. See those trees on the edge of this field? There are fifty of you soldiers, and there are fifty trees with a nail driven halfway in. Each of you should go and locate your tree with a nail, then pace off fifty steps and fire at that nail. Those nails are the buttons of a Redcoat." With a slight smirk, he added, "Each of those nails must be driven into those trees until they come out the other side."

"That's impossible," shouted Wade.

"It can't be done," said Humphries, shaking his head.

He waited for our incredulous reactions to subside. "Seriously, anyone who can drive their nail clear into the tree trunk will be the first in line for meals during trainin'. Now, go shoot those buttons."

I did not hit the nail once but dug a hole in the tree around the nail. Ben hit the nail once, but otherwise also scattered his shots around the nail. We shook hands and congratulated each other on our fine marksmanship.

The third day of training, Captain Gwatkins instructed us. "You've improved your shootin', but you were standin' still, or lyin' down. Ya have got to be able to shoot on the run. Today, I want you to go to those same trees with nails and back up about thirty paces. Then run toward the tree and fire on the run. You should still be able to hit the nail."

After that exercise, Captain Gwatkins called us together. "Now that you have learned that you can shoot that rifle and hit a nail head and that your brothers can do the same, I want you to pair up, and each one of you take one of these barrel staves. Then pace off fifty steps. Hold the piece of wood to your side while the other shoots six holes through it. Then change places and let the other do the shootin'."

I counted off fifty paces then held out the board for Ben to shoot. He put six shots through the board. Relieved, I held up my Pennsylvania long rifle and, with confidence and in rapid succession, put six shots through the board. This exercise, and indeed the training for the whole week, built confidence in both myself and my comrades.

Toward the close of the afternoon, Captain Gwatkins gathered us together and motioned for us to sit down in the field. "Men, I'm proud of all of you and impressed with your skill and your hard work. I'll be proud to march into battle with you. In battle, there can be any number of outcomes. First, we could win the battle and take captives. That's what we train for. Second, we could lose the battle, and many will die. The rest of us might be taken captive. Any of us could become a captive of the Indians or a become a captive of the British. I hear that the Redcoats deprive their prisoners of the necessities of life, hopin' they will die. The British consider us traitors who deserve to die, in some cases by the hangman's rope. In other cases, by starvation or disease. Faced with those options, they may ask you if you want to enlist in the British forces and live. What will your response be?"

There was silence.

"I am still waitin' to hear your response."

"I say what Patrick Henry says, 'Give me liberty, or give me death,'" Richard Wade said.

"I'll take a hangman's rope before I will fight for the British," Arabia Brown yelled.

"I'll never fight for the Redcoats," shouted James Morton, a twenty-one-year-old, with wavy blond hair.

"Fightin' for the British would be worse than swingin' from a rope, starvin', or the firin' squad," yelled Ansel Goodman, a newly married twenty-five-year-old, who was determined to finish his military duty as soon as possible and return to his wife.

I was about to say, "Fightin' for the Brits would be traitorous," then someone from behind shouted, "Liberty Forever."

James Morton stood up and thrust his right fist in the air. "Yeah!"

We all stood with raised fists, "Liberty Forever."

"We are united then," Gwatkins continued. "United, we have a better chance of comin' back home alive. Unfortunately, it's likely that we will not all return to our families. Some of us probably will die. For that reason, you might ponder whether you need to set anything right before you leave."

There was silence. I reflected on this for a moment. The possibility of death closed in around me like a shadow. But surely it could not happen to me. No. No. I would be alright. I did not know how to think about death so I consciously pushed the subject aside.

Gwatkins waited several seconds, then continued. "We'll meet here on Monday morning at ten o'clock. Take the next two days to spend with your families and say your farewells. Get some rest. It's a six-week march to Boonesborough."

On Saturday, our whole family, including Rex, piled into our wagon for a day of swimming, games, and picnicking at the James River. Ma and Pa acquired their seats in the front of the wagon, while the rest of us sat or laid on a bear skin in the back. Under the August sun and a blue sky, Henry and Millie pulled our wagon at a lively, efficient pace. We admired the tall green chestnut oaks and red maples along the road. A variety of birds flew into their branches and sang a chorus of songs, while a blanket of silence hung over our wagon of Asburys. The usual laughter and teasing among us kids had departed. The one thing on everyone's mind was the one thing we did not talk about.

Finally, James found his bilbo stick to occupy himself.

Attached to the stick by a string was a wooden ball with a hole. He swung the ball into the air and attempted to catch it with the point of the stick into the hole. On about the tenth attempt, he caught it, and said, "I did it!"

"Let me try," Patsy said. "I bet I can do it."

"Here," James said. "You only get ten tries, then let someone else do it."

Patsy attempted ten times to catch the ball without success.

"Let someone else try," James said. "It might be easier if you spin the ball on the string before swinging it into the air."

"I wanna try," Molly said.

Patsy handed the bilbo stick to Molly. She almost caught it once but missed it.

"I give up," Molly said. "Daniel, you try,"

She passed it to me. I spun the ball and swung it in the air. On the fourth try I caught it.

"Yay Daniel," shouted Elizabeth. "You did it."

We occupied ourselves with the bilbo stick for most of the trip, with not a lot of success. When Nancy crawled into my lap, I stopped trying.

After the two-hour wagon ride, we approached the river. Pa directed Henry and Millie into the shade of a sprawling sycamore tree that stood alone in a meadow by the river. The river, deep in places, flowed at a slow pace around an island. Pa unhitched the horses so they could graze and rest from the labor of their journey. We were lucky to have the place to ourselves.

"Let's go swimming," shouted James.

"Yeah," answered Molly.

"I am going to swim to the island," said Patsy.

"First, you must learn how to swim," Pa said. "But before we get in the water, I want everyone to gather firewood and bring rocks from the river for the fire ring. We're goin' to build a fire for our picnic."

We roamed through the woods gathering firewood and

hauled rocks from the river. Pa started the fire using flint and steel to get a spark to light some dry dead grass and dead pine twigs. We watched the fire build from the small flame of two pine twigs to several large dead cedar and oak logs set ablaze.

"Now let's go swimming," Pa said. "No one goes in without a swim lesson. The river can be deep and the current can carry you to areas over your head. Everyone put on your swimming attire then gather along the shore."

Ma tended the fire, spread the bearskin on the ground, and played with Nancy.

Only Elizabeth knew how to swim. The rest of us had only gone into shallow creeks near our farm. None of the creeks had water over our head. Elizabeth, Molly, Patsy, Genny, James, and I lined up on the shore of the river with our feet in the water awaiting Pa's instructions. Rex jumped in and swam into deep water, without waiting for Pa's instructions.

"If Rex can do it, then I can do it," James hollered.

"Let's move into the water up to our waist. No deeper," instructed Pa. "Now, take a deep breath and hold it like this." Pa demonstrated holding his breath, and we followed his example. "Now let's do it again. Lay face down in the water. Then pick up your feet up so that you float." Pa lay afloat face down. We all attempted it, but only Elizabeth and Molly did it well. Pa continued, "Now let's hold our breath and then lay on our backs and pick our feet up. See how long you can float."

I held my breath, laid back, lifted my feet up, then sank to the bottom.

"Keep practicing your floating." Pa said.

I attempted again to float face down and pushed off with my legs a little. I moved across the surface into deeper water. I turned around and floated back to shallow water.

Patsy was four feet from me. "Help!" she hollered. "It's over my head. I can't touch bottom."

I reached over and clutched her arm. Then the current

carried both of us. My feet reached for the bottom but could not touch. I sank before I could get another breath. Patsy's arms thrashed in the water. Her head went under. I could save neither Patsy nor me. I felt the bottom and jumped straight up. When my head surfaced, I gasped for air, but sank again. Patsy pushed against me and managed to break the surface.

Then, an arm around my chest lifted me up and I breathed in a full breadth. Pa carried me to shallow water. Elizabeth held Patsy and walked her back to shore.

"You alright, son?"

"Yes, Pa. Thanks for helping us."

Patsy, sat with me on a large rock by the river. "I don't think I like the water, Daniel."

"Yeah. Me neither. I am glad Pa and Elizabeth were close enough to pull us back to shore."

The others were not so eager to jump in. Only Elizabeth and Molly, who was making progress, continued to swim. We all watched Pa and Rex swim across the river to the island and back.

After a couple of hours at the river we gathered around the fire for our picnic. Elizabeth, Molly, Patsy, and I shaved the kernels from ears of corn into a large cast iron pan. Ma placed some butter in the pan and cooked the corn over some red-hot coals. Ma served the corn with slices of ham.

I sat beside seven-year-old Genny as we ate our food. A tear rolled down her cheek. She looked up at me. "Daniel, I wish you weren't leaving us."

I placed my arm around her. "I know, but I'll be back in a year."

"Daniel, tell us about your training," James said.

"We learned to shoot at the head of a nail and drive it into a tree. We learned to shoot on the run. We learned to load and re-load fast. Captain wanted us to developed confidence in each other's ability to shoot accurately. We held out barrel staves for another to hit. Then we switched places."

"Those are all important so that you can fight as one unit, not fifty individual men," Pa said.

"We learned to throw a hatchet," I continued.

"Very important. The enemy may be upon you and there is no time to reload," Pa said.

There was a lull in the conversation as we stared at the dancing yellow flames and red-hot coals.

"We're going to miss you for sure," Molly said. "Promise you won't do anything stupid. Be safe."

"I'll be alright," I replied. "There's fifty of us. We look out for each other. I must go to fight for our country's freedom and protect our family's future."

"Without me, who will cut your hair?" Elizabeth said.

There was a long pause in our conversation.

"Captain Gwatkins asked us what we would do if we were captured," I said. "And the British offered us freedom if we would fight for them. Everybody agreed with Patrick Henry 'Give me liberty or give me death.'"

"Well it's one thing to be patriotic," Ma said. "But sometimes you must be practical. Life should not be given up lightly. One's life is very precious."

"Captain Gwatkins told us something like that," I replied. "He said it's likely not all of us will return alive. He said we should consider whether there is anything we need to set right before we leave. What did he mean by that?"

"If you owe someone money, you need to pay 'em before you leave," Pa said. "If you have hurt someone, you need to tell 'em you're sorry."

After a silence, Ma placed her arm around my shoulder. "That's true, Daniel, but there is something else." Ma paused. "There is one other person that we must all make amends with before we leave this earth: the Almighty. We must set things right with Him before we die."

I did not know how to respond to Ma's statement, and apparently, neither did anyone else.

After a long silence Pa stood with a grunt and challenged us to a game of horseshoes. Molly and James were the champions. Later in the afternoon we began our journey home, arriving as the sun set.

After church on Sunday, Ma gathered the whole family together to pray for me. We all sat down together around the table and Ma placed her hands over mine, "Heavenly Father, we acknowledge You as our all-powerful, sovereign, loving and caring Father. We ask that You hold our precious Daniel in Your protective hands. We ask that You protect him from the dangers of the war and the wilderness. Protect him from injury and disease and the brutality of evil men. Protect Daniel so that he can serve You and glorify You. We ask that You return him safely to us after he completes his year of service. We continue to pray for George, that You return him safely to us. We ask this in the powerful and loving name of Jesus."

Everyone was silent after Ma's prayer. Finally, Ma spoke. "Daniel, I've prayed for George every day and I'll pray for you every day until you return safely to us." Even though I did not pray myself, and did not really believe it made a difference, Ma's prayer reminded me of her love for me, and was a comforting memory to leave home with.

My sisters and brother came around me. Elizabeth spoke for them. "Daniel, I don't know what kind of mail service you will have out there in the wilderness of Kentucky, but we want you to write us."

"We want to hear about Boonesborough," Molly added.

"Are there any kids our age?" Patsy said.

"Tell us about the Indians," James interjected.

"We bought you something to help you with our wish," Elizabeth continued as she presented me with a handsome wooden case, about eight inches long, painted red.

I opened the case to find an exquisite quill pen, the feathers trimmed, except for the end. I smiled, tears welling up in my eyes.

"Thank you so much. It's a handsome gift. I shall treasure it and use it. And I'll write to you and tell you all about Kentucky," I responded.

Patsy stepped forward, pulled something from behind her back, and offered me a black ceramic jar, with a cork stopper. "Of course, you must have the finest ink to go with the pen."

James thrust forward a leather satchel. "And you must have paper to write on." As James spoke, I tried to smile but was thwarted by the lump in my throat. I reached out and gathered all my sisters and my brother into a gigantic hug, each with a stream of tears on their cheeks. Ma and Pa came over and joined us. I don't know how long we stayed there, but I wished it would never end.

As we broke apart, Pa said, "Come on, son, let's take a stroll before we go to bed." We walked out to the cornfields. The waning sunlight and crescent moon showed us the way.

"Daniel, I know you don't like being told what to do, but part of growin' up is learnin' how to take orders. We all must learn this. If it is not your Ma and me, it'll be someone else. You're joinin' the militia, and you'll have to take orders. Captain Gwatkins will be your commanding officer, and you'll have to follow what he says. Others are depending on you doing your part. If you don't, things'll go poorly for you."

"Pa, I don't know what makes me want to go against what you and Ma tell me. I want to be my own man. To plough my own field. Decide where I am going and when. I can't do that on this farm—your farm. And I want to see what's out there, and I just can't stay here. I know you and Ma love me. I love you, too. You're right. I'll follow Captain Gwatkins' orders.

"I know you will," replied Pa. "One other thing. Learn that rifle of yours. It's your friend and it will save your life. Take target practice when you can and learn from the other men in the militia, anyone who's better than you."

"Yes, Pa," I replied. "I learned that lesson on our bear hunt. I've been practicin'."

"Okay," Pa replied, his eyebrows drawing together as he rubbed his neck. With a smile and a chuckle, he continued, "I kinda wish it was me goin' instead of you."

"Don't say that. You gotta take care of the family. After I finish my Kentucky adventure, I'll be back, I'll be stronger, and I'll help you."

Pa laughed and placed his arm around my shoulders as we strolled back to the house.

The next morning, September 1, 1777, the day I would report to duty, I was awakened by Rex's familiar licks on my face. "What do you say, Rex? One last morning of chores before I head out." Rex replied with his excited panting.

We did our chores and then we strolled together to the forest, just past the cornfields, and sat down together. Rex sat on his hind haunches. There was a sadness about his demeanor—as if he knew I was leaving. I wrapped my arm around his neck as he gazed forward into the forest. "Rex. I'll miss you. I will miss you runnin' by my side, watchin' you herd the cows, and wakin' me up in the mornins. Take care of the family while I'm gone. I'll be back."

Ma, Pa, and I rode to the county office in New London. I hugged Ma and Pa, then gathered my sack and my gun and joined the others. Everyone was there, including Huddleston and English. The sight of those two put a knot in my stomach and I kept some distance from them. After about an hour,

Captain Gwatkins read off our names and each man answered "here". We lined up two-by-two for our westward march. We would march along the road to Big Lick, right by our house. At Big Lick, we would take the Wilderness Road southwest, cross over the New River, and continue westward toward Cumberland Gap and Kentucky.

As Judge Lynch looked on, he thrust his right fist above his head and thundered, "Liberty Forever!"

In response, we all raised our fists in the air and shouted, "Liberty forever!"—all except Huddleston and English.

CHAPTER THREE

THE WILDERNESS ROAD

SEPTEMBER 1777

Our company of fifty men, including three that rode on horseback and four pack horses, marched southwest. The pack horses carried much-needed ammunition and salt. One horseman scouted for our next campsite and maintained constant vigilance for possible attacks from Cherokees and Shawnees. Two others roamed ahead on horseback, hunting for game such as deer, bear, or buffalo, to feed the men.

On the afternoon of the third day of our march, we stopped for a rest. Desperate for shade, I leaned back against a large oak tree, and took a few sips from my canteen as a drop of sweat ran into my eye, with a sting. As I rubbed the sweat from my eye, I heard someone whisper from behind the tree.

I glanced at Ben and whispered, "Did you hear that?"

"Hear what?" Ben replied in a normal voice.

I placed my forefinger to my mouth and whispered, "Listen."

We both listened. Among a string of whispers, I recognized the word, "Gunpowder."

Then there was silence. I motioned for Ben to stay seated as I rose and walked away toward a group of men seated on the ground, where I figured I could see the whisperer. I turned back, but there was no one by the tree, except Ben. I returned to Ben and said in a low voice, "Someone whispered, 'gunpowder.' Where's English and Huddleston?"

"I heard nothin'. You may be imaginin' it," Ben replied.

"I didn't imagine it, but there was no one on the other side of the tree."

"Men, let's march," shouted Captain Gwatkins.

We assembled in formation and resumed our march into the wilderness. As we marched, I said to myself, *I'll bet those two Tories are up to something.*

As the afternoon sun fell below a distant mountain peak, we approached a grassy area with a stream. Captain Gwatkins raised his right fist, "Halt. We will make our camp for the night here."

We each began our respective duties to cut wood, build campfires, and erect tents. Our tents slept six men, and each tent had its own campfire to cook supper. I was assigned to a tent that included Richard Wade, William Humphries, Ben Kelly, Samuel English, and Paul Huddleston. I had hoped to avoid English and Huddleston but it did accommodate my goal to listen in on their conversations.

Each morning, we received our ration of food for the day, which consisted of flour that we mixed with water and spread out on a rock set upright by the fire. The outside was often charred, while the inside was still gooey. We were so depleted at the end of a day that even that pile of charred dough resembling bread tasted terrific. Our meal also included meat—shot that day by the hunters or left over from a previous day.

About an hour later, the three hunters rode in. They led a horse that carried a headless bear, the blood still dripping from its body. Benjamin Kelly, Richard Wade, John Brown, Paul Huddleston, and I lifted the bear off the horse and carried him to an area near the fire, to remove the skin and cut the meat for our supper. Sam English stood nearby, still recovering from his thumb hanging.

Richard instructed us, "Let's first remove the skin. Turn him face toward the sky."

"No, No, No," English broke in. "That's not how you do it. Ya tie off his paws, then stretch him between trees and slit him down the middle."

"It's not necessary to stretch him between trees," Richard said calmly.

English marched over to Richard, loomed over him, and bellowed, "It's the way we do it in New York and it's the way we'll do it now."

"Either way, we skin that fella," Richard replied. "This'll make somebody a nice blanket."

"I claim the skin since I'll be doin' the skinnin'," shouted English.

Captain Gwatkins walked up. "The bearskin goes to the fella that shot him. I believe that's Arabia Brown. English, please ensure that Brown gets it. Asbury, report back to me to verify that Brown got his skin."

"Yes, sir," I replied.

English was silent.

We skinned the bear and salted the hide. "Now let's take the skin to Arabia," I said.

"Hold on," replied English. "I'll stretch it out for him overnight." He gathered the skin and walked away.

I jumped up and trailed behind him at a distance. I would see how honest his intentions were. A twig snapped under my foot.

English turned around and hollered, "What do you want?"

"My assignment is to verify to Cap'n that Arabia receives his skin. I am just following his orders."

"Well, it ain't gonna be today, so you best run along."

I turned to walk away, but stopped. I turned back to English,

"You'll give it to Arabia now, or I'll report your actions to Captain Gwatkins."

English stomped over to me and pushed me up against a tree. His breath reeked, making me turn away. "I will give Arabia the skin when I'm dang well ready to."

"Very well," I replied, trying to sound confident, despite my quivering legs. English was not likely to hit me in front of so many soldiers.

He let go of my shirt and proceeded on his way. I marched immediately to Captain Gwatkins' tent.

"Captain Gwatkins," I shouted.

"Yes. Come in."

I entered to find Captain Gwatkin as he studied maps. "Sir, English has taken the skin and hasn't yet given it to Arabia."

"Is it ready?"

"I believe so, sir."

He sighed and stood. "Come with me," he said, as he walked out of his tent.

"Wade, Humphries, Brown. Come with me," Gwatkins commanded. The three men sprang up and fell in line with me.

We walked over to where English was seated at the fire with Huddleston. "English," Gwatkins barked. "Where's that bearskin?"

"Right here. I was gonna stretch it out overnight."

"I ordered you to give it to Arabia. If it needs to be stretched, he can do it himself. I expect my commands to be carried out immediately. Get up. We'll all make sure Arabia gets his pelt."

English stood with a grumble and scooped up the bearskin. As Gwatkins turned toward another fire, English glared at me. He followed Gwatkins and the rest of us marched behind.

"Arabia Brown," Gwatkins yelled.

"Yes, sir," Arabia returned, jumping to his feet.

"English has something for you."

"Here is your bearskin," English muttered as he tossed the

pelt at Arabia's feet. "The skin goes to the fella that shot him." As English turned away, he glared at me again, his fist clenched.

We pressed on, traveling ten to fifteen miles a day. Whenever we stopped for a rest, I positioned myself near English and Huddleston to listen in on their conversation. Though my ear was attentive to their conversation, I kept my distance, for I feared what English would do if he caught me eavesdropping.

We continued southwest on the Wilderness Road until we arrived at the New River and Ingles Ferry. The flow of the river slowed as it deepened and widened so that there were no rapids. I spotted a ferry boat, along with several buildings—a house, tavern, general store, and barn. The forty-foot flat-bottom ferry boat could carry a team of horses that pulled a wagon. The ferry operator pushed against the river bottom with a long pole to propel it across the river.

"Halt." Captain Gwatkins shouted, raising his right hand. He turned to us. "We will camp here two nights to replenish our supplies and rest. Set up camp over by the river in that flat, grassy area."

We pitched our tents and built our campfires, then roasted our meat and baked our "bread" while the daylight faded and the stars revealed themselves. While we ate, English and Huddleston moved away from the group, over near some trees. I laid my hand on Ben's arm to get his attention. I nodded my head toward them. We rose and snuck toward them hiding behind some bushes.

"This is the right moment," English whispered. "We can get empty barrels from the storeroom for Ingles Ferry and fill them with rocks. Then, switch them for the gun powder and ammunition barrels tomorrow night after everyone's asleep."

Ben and I turned to the other with wide eyes. Ben pointed

his head toward the river, away from English and Huddleston, away from anyone else, where we could sort out this treacherous conversation.

"Daniel, you were right," Ben whispered.

"Yeah, we must tell Captain Gwatkins at once," I replied.

"Let's not draw too much attention to ourselves," Ben cautioned.

We crept away, keeping low, and walked casually toward Captain's tent and the guard who stood nearby.

"We request permission to speak with Captain," I said to the guard, Willie Staggs.

"Captain has requested that he not be disturbed under any circumstances," Staggs replied.

"But sir, this is about the safety of our expedition," Ben responded.

"I am sure it can wait until tomorrow," Staggs replied.

"What time?" I inquired.

"An hour after sunrise."

"We will be here then," Ben said.

Ben and I ambled to the circle around our waning campfire. English and Huddleston both eyed us with prolonged stares.

"What you boys doin' over by the captain's tent?" English asked.

"Just catchin' up with Willie Staggs, an old friend from New London," Ben replied.

English and Huddleston both grunted, returned their gaze to the fire, but said nothing.

Ben and I rose just before daybreak and washed and shaved by the river without much conversation. An hour after sunrise, we stood outside the captain's tent. Soon the captain parted the flaps of the tent and emerged.

"Captain, we must speak with you," I stated.

"Fine. Go right ahead and speak," he replied.

"Sir, we would like to discuss this in private, inside your tent," Ben answered.

Gwatkins hesitated, raised his right eyebrow, then said, "Alright. Let's go inside."

We followed Gwatkins inside the tent, as he closed the flaps.

"Captain, we discovered a threat to our expedition," I explained. "The two Tories are up to something. We heard them talkin, sayin' they were gonna steal our gunpowder and ammunition so the British could use it. Tonight, after everyone is asleep. We are both witnesses of this treacherous plot."

"Ordinarily, I'd say you boys are imaginin' this," Gwatkins answered as he stroked his red beard. "But I've tasted a smidgin too much of their sour attitude. I'm inclined to believe you. I'll place extra guards around the ammunition tonight. You boys go about your normal business today. Don't do any snoopin' around."

"Yes, sir," we said in unison.

When we emerged from the captain's tent, my eyes fell on English and Huddleston washing in the river. English looked our way. I averted my gaze as we strode toward our tent.

"Let's go fishing. Get our minds off the treachery," Ben suggested.

"Yeah, let's catch our supper," I said. "It's got to be better than what we've been eating. We can get some fishing tackle at the Ingles Ferry store."

On our way to the store, we encountered Richard Wade, James Morton, and Adam Wiley.

"Let's go fishing. We're headed to Ingles store to get some fishhooks and line," Ben said.

"Sounds good. We'll join you," responded Morton.

Inside the store, behind the counter, was a thin middle-aged woman with a pleasant countenance. She greeted our entrance with a smile.

"Good morning. Welcome to Ingles Ferry. I understand you fellas are from Bedford County. I used to live there."

"Are you Mary Ingles?" I asked.

"Yes."

"My ma told me about your experience with the Indians. How they captured you. And then you escaped."

"I nearly died of starvation trudging through the wilderness to get home," she replied. "But I never gave up hope of seeing my family again."

Mary Ingles story—the terror of her captivity, the loss of her children, and her courageous trek through the wilderness—dwelled in my thoughts for the rest of the day. I was glad to have met her.

We obtained the fishing tackle we needed, dug up worms along the shady riverbank, and fished for trout in the New River. We caught ten eating-sized speckled trout, a welcome change from our normal diet.

That night, everyone went to bed early in anticipation of the ferry crossing and long march the next day. Ben and I pretended to sleep while Wade and Humphries snored. English and Huddleston lay quiet and still. Eventually the traitors rose from their beds and slipped out of the tent.

Ben and I looked at each other and crept out of the tent without a word.

We sat down by a tree, about fifty yards from the guard and ammunition, to watch the caper unfold. The silhouettes of Huddleston and English were down by the river. The hollow thump of rocks falling into empty barrels was the only sound. Once they filled them, they rolled the barrels up to the ammunition tent.

Just as English was about to open the flap, Captain Gwatkins' gruff voice cut through the silence, "You figure we wouldn't notice our gunpowder had turned into rocks?" Both traitors froze as two guards seized them from behind. "Guess you were fixin' to deliver the real ones to the Redcoats. Tie 'em up, Staggs."

I poked Ben in the side. "Let's go back and get some sleep."

"I'm for that."

Before I turned around, I saw English glaring daggers at me.

The next morning, we packed up for the river crossing, Captain Gwatkins gathered us together. "Men, we had an incident last night where two of our own attempted to steal our ammunition. Thankfully, our guards apprehended them in the act, but English and Huddleson will bear the penalty for their actions. They'll be treated as prisoners. They can't carry rifles, nor any weapon, and will be tied up at night. They'll be separated, so they can't conspire together for another treacherous act. Both will have men assigned to watch their actions to ensure they don't damage our enterprise. When we arrive in Boonesborough, Samuel English and Paul Huddleston will be placed in the jail." Gwatkins paused, then continued, "Now, the ferry is waitin' for us to load up. It'll take a few loads for us all to get across, so let's get movin'."

As soon as the captain dismissed the men, he called out, "Asbury and Kelly." We walked over to him. "I commend both of you for bringin' this treachery to our attention. I'll make a note in our records of your role in this matter."

"Thank you, sir," we replied in unison.

"Now, let's get on with crossing the river."

"Yes, sir," we answered.

Ben and I departed to carry our packs and supplies toward the river. Then, from behind me, a voice called, "Asbury."

I turned around. Samuel English stood five feet from me, still bound and guarded, and said, "I know it was you that tipped off Cap'n about our plans. I am not one that forgets those that hurt me. You'll have a short life on this earth, so you better get your affairs in order."

"Those plans were traitorous and doomed for failure," I said, as I turned away and hurried toward the company of my friends William Humphries, Richard Wade, and Ben Kelly.

Days turned to weeks as we marched deeper into the wilderness. We passed Fort Chiswell and continued down the valley. We crossed streams and rivers, climbed hills, and admired the first emergence of the crimson, yellow, and orange leaves. We continued southwest from Martin's Station, and viewed the majestic and imposing Cumberland Mountains, marked by the numerous white rocks on their slopes. At the southwest end of the mountain ridge, the rugged terrain descended to form Cumberland Gap before rising again to render yet another obstacle to westward travel.

We crossed over Cumberland Gap into Kentucky and marched along the road cut by Daniel Boone and thirty-five axmen two years earlier. One could not call it a road, though. It was just an improved path to accommodate single-file walkers, horses, and pack animals, not wide enough for a wagon.

Near the crest of a hill, Captain Gwatkins stopped and raised his arm. "Men, we'll camp here tonight. We have arrived in Kentucky. Behold the land," and pointed westward to an opening in the trees. "Enjoy its beauty but beware of its peril. We're deep into Shawnee country, so we'll douse our fires early and have double the guards tonight."

The beauty of the land exceeded the stories we had been told —the rivers and streams, the trees and meadows, the buffaloes, and deer. A half-dozen turkeys foraged the ground for food.

We pressed westward into Kentucky. Captain Gwatkins marched at the front of our line; his long, dark red hair streamed behind him in the breeze. English marched near the front, and Huddleston in the middle. I was still farther back in the line, behind Adam Wiley. As sweat ran from my forehead down my cheeks, I heard only the sound of fifty soldiers trudging along the path, the chirp of a cardinal, and the whistle of wind through tree branches. I was focused on Adam Wiley's back when, from behind a tree, an arrow flew through the forest.

"I'm hit," screamed Adam Wiley as he tumbled to the ground with the arrow protruding from his chest.

"Attack!" I shouted. "On our right!" then dove behind a tree. My heart pounding, my stomach tightened.

"Find cover," Captain Gwatkins commanded. "Shoot to kill."

Bang, bang, bang. Rifle shots followed the arrow, and another soldier dropped.

After the shots, smoke drifted away from a bush. I aimed and shot toward the bush, along with five others. One of our attackers flopped to the ground. *Did I hit him?*

Gwatkins motioned to five men on the hill, "Circle around behind the attackers."

Then, he turned toward us near the back of the line, "Circle around from below."

We crept away and stayed low, my heart still pounding. I reached the cover of a tree and took two deep breaths. Several more rifle shots rang out through the forest. When silence followed, I darted to another tree. Our militia occupied the enemy's attention while we dashed from tree to tree.

Before my third dash, a bullet whizzed by my ear. I did not have a second to be scared. Propelled by that bullet, I shifted from a fast jog to a sprint.

Our group reached the back side of our attackers, and the group that had circled from above were in position. We surrounded the enemy. I fired my rifle at an Indian, and our foes fled.

Captain Gwatkin shouted, "Go after 'em."

One fled through a gap in our line, near where I stood. I chased after him, but hesitated. *I just fired my rifle. I had no other weapon. Do I continue the chase? Or do I reload? He's an older, stronger man. I need my rifle loaded.* I stopped and grabbed my powder horn. I poured the powder down the barrel. I placed the patch and ball over the barrel and rammed them to the bottom.

The Indian stopped and turned around. He charged me with his knife in one hand, ready to throw, and his spent rifle in the other.

He was twenty-five yards from me. I placed some powder in the pan, cocked the hammer, and aimed.

He threw his knife. I jumped to my right, but it grazed my side. I aimed again. He was five yards from me. I pulled the trigger. Though I had fired it many times, the recoil threw my shoulder back. He dropped his rifle, leapt, and hit me in the face. I fell to the ground under his weight. As I braced for more blows, he wilted and collapsed on my face. The odors of dirt, sweat, and blood filled my nostrils, though I could barely breathe. I pushed him off as his blood poured out of his chest onto mine. He lay still. I stood shaking. I quickly looked away from his face but saw it so clearly. He was young. Handsome too, with straight features and clear skin. He did not look afraid or at peace or anything like that. He just looked dead.

I turned away as I caught my breath. I just took a life. A human life. But it was him or me. I had to protect myself. I'm not just fighting for myself but for all thirteen colonies.

In the hours, days, weeks, and months that followed, I grappled with having killed another human. I had no problem killing a deer or a bear to feed the family, but this was different. This man had a life. He probably had a wife and children. Not only did I hurt him, I hurt them as well. I was not so sure I could do that again. Was it right to just let him kill me? Still, this brought guilt that I had not anticipated when I signed up for the militia.

I examined the knife. Its sharp point and shiny blade drew

my admiration. The blade had a slight curve with sharp edges on both sides of the blade. The knife was magnificent, about fifteen inches long including the handle. The bone handle was polished smooth and shiny. Around the Indian's waist was a leather belt with the knife's sheath. I gathered the belt and sheath, along with my rifle. I started back toward the others when the sting in my side caught me. I felt my side, then saw the blood. It covered my hand.

Adam Wiley screamed, "Oooowwwww," as the medic pulled the arrow from his chest.

The medic turned to me and said, "What's your wound from?"

"A knife grazed me. It's not deep but is bleeding."

He handed me a bandage. "Wash that wound and keep pressure on it."

Finished with Wiley, the medic wrapped a wide belt around my waist to secure the bandage against my wound.

The Indians had killed two of our men, including Huddleson, and wounded five others. We had killed three Indians.

The scouts and hunters, who were ahead of us, arrived leading a pack horse loaded with buffalo meat. One scout spoke to Gwatkins, "There's an agreeable place to camp with a spring just a half mile down the trail."

Gwatkins spoke to the men, "After we bury our dead and treat the wounded, we'll make camp about a half mile from here. You five men there." He pointed to five men near the bodies of the men. "Dig the graves for our two brothers who've passed. You three men, go tend to the bodies of the dead Indians. My guess is that they are Shawnee, as they come to Kentucky from north of the Ohio River to hunt and attack settlers."

They buried the three Shawnee bodies without ceremony.

Once the others had buried our two fallen, we gathered around the graves. Captain Gwatkins conducted a brief ceremony to honor our men. We all removed our hats as our captain spoke. "Let us all bow our heads in prayer. Lord, we commit the souls of David Eubank and Paul Huddleson into Thy care. They were brave soldiers and fought for the freedom of their countrymen. We plead on their behalf that Thou would grant them mercy and forgiveness for the wrongs they have committed. Thou gave them to us for a short while, and we give them back to Thee for the rest of eternity." Though Paul Huddleson was not a patriot, Captain Gwatkin gave him the benefit of the doubt in his prayer.

We trekked toward our next campsite in the late afternoon. The campfires blazed as the scouts roasted the buffalo meat and "bread" for our evening meal. As I waited for supper, I admired again the knife that the Indian had thrown at me. Along the polished bone handle were three diagonal green lines. What history did this knife know? Who had owned it? Since it was superior to my own knife, I decided to wear the sheath and knife and use it as needed.

Darkness fell during supper. I ate my fill of buffalo and "bread" and lay back on my blanket. As there was no moon and no clouds in the night sky, we did not pitch our tents. The crickets began their nightlong chorus accompanied by a nearby hoot owl. The clearing in the trees revealed the vast array of stars. As I gazed upward, the memories of Ma, Pa, and my brothers and sisters filled my reflections. I missed them but was comforted when it occurred to me that those same stars also watched over them.

Reflections on the five men who had died, two from our militia and three Indians, filled my mind. *Where were they now? Were they up in the stars?* Whatever happened after this life, now they knew about it. How close I had come to death. Two times that day, death had called my name. First, the bullet that pushed the air near my ear. Then, my fight with the Indian could have ended my life. Two seconds slower reloading my gun, and he would have killed me. Then, I wondered about my brother George. *Was he still alive? Was he taken captive?* I had to bury those thoughts, for tomorrow I had to rise early to march deeper into the wilderness.

On October 12, we were slowed by a cold, heavy rain. Our feet slipped in the slick mud, burdened by the added weight of rain-soaked clothes and packs, and chilled from the cold rain against our bodies. We trudged up a hill. When we reached the crest, the rain stopped, and the sky cleared. Fort Boonesborough lay before us in the vale, with the Kentucky River behind it. A rainbow arced across the distant hills. Cheered by the site, our pace quickened.

At the fort, the guards opened the door, and there to greet us was the commanding officer, Captain Daniel Boone.

CHAPTER FOUR

BOONESBOROUGH

OCTOBER 1777

As the guards closed the gates behind us, Daniel Boone greeted us with a huge smile and arms opened wide. "Welcome to Kentucky. I am Captain Daniel Boone. I trust your journey was safe."

"Thank you, Captain Boone. I'm Captain Charles Gwatkins. We're the Virginia Militia from Bedford County. We've admired the beauty of Kentucky these past two weeks. However, you are not the first to welcome us. A band of Shawnees greeted us some five days back. They killed two of our men."

"Sorry to hear that," Boone responded, shaking his head. "The Shawnee have been quite pesky here, too. They've burned our cornfields and killed our cattle and horses. They're a constant threat here, forcin' us to stay within the walls of the fort except to hunt for food and retrieve water from the springs. The women and children, and all of us, are in constant distress from Indian attacks. Your men are a long-awaited and pleasurable sight, fetching us hope that we'll indeed endure the threats surrounding us outside these walls." Boone craned his neck to get a better view of our numbers, then continued, "I'm surprised they attacked such a large group of soldiers. They usually attack smaller groups they're likely to overpower. The Indians are all around us here in these forests, but there aren't enough of 'em to attack a group this large."

"Any news of the war?" Gwatkins asked.

"We don't get a lot of news out here, but I did hear Washington's army lost the Battle of Brandywine Creek and lost Philadelphia. We may have lost a battle, but there are many more to be fought." Boone pointed to the large man to his right. "This is Jacob Starns. He'll show you to your quarters. After your men are settled, we'll talk further."

"Captain Boone, we have one prisoner, who must stay in jail for his attempted sabotage of our mission," Gwatkins said.

"Starnes can show you the jail," Boone replied. "But you'll have to supply your own guards."

With the men we brought from Virginia, there were 120 living in Boonesborough, including twenty-four women and twenty-nine children. The fort was rectangular with a blockhouse on each corner, where guards stood watch day and night. In the center of the fort was the important blacksmith shop, where we tended to congregate for conversation. Our meals did not have much variety, usually just meat and occasionally some bread, just like we had on the trail.

Our quarters were log cabins built into the wall of the fort. The roof was equipped with bark gutters to capture rainwater in barrels, as there was no well or cistern in the fort.

In the center of our cabin was a slab table surrounded by several hickory chairs with deer-skin seats. Around the perimeter of the room were buffalo beds. Deer antlers hung on the walls to hold rifles, powder horns, and fishing poles. The shelf over the fireplace held a whiskey jug, a tinder box, the Bible, and a copy of *Pilgrim's Progress*.

Ben Kelly, William Humphries, and I were in the same cabin. As we settled in our quarters, Captain Gwatkins stepped inside our cabin and said, "Asbury and Kelly. You will be on guard duty this evening. You will each stand watch with an experienced guard. Asbury, you will be on the Southeast corner, next to the river. Kelly, you will be at the southwest blockhouse. Report there just after sundown this evening."

The bare room of the blockhouse had trivial comfort to offer the guards except for the confidence that the log walls were thick enough to stop the lead balls fired from the trees. The numerous small openings provided the means to scan the surroundings and to poke a gun barrel through. Andrew Johnson was my mentor for the evening, a small man in his thirties and an experienced woodsman. He was a quiet man but with a wit that made him enjoyable to be around.

"Make your rounds to all the lookout holes and check for lights," Johnson instructed. "During the day, look for movement, usually close to the ground. They'll crawl up close to the fort if they think no one's looking and try and set the fort on fire. Listen for sounds that resemble nature but are made by people imitating nature. They signal each other and coordinate their positions. They reckon we won't figure it's them comin'. Try to figure how close they are. If you see or hear something within fifty yards, shoot at it.

We made our rounds as the fort settled down for the evening. There was quiet now, which made the forest sound loud.

"Hoo-hoo-hoo-hoo," an owl hooted.

"I can hear the hoot of an owl out there, not far away," I remarked.

"Them ain't owls you're hearin'," Andrew responded.

"What are they?"

"Them's Shawnee birds," Andrew replied, with a sly grin.

"A real owl will studder on the second hoo. Like this, 'Hoo-h'hoo-hoo-hoo'. That hoot you heard had no studder on the second hoo. Indians also make the sounds of turkeys and other birds, and the scream of a panther. Learn the difference between the real sounds of the forest and humans tryin' to imitate it."

The forest quieted during the night. A couple of hours before sunrise, the doors of the fort opened, and a lone rider on horseback, leading a pack horse, departed.

Andrew explained, "That's one of our hunters. They leave before sunrise and return after dark. They ride many miles to get clear of the Shawnee around the fort. We'll eat the meat they bring back tomorrow."

The next day, we did indeed eat the deer meat they shot and hauled in on a pack horse. We ate meat every day, and only about every three days did we get bread.

One November afternoon, Captain Gwatkins informed us, "Captain Boone will write a letter to Virginia (legislature) to ask for salt and some other supplies. If you want to send a letter to your families, get 'em to me by this evening."

I used my new quill and paper to write my family and let them know I had arrived in Boonesborough.

Our life in Boonesborough became routine and boring. The constant threat of Indian attacks kept the Boonesborough residents confined to the fort. Keeping watch during four-hour shifts at one of the blockhouses was our primary duty. Occasional trips to the nearby river and springs for water required several men to stand guard. We spent the remainder of our time playing cards, pitching horseshoes, throwing hatchets at targets, and reading whatever books we could find.

After a month in Boonesborough, a group of us sat in a circle eating our ration of buffalo meat. Captain Gwatkins stepped toward us and interrupted our conversation. "We need other food as well. The Indians don't allow us to grow much, though. However, there's some corn left over from last year's harvest at some of the nearby plantations. The Indians have left those there, hoping we'll come get them. They'll pounce on us if we do. I propose a dangerous mission for six volunteers.

This is not mandatory for any of you. Six will mount horses and leave before daybreak tomorrow morning when the hunters leave, seize the corn from the cribs, and then bolt back. There'll be a nice moon tonight to help you find your way."

Ben Kelly, William Humphries, Jacob Starns, Andrew Johnson, Adam Wiley, and I volunteered immediately. "Anything to get out of this fort, if only for a short time," Humphries said.

"Good," Gwatkins said. "Johnson and Starns know where the plantations are. Starns, you wake everyone up during the night."

"I think we should divide into two groups," Johnson said. "One will go to the Thomas farm, the other to the Smith farm. We grab the corn and stuff it into sacks as quick as possible. Then high tail it back before the Indians know we left the fort."

"Agreed. The faster the better," Humpries said.

The nearly full moon, hung high in the cloudless night sky, provided suitable illumination for our mission. The hunter, who would travel many miles away, joined us at the gate.

Captain Gwatkins stood at the gate holding the reins for several horses. He handed me the reins for a spirited, tall, muscular horse with a black mane, legs, rump, and tail, with black, white, and grey splotches covering his body. "His name's Pepper. Good luck, Asbury," Gwatkins said.

"Thank you, sir," I replied, taking the reins.

We mounted our horses and without a sound, slipped through the gate. We kicked our mounts to hurry through the open, vulnerable area surrounding the fort to the cover of the forest. Ben and I followed Johnson, while Humphries and Wiley followed Starns. We grabbed the dried corn by the armfuls and stuffed our bags. After about three minutes, a screech or scream sounded from the nearby trees.

"That's a panther," observed Ben.

"That ain't no panther," responded Johnson. "That's an

Indian, tellin' the others we're here. Get a move on before they all descend on us."

I gathered an armload, shoving the corn in my sack, when a gunshot shattered the stillness of the night, and splintered some wood beside us.

"Let's git now," Johnson exclaimed.

We threw our bags over the horses' necks, swung into the saddles, and kicked our heels into our horses' sides, shifting them into a gallop. I led the way, wind rushing past. I leaned into Pepper's flying black mane and whispered in his ear, "Carry us back to Boonesborough, Pepper, as swift as you can," with a pat on his neck. Seeming to grasp the urgency, Pepper raced along, climbing hills, descending the valley, and leaping over the creek without a splash. A gunshot sounded when we reached the clearing around the fort. Pepper's muscular legs surged. He ran even faster, as though the finish line lay ahead, and he was determined to win the race. The nightguards of Boonesborough opened the door, and Pepper sprinted into the safety of the fort.

I dismounted and wrapped my arms around Pepper's neck. "Thank you, Pepper. Thank you."

Another rifle shot rang out as Johnson and Ben raced into the fort. Laughing, Johnson said, "Daniel, I've never seen Pepper run that fast. Solomon could barely keep up." He and Ben dismounted and grabbed the bags from their horses' necks.

"Yeah. Pepper is a mighty fleet animal. I am much obliged for his rapid return to Boonesborough." I replied. I looked around the empty courtyard. "Have the others returned?"

"Not yet," Johnson observed. "I'll look for them now."

I fastened Pepper to a hitching post and followed Johnson to the blockhouse. Johnson turned and suggested, "Bring your rifle."

I returned with my rifle to join Johnson, Ben, and John Brown in the blockhouse.

"Be ready to shoot if any of those Indians show themselves,"

Johnson instructed. "I'll shoot first, but if I miss, you follow with your shots."

"Here they come," Johnson shouted. "They've just cleared the hill—Humphries and Starns, followed by Wiley."

Humphries and Starns raced for the fort. As Starns entered the fort, another shot was fired from the trees. Humphries' horse stumbled. Humphries lept from his horse as it fell, landing on his feet and sprinting without missing a beat. He ran with long strides, like a deer being chased by a wolf. My heart was in my throat as another shot sounded from the forest, but the ball missed its target, and Humphries dashed inside.

A gunshot rang out from the forest. Wiley fell from his horse. He quickly recovered and limped toward the fort. At the second shot, Wiley fell to the ground and did not move. Just then, an Indian emerged from the forest and ran up to Adam. The Indian slit his throat and grabbed his hair. He looked like a figure from a nightmare, not what I thought of as a soldier. With his knife, he slit a gash in Wiley's head, just above the ear, and in three quick motions, cut around the top of his head. He yanked and lifted Wiley's hair off his head. The thrill of Pepper's swift gallop back to Boonesborough vanished as the Indian waved Wiley's scalp into the air and released a howl we could hear at the fort. This all occurred while Johnson took aim and fired his shot. The shot missed, and I was not surprised—it seemed like the Indian was the devil himself. Then Brown fired his rifle, and the Indian collapsed to the ground on top of Wiley, just a man.

"We've got to go get Adam," I screamed. "We can't leave him out there."

"Let's wait a while to let things settle down, maybe an hour or so," Johnson said. "They'll have their guns cocked and aimed in case we rush out there. Adam is surely dead. I saw the Indian slash his throat."

"Two men need to go," Starnes said. "Every gun hole in the

blockhouse needs a gun aimed at the woods, with a second gun loaded and ready to fire. When a gun from the trees fires, shoot back at it."

"Whoever goes should take a barrel lid as a shield," Humphries said.

"I'll go," I shouted.

"I'll go too," followed Ben.

"It'll go faster if a third person picks up his feet. I'll do that," Humphries said.

After about an hour, the three of us gathered at the door of the fort to retrieve Wiley's body, each with our wooden barrel lid. The door opened. We rushed to the slain patriot's body and carried him back to the fort. No shot was fired from the forest.

Inside the fort, gazing at Wiley's body, seeing his blood pour off his scalped head, my stomach tightened and ached. The memory of the horrifying sight of the Indian yanking Wiley's hair off his head haunted me. I bent over and hurled vomit.

"This is terrible," Ben said as he stood beside me. "Adam was our age, too young to die. I feel sick too."

As light dawned in the eastern sky, some of the women wrapped Wiley's body in linen and placed it in a crude wooden box. Captain Gwatkins conducted a burial ceremony like the one he conducted on the wilderness road.

Shocked by the loss of Adam Wiley, I staggered back to my cabin and found my bed, but I could not sleep. I wept. Why did it have to be Adam who died? Why wasn't it me?

One cold day toward the end of November I kept watch in the southwest blockhouse. I discerned a single horse and rider, waving as he cantered toward the fort. I yelled down toward the gatekeeper, "A lone horse rider is approachin'. Open the gate."

The gatekeeper unbolted the door and opened it as the rider

hurried inside. After my watch duty, I joined a group of men that included Boone, seated around the blacksmith's shop. The rider reported news of the war.

"We lost the Battle of Germantown in October, and many men died, some were taken prisoner."

I wondered if George was in that battle and if he survived.

The messenger went on with other news, "Some scoundrels at Fort Randolph murdered the great Shawnee Chief Cornstalk. He'd come in peace, but they locked him in jail. They also jailed his son and two other Shawnee."

"Why'd they murder him?" asked one listener.

"Well, some of the militia from the fort had gone huntin'. Some Indians, not Shawnee, shot and scalped one of the men. The Americans brought the bloody body back to the fort and declared, 'Let's kill the Indians in the fort.' The fellow hunters rushed up the hill in a rage, guns in hand. They stormed past any that would dissuade them from their mission and threatened them with immediate death. Then, they murdered all four of the captive Shawnee. None of the murderers were brought to justice."

"Dem Indians are barbarians," said one fella as he pulled his poker of buffalo meat from the fire to examine it. "They deserved it."

"Naw. They didn't deserve to be shot for something they didn't do," another added.

"Well, not only was it cruel and unjust, it was half-witted," Boone said. "Cornstalk sought peace with the Americans. The Shawnee revered him as a great chief. He went to Fort Randolph in peace. First, those dang fools locked him up. Then they put a lead ball through his heart. The Shawnee know the murderers will not be properly reckoned with for their crimes. Now, the whole Shawnee nation will crave revenge. Their drive for justice will not wane until they get it. And . . . " Boone paused for a few seconds, and we all waited for him to finish.

"It won't matter who they take revenge on. Many innocent Americans will now die. That was a foolhardy and reckless act."

As I walked back to our cabin I thought about this story regarding Cornstalk. This incident was different from my previous experiences. Unjust Americans murdered a peace seeking Indian chief. I did not know what to do with this information.

I arrived at our cabin to find Humphries laying on his bed, his eyes darted at the ceiling and then around the room. He sat up, rubbing his arms and biting his lips. He held a letter in his hands.

"Daniel," he said. "I just received a letter from my wife, Mary. She had to move our family to Richmond."

"What happened?"

"I had arranged for my brother to help her with our farm, but he got the call to serve in the army too. She couldn't manage it by herself, so she moved to be near her brother."

"I'm so sorry to hear that," I said. "It must be difficult to be so far away and not be able to help her."

"I think she and the boys are safe, but I can't wait for this Kentucky mission to be finished so I can get back to them."

"Yeah, it'll be over soon," I said. "And you can git back to them."

"I sure hope so."

December blew into Kentucky with cold and snow, resulting in fewer successes for our hunters, which added to our mounting distress. Around the middle of December, Captain Gwatkins entered my cabin and delivered added pain. "Asbury. It's your turn to watch over our prisoner. Report to the jail to relieve Goodman. You'll watch him for four hours until you are relieved by the next guard. Goodman will let you know what ya have to do."

"Yes, sir." I tried to conceal my dread.

"Asbury," Gwatkins added, "your time to guard English came up twice before since we have been in Boonesborough, but I spared you. Now it's time you take your turn."

"Yes, sir. Thank you, sir. I'll do my part."

"You're a good soldier, Asbury," Gwatkins said and departed.

Ansel Goodman sat outside the cabin that served as the jail. I approached. "Howdy, Ansel. Here to relieve you of your guard duties."

"A welcome sight you are, Daniel," replied Ansel.

"Cap'n said you'd explain my duties."

"Not much to it. You sit out here. Have your gun ready and loaded. Take him some food when it's time to eat. That's about it," Ansel replied as he departed.

"Is that Asbury out there?" English hollered. "Come in here. I want to talk to you."

"I'll be in to see you when your food comes."

"That's hours from now. Come on in. You ain't got nothin' else to do."

"You'll have to wait."

I sat in the chair outside the cabin jail until the food came for us, a small morsel of venison. I opened the door to find English lying on the bed, looking up at the ceiling.

"Well, Asbury, you've finally come to interrupt the boredom, have ya?" English said. "Come right into my palace and let's partake of the feast."

The cabin was bare, except for English's bed, a chair, and a fireplace with no fire.

"Here's your supper," I said, as I handed him the plate.

He grunted in acknowledgment as he received the food. My first instinct was to leave as soon as possible, but I stayed to give English some company while we ate our supper. English sat on his bed, and I sat on the chair.

"What's it like out there, beyond the walls of the fort?" English said.

"The Indians are scattered out in the trees, ready to shoot anyone they see leave the fort," I replied.

"Well, ya don't have to worry about me escapin', cause I got nowhere to run."

"That's right. You're safer sittin' right here in jail than anywhere else," I replied.

"Yeah. The Indians would shoot me for sure. They don't know I'm on their side."

I changed the subject, curious to know further details about English. "Sam, how long you been livin' over here in the colonies, so far from the country that you love?"

"About five years, I'd say."

"What brought you here?"

"Well, that's a long story, and I won't bore you with too many details. When I was fourteen, some thugs murdered my parents. I worked on the docks. When I came home, I found them, stabbed to death and lyin' in a puddle of their own blood. Took everything we had. The constable never found the offenders. They were rebels and they should'a hanged for what they done. Left only me and my older sister. We nearly starved, but for our aunt and uncle. I kept workin' the docks for years. Then, about 1772, I caught a ship bound for New York."

"Sorry about your parents," I said. "But now that you're over here, how can you fight against your neighbors and fellow countrymen to live under the tyranny of the king?"

"Young fool. The Crown is the rightful authority of the land. You all deserve to hang. If I could, I'd hang every one of you rebels."

"We're battlin' for what's right and just," I said. "The king's unjust. We can't bear to live under his cruel iron rod any longer."

"We live in a crazy world. I have lived on both sides of this war—with those loyal to the Crown and with those fightin' the Crown. The Crown says those that rebel should hang. Your destiny, young Asbury, is to dangle from the end of a rope, kicking your legs until you ain't got any kick left."

English said this with a half-smile, and a twinkle in his eye, as though he did not believe it.

Nevertheless, I did not want to hear any more talk of hanging. I was ready to leave. "You're in no position to make such predictions, English. Now, as you can see, I've finished my supper and I will take me leave."

I turned and opened the door.

"Thank you for bringin' my food and for the conversation," English said.

"You're welcome. Just doin' my duty."

I closed the door behind me and replaced the board across the door, locking it.

CHAPTER FIVE

THE SALT MAKERS' MISSION

JANUARY 1778

With the onset of cold temperatures, ice, and snow the Indians retreated from the Boonesborough area to spend the winter elsewhere. But Boonesborough was desperate for food. Hunting was difficult in the winter, and we had run out of salt to preserve the little meat that the hunters brought back.

Captain Gwatkins gathered his men in the center of the fort, and announced, "As you know, Boonesborough needs salt. The Virginia General Assembly has not responded to Captain Boone's requests. The only alternative is to make it, by boiling water from salt springs. Captain Boone thinks now's the best time to send men to make salt for the town. There are fewer Indian war parties in Kentucky during the winter. We'll send a group of thirty men to Blue Licks on the north side of the licking River, fourteen of whom will come from our ranks." Gwatkins read the names of those selected for the mission which included Arabia and John Brown, Ansel Goodman, William Humphries, Ben Kelly, James Morton, Richard Wade, and me. Gwatkins continued, "This will also include Samuel English. He gets the opportunity to earn his keep choppin' wood and keepin' the fires burnin'. You'll report to Captain Boone tomorrow morning before dawn."

As we trudged along rocky Kentucky terrain, I smiled at the sight of Pepper as he carried one of the hunters riding ahead of us. Our winter trek was slow. Weakened by a lack of nourishment due to the scarcity of food the past three months, we stopped for rest and water often and covered less ground each day. On the fifth day of what was supposed to be a three-day march, we followed a wide road made by the buffalos that came to the salt springs in vast herds. I examined the terrain in all directions eager to see a herd of buffalos but witnessed none. So trampled was the road that dirt over the roots of trees and rocks had been worn away, exposing them above the ground. These roads came from the north, south, east, and west and met at the springs. The buffalos had trampled out the weeds, bushes, small trees and undergrowth and left only tall trees.

"This place makes the hairs on your arm stand up," Morton said.

"Yeah. It feels like this place belongs to someone else," Wade replied. "Someone immense and ornery, and we're trespassin'."

"Yeah. And they are due back soon. It's like you can smell trouble here. I wanna make our salt and git back to Boonesborough promptly," Humphries said.

We unloaded our gear and set up camp. Everyone gathered and chopped firewood. Once the fires were going, we filled large iron pots with spring water and boiled off the water all day and all night. The water left behind a film of salt on the walls and bottoms of the pots.

Samuel English's time in jail did not cure him of his disagreeable manner. The second week at Blue Licks, Daniel

Boone rode into camp and hollered to English, "Sam, I found a large fallen tree about two hundred yards toward the top of that hill yonder," pointing behind him. "That tree'll make an admirable fire to boil our spring water. Take an ax and saw and Pepper. Go chop it up and put a load of it on Pepper's back."

"It's too late in the day to start a project like that. I'll do it tomorrow," replied English.

Boone dismounted his horse and rushed to English, stopping about six inches from him. English stepped back a foot.

"You'll do it now. Look at our wood pile. It'll last us only two hours. You best commence your work, or we'll find you enough work to keep you busy all night."

English stepped forward, closed the gap between Boone and him, and pulled his fist back to hit Boone. Johnson and Wade grabbed English's arms and pulled him away from Boone.

"You best change your arrogance in a hurry, or you'll find yourself wishing you had," Johnson said as he wrestled with English's arm.

English lowered his arms and relaxed the tension on his face. Without a word, he picked up an ax and saw, seized Pepper's reins, and trudged up the hill toward the fallen tree.

A rare balmy day boosted our spirits and offered a reprieve from the constant battle with snow and cold winds. As the sun lowered in the sky, we rested from the labor of the day with an optimistic view that our salt-making mission had progressed as designed. We made about ten bushels a day and about one hundred fifty bushels since the operation began. The three hunters, Boone, Wade, and Flanders Callaway, all labored at cleaning their rifles. Callaway was Boone's son-in-law, having married Jemima Boone in the last year. Several of us chopped and gathered firewood and tended a buffalo steak as it roasted over the flames. Sam English sat by himself, leaning against a tree with closed eyes.

"The hunters did well today, bringin' us this buffalo," remarked Humphries.

"Yeah, we're fortunate. This was the only thing we saw today we could shoot at," stated Wade, as he leaned his rifle against a tree, then moved closer to the fire while Flanders and Boone continued to clean their rifles.

English rose and moved into the shadow of a tree, near where Wade had been.

"Where'd you find the buffalo?" Ben asked.

"About two miles north of camp," Wade answered.

My eyes turned from where Boone, Wade, and Callaway stood to where English stood. He was aiming Wade's rifle. I grabbed and threw a rock at English and hollered, "Stop!" just as he pulled the trigger. Morton and Humphries, who were not far away from English, grabbed him. I turned my head in the direction of English's aim. There, thirty feet away, was Daniel Boone. English's shot knocked bark off a tree about eighteen inches from Boone.

Boone glared at English.

As Morton and Humphries held the man, Boone rushed over to English and said, "English, you just lost your freedom. You'll be tied to a tree all day long, every day, until this mission is completed. Then you'll return to the jail in Boonesborough."

"You look surprised," English replied. "Did you forget that I fight for the Crown? If I can kill the leader of the Kentucky frontier, I can help the British. You would be dead right now if someone hadn't thrown a rock at me just as I fired the rifle."

"Who threw the rock?" Boone inquired.

Humphries pointed at me. "Young Asbury, yonder."

Boone turned to me. "Daniel, I knew you were a fine soldier the first time I saw you. Thank you for your alert action."

"I'm just glad he missed and that you're still alive," I replied.

Boone turned his attention back to English. "Tie him to that tree yonder."

English glared at me until Humphries and Morton ushered him to his new jail by the tree.

The third week of our camp at Blue Licks, Daniel Boone announced, "By the end of today, we'll have enough salt made to send back to Boonesborough. Three of you'll pack up the salt and leave early tomorrow morning for Boonesborough. Today, Flanders, Asbury, and I will hunt and scout."

Boone turned to me. "Choose your horse, Daniel."

"I choose Pepper. He's my favorite," I said with a smile.

"Pepper's yours. I'll take Chestnut here."

Callaway, Boone, and I rode to the crest of the hill above the camp. We paused to gaze back at the camp, the fires ablaze and the pots boiling.

"You go south and east, farther upriver," Boone instructed Callaway. "Daniel and I will head north. Good luck."

"Right. And good luck to you," Flanders replied with an optimistic smile, turning his horse to the east.

With those parting words, we traveled toward our respective hunting grounds. Boone and I followed a buffalo trace heading north, then traveled along a stream. We tied off our horses and hiked along the stream another hundred yards.

Boone turned to me. "Let's sit over here by this bush and hide. Daniel, do you ever use deer calls when you go huntin'?"

"No, sir," I replied.

"In the winter, we're apt to get a buck. Call them by making a snort sound. Put your teeth together, then press your lips together and blow through them, making a kind of buzzin' sound. Like this: *buzzzz*," Boone explained.

"OK, like this? . . . *buzzz.*"

"Yes, that's close. When you see the deer, wait 'til he is not looking toward you, then make that sound. But not often. Let's separate. You stay here, and I'll go over near that rock," Boone said, pointing toward a large rock above the creek.

He trotted up to his hiding place, and we waited for a deer. Every half hour or so, Boone would make his deer call. After a couple of hours, we moved upstream and found a new place to wait. Boone made his deer call, then I added my version intermittently, not convinced I had called a deer. After another couple of hours, I spotted a six-point buck. I waited and then sounded my deer call again. Boone pointed to me and gave a short nod. I breathed deeply and raised my rifle. I gave my deer call again and the buck moved closer. He was close enough to take my shot. I took aim. My shot sounded through the valley, and the buck stumbled back—I hit him. But he ran. We both raced after him, following his trail of blood. We chased him, staying low and behind cover. He leapt over the creek, then ran up the valley, turned to climb to the crest of a hill but paused for an instant. Boone had already taken aim. His shot hit the deer midway between his eye and ear, dropping him to the ground.

Boone smiled and shook his fist in celebration. I shouted, "You got him!"

As we climbed the hill to retrieve our deer, I admired Boone's marksmanship and skill as a hunter. However, I stared at the ground as we walked and slowly shook my head. Boone's skill revealed my ineptness. Though I hit the deer, I did not drop him to the ground. The deer suffered and might have suffered more if Boone had not shot him in the head. Boone's example became my aspiration.

We skinned and dressed out the deer as darkness descended. Boone took a moment in the darkness on the crest of the hill to look around for Indian campfires. Satisfied that there were none, we retrieved our horses and made camp near a spring.

As he took his knife and extracted the heart from the carcass, Boone said, "To celebrate our success, we're having roasted heart cutlets tonight." He sliced the heart into smaller pieces and then poked two sharpened green sticks through the cutlets for roasting. While waiting for our supper to cook, we constructed a lean-to, with the open end facing the fire and the sloped side, covered with pine branches, facing the wind.

Then Boone said, "Tonight's a beautiful clear night, but you never know when a storm can blow in and make things uncomfortable. It also helps to hide the light of our fire on this side."

As we enjoyed the roasted venison, Boone said, "Tell me 'bout your family back in Virginia. Bedford County, is it?"

"Yes, our farm's about five miles out of New London. Moved there about ten years ago from Fairfax. There's my Ma and Pa, then I have six sisters and two brothers. My oldest brother, George, served in the Continental Line in Pennsylvania. He's twenty-two. My other brother, James, is only ten. My oldest sister, Elizabeth, is twenty-four. She was to be married this past November. I wish I could have been there. My other sisters all live at home and help on the farm. Then, of course, there's Rex, my dog. He is the best cow dog you ever saw. I don't have to lift a finger to round up those cows. All I have to say is: 'Go bring the cows home, Rex.' And he brings them in."

"Why did you join the militia, Daniel?"

"My father was drafted, but if he left the whole family would be in danger. I went in his place. Besides, I wanted to get away and see the world. See the wilderness."

"I love the wilderness, but it is also dangerous," Boone replied. "My oldest boy was about your age when he died. About five years ago, a group of us first attempted to settle Kentucky. Because travel over the mountains was slow, I sent my son James and others back for supplies. They had near made it back when some Delaware and Shawnee ambushed and murdered them. Losing James was the hardest thing I ever dealt with. I think about him every day. Given the Indian threats we figured it best not to continue into Kentucky. They took Jemima two years ago, but we were able to retrieve her before they got over the Ohio River. It can be a hard and hazardous life livin' in the wilderness. But I do love it out here."

"Yes, it's much harder than I ever imagined. My family tried to warn me, but I was determined to get away from Bedford County and see the world. I was ready to make my own decisions, rather than just following what Ma and Pa said."

"Well, I understand that, Daniel, but there'll be plenty of time for you to be on your own."

"Captain Boone, have you ever been captured by Indians?" I asked.

"Aye, a couple of times. The first time, my sister's husband, John Stewart, and I were robbed of our furs and horses, but let go with a warning never to come back to Kentucky. John and I went right back after 'em to get our horses. During the night, we stole 'em back, but two days later they re-captured us. They held us for 'bout a week while traveling back to their villages above the Ohio. But one night, before we got to the river, we escaped."

"Wow. I would've never tried to get the horses back, but I admire you for tryin'. I'm glad you got away."

"I'm glad too," Boone responded with a smile. "Another time, while exploring Kentucky alone, six Shawnee cornered me against a cliff overlooking a small river. The lone way to escape was to leap off the cliff, some sixty feet above the ground. Being captured was not a notion I gave much pleasure and might mean death. So, I jumped. Landed in a small sugar maple tree. The small limbs let me down nice and easy to the ground. I swam across the stream and was soon out of sight," Boone chuckled. "They didn't follow me."

"That was a daring escape. I wouldn't have followed you either. Have you ever had to fight an Indian?" I asked.

"Aye to that also. But I am not an Indian hater. The Indians are just tryin' to keep their lands for hunting and living, so their attacks are understandable. Some are noble and fair, and show mercy, trying to avoid bloodshed. Others are violent and cruel. Same with Americans. Same with the British. I always try to treat them with honesty and fairness and to do what is right in each situation. I don't seek revenge on one man for the cruelty of another. My dream is that we Americans could live in the wilderness at peace with the Indians. I'm afraid there's too much greed, distrust, and fear for that to happen."

Boone reached into his pack and pulled out a book. He lay close to the fire so he could read.

"What are you reading?" I asked him.

"I'm reading one of my favorite books. My folks taught me to read from the Bible. It gives me comfort. God's everywhere, even out here in the wilderness, maybe more so, if that can be.

"My mother's religious, but my Pa's not. I don't think about God much," I replied. "What part are you reading now?"

"Psalm 23, 'The LORD is my shepherd; I shall not want. He maketh me to lie down in green pastures: he leadeth me beside the still waters.' I read that Psalm often when I am out on a hunt. My other favorite book is *Gulliver's Travels*. I'll read that one to you next time."

With that, I put another log on the fire and wrapped up in my blanket to sleep. There was no moon, but thc stars were a brilliant sight, as though they wanted to speak their secrets to the world but were hushed by the silence of the winter night, disturbed only by the howl of a distant wolf, the occasional rustle of a bare tree limb in a gentle breeze, and the crackle of a dying campfire.

February 8, 1778, Sunday, started out quiet and sunny. It was midday, and we reclined on our blankets, warmed by the sun, despite six inches of snow on the ground. The rising water flooded the springs and caused a temporary halt to salt making.

"Here comes Captain Boone," Wade called out. "He's got Indians with him."

I reached for my rifle as Humphries raised his.

Boone lifted both hands and yelled, "Don't shoot! If you do, all will be slaughtered!"

I stood up. A line of Indians walked single file behind Boone into our camp. The line included Chief Blackfish and a black man named Pompey, who had lived among the Shawnee many years. Over a hundred warriors filed into our camp and surrounded us.

Boone stood before us. "They captured me yesterday. Chief Blackfish has promised not to kill us, but only if we surrender without a fight. Stack your guns over by that tree. Our choices are fight and be killed or surrender and survive."

"I don't want to die today," Wade said. "Let's do as Captain says."

Despite Wade's sentiment, no one moved. What had Boone done to us? We trusted him as our leader and now we were captured. What did this capture mean? Slavery? Death? Then, with pained faces and shaking heads we each dropped our rifles in the snow by the tree.

"They seek revenge for the murder of Cornstalk," Boone explained. "They already knew you were here, and they wanted to kill us all and then attack Boonesborough. I negotiated our surrender and convinced them it would be better to take Boonesborough in the spring."

Three dogs scampered into our camp. One of them had the same color and similar markings as Rex. Several of the Indians approached us with smiles, shook our hands, and said, "howdy-do." Many of the Ohio Indians knew the basic greetings in

English. The Indians motioned for us to move away from our campfire and sit under an oak tree. Armed with rifles and tomahawks, they surrounded us. The dog that resembled Rex wandered near us. I held out my arms to beckon him. He strutted toward me, and I wrapped my arms around his neck. He licked my cheek, and I dared a slight smile. An Indian wacked my arms with the butt of his rifle to separate us.

The Indians gathered in a circle around the fire and sat on the ground. Boone was allowed to join them. One by one, different speakers rose to their feet and made passionate speeches. The tall and muscular Pompey sat beside Boone and whispered to him as each warrior spoke. I assumed he was translating and wished I could hear. The Indians spoke with great passion and displayed their anger toward us. Others spoke with no hint of anger, but instead displayed welcoming gestures. Blackfish motioned for Boone to speak. Boone rose and stood in the middle of the circle. Pompey stood beside him and interpreted. As Boone spoke, the gravity of our situation became clear, like a wildcat that emerges from the shadows on the path in front of you.

> Shawnee Brothers! I can accomplish my pledge to you later in the spring when the weather is warm, allowing the women and the young children of Boonesborough to journey to the Shawnee towns. Then we can live together as one people. You have captured my men. If you kill them, as some of you propose, then the Great Spirit will be unhappy. Then you could not anticipate victory in either hunting or battle. If you show mercy to them, they will protect and defend your towns from those that threaten you, and will make superb hunters to provide food for your women and children. These men have not threatened you. They were occupied in peaceful endeavors and surrendered to you when I advised them that no harm would come to them. I agreed to their surrender on the condition that

> they be treated favorably as your prisoners. I urge you, as fellow human beings, to spare them. If you do, the Great Spirit will be pleased with you.

I gasped for my breath. It was either be a captive or die. Those words whacked like a judge pronouncing my sentence. Neither choice was a desirable fate—both seemed dark, dreadful, and hopeless. Even so, I knew which one I hoped for.

Boone and Pompey returned to their seats in the circle. Blackfish rose and stood in the center of the circle of 120 warriors. He spoke a few words and called upon each man to declare his vote. Twenty-six of us captive defendants sat under our oak tree as our captors debated and now voted to decide our fate. One by one, Blackfish called a warrior's name, and the warrior announced his vote. The first few warriors voted: "*Nepoowe*." Ben made a mark on the ground for that vote. Others voted "*lenawewi*!" This went on, Ben tallying votes between the two unknown words, and it drove me crazy not knowing which was which. The knowledge that many votes were for our death was like an arrow to the heart. The voting process was like a long, drawn-out snuffing of a candle. The memory of my family's hugs before I left for Kentucky and Ma's loving prayer for me flooded my mind. Tears trickled down my cheek. I fought to hold the tears back. Silent faces surrounded me. A drop of sweat fell from Wade's chin. A tear ran down Ben's face as he continued to tally the votes. Some hid their faces, heads bowed between their knees. We faced death but were powerless to fight for our lives. The vote proceeded around the circle until the last two warriors.

Ben whispered, "The vote is 59 to 59."

The next warrior voted: "*lenawewi*." Then the last warrior: "*lenawewi*."

The vote was 61 to 59. But which was it?

The warriors arose from their seats and gathered around us.

They smiled. They shook our hands. They slapped our backs and said, "Welcome," and "We brothers."

We were to live. We were to become Shawnees, adopted into the tribe.

Time in Captivity: 1 Day

CHAPTER SIX

THE GAUNTLET

EARLY FEBRUARY 1778

Boone made his way through the crowd to us. "Men, we were one horsehair away from meetin' our Maker. For those of you who're religious, you might offer a prayer of thanks. We'll be adopted into their tribe. They might sell some of us to the British. Gather up your things and prepare to march. We face a several-days trek in snow, north to the Shawnee towns across the Ohio River."

Rex's look-alike trotted toward me. I knelt and wrapped my arms around his neck. "Hello, friend. I'm gonna call you Buddy."

The Indians got busy gathering the plunder of our camp, including large kettles, guns, axes, and some of the salt we had made. They scattered the rest of the salt on the ground. It was too much to carry all of it, but they did not want the Americans to have what was left. As I hoisted up my pack, a warrior shoved a large iron kettle at English. English thrust it right back at the Indian with a force that knocked him down. The Shawnee warrior lunged at English with his tomahawk raised. Boone rushed over to English, seized his arms, and stared him in the eye. "If you don't pick it up, you'll be killed."

Scowling, English shook free of Boone's grasp and bent down to retrieve the pot.

One of the Shawnees came up to me and spoke. He was short, his hair was graying, and he walked with a slight limp. His left eye stood still when his right eye moved. He pointed to his chest, "*Skesaquey*." I took that to be his name. He spoke again, pointing to me.

I said "Daniel."

He shook his head and repeated "*Skesaquey*" pointing at my mouth.

"Oh, *Skesaquey*," I said and pointed at him.

He nodded. "Yes." He pointed to me. "You."

"Daniel."

"Daniel," he repeated.

I nodded.

Skesaquey grabbed my pack from my arms and searched through its contents. He retrieved the quill and ink. He examined them and then placed them in his own pack. It was as if he were taking my family away from me. I wanted to snatch them back but knew better. At least he left the pack of paper. He also took my knife—not the knife from the dead Shawnee since I now wore that knife.

Pompey, who stood nearby, approached us and spoke to *Skesaquey*. He turned to me and said, "I see you have met *Skesaquey*. He can be ornery. His name means Crooked Eyes, because his left eye doesn't move. Do what he says and you will survive."

"Thank you," I responded and then he left.

We marched that day, each soldier placed between two Shawnee. Each of us had a Shawnee guard assigned to him. Crooked Eyes was mine.

When we stopped to make camp, several Indians started clearing a path in the snow about a hundred yards long. Daniel

Boone and Blackfish, with Pompey, stood beside the clearing. I walked over to listened to their conversation.

"We made this clearing for the gauntlet," explained Blackfish via Pompey's translation.

Boone sounded perplexed. "You agreed that my men wouldn't have to run the gauntlet."

"This gauntlet is not for your men." Pompei translated for Blackfish. "This gauntlet is for you." Blackfish pointed at Boone's chest. "When we captured you, we made no such agreement."

Boone jerked his head back and winced, though he said nothing. He accepted the challenge.

The Indians lined up on both sides of the path, each holding a club, stick, or tomahawk. Boone stripped to his deerskin shirt, leggings, and moccasins and crouched in a running position. Pompey kicked Boone in the rear, signaling the start of the gauntlet. He shot down the lines as fast as he could. He moved toward one side to limit the range of their swings, then switched to the other side. One tomahawk blow hit Boone on the forehead, staggering him and drawing blood. Near the end of the line, Crooked Eyes stood in the middle, between the lines, ready to deliver a whopping hit. Boone came at him full force, lowered his head behind both forearms, and hit Crooked Eyes square in the chest, knocking him over on his back, passing over him unhurt. The Indians erupted into a celebration of Boone's "victory." They clapped and raised their arms. They shook Boone's hand and said "good sojer."

Many of the warriors even ran over to us and shook our hands.

Some pointed at Crooked Eyes, still lying on the ground, and said, "*Quiawaw* (woman)."

Crooked Eyes kept his vigilant right eye on me. I celebrated Boone's success in silence. Being careful not to upset Crooked Eyes.

The warriors built a fire and distributed food to the captives. Ben's guard, whose name was Ran in Thorns, gave him a sizable morsel of buffalo meat. Ran in Thorns was a tall, muscular man of middle age. He seemed to have the respect of his fellow warriors, including Crooked Eyes. He treated Ben with kindness.

I sat next to Andew Johnson as I was anticipating my own much-needed morsel. Crooked Eyes sat down next to me with a handful of meat and proceeded to eat the whole thing in front of me. Upon finishing, he yelled some Shawnee words at me. After Crooked Eyes walked away, Boone took his place and handed me a small portion of his allotted meal.

"Much obliged, Captain" I said. "But don't you need it?"

"No," replied Boone. "They gave me a very big portion. I don't want any of my men to go without." He then left to talk to Wade.

"That was kind of Boone to share his supper," whispered Johnson as he leaned toward me. "Keep this between me and you. I'm gonna trick these Indians. I intend to act like a simpleton and a fool, so they won't guard me closely. When I sense they've stopped watching me, then I'm gonna high tail it back to Boonesborough."

"Do you really think you can fool them?"

"Shushh. Not so loud," whispered Johnson. "Yeah, and you can help by laughing and playing along with me, when you can." Johnson moved to the other side of the fire.

I sought out Humphries, who sat in silence eating his portion of food.

"So sorry this has happened," I said. "There's no way to get word to your wife."

"Yeah. But that's true for all of us. Who knows how long before we can escape."

"Maybe Captain Boone can help us," I said. "He's been captured before and escaped."

"I sure hope so."

Crooked Eyes returned and stood by me. As I considered the day's unfortunate events, Buddy came to me nuzzling my arm. I wrapped my arms around his neck for all the comfort I could extract. I glanced at Crooked Eyes and caught his disapproving glare, sapping the joy of Buddy's presence.

When bedtime came, the warriors tied buffalo-hide ropes to our wrists. After tying my arms, Crooked Eyes jerked the ropes so they cut into my wrists. I cried out, and Crooked Eyes made a satisfied nod. He tied each rope to a tree, making me lie on my back with my arms outstretched. A warrior lay on each side of us, on top of the ropes. They were free to move or change sleeping positions during the night, while we had to sleep on our backs without moving. I lay on my back that night and gazed at the bright moon and stars. I contemplated the consequences of the day's calamity. That morning, I woke up a soldier serving my country. That night, I lay down a captive of a strange people who spoke a strange language. I was not prepared for such a change. But here I was facing it. It was like Boone's story of standing at a cliff edge surrounded by Indians, except that freedom was not in front of me. Only the unknown. What would life among these people be like? Could I eat their food? Would I be enslaved? Would I become a callous brute like Crooked Eyes? Would I ever see my mother, father, brothers, sisters, and Rex again?

The next morning, a familiar but forgotten sensation awakened me. Buddy licked my face. Crooked Eyes untied my arms without inflicting additional pain. Arising, I took a deep breath to muster strength for the day's march. Then, the laughter of the Indians demanded my attention. Andrew Johnson, his arms stretched in front of him, walked in circles as though he did not know what to do or where to go. An Indian gave him a pack to carry. Another placed a pot in his arms. Another grabbed his shoulders and pointed him in the direction of our march. All the

Shawnees laughed. They received a great deal of amusement from Johnson's display of simpleton-like behavior. To us Americans, Andrew Johnson was no simpleton.

Then, a warrior shoved a huge, heavy kettle into Ansel Goodman's belly. Goodman yelled, "No, no, no."

The warrior cocked his tomahawk, ready to strike. Goodman responded by taking off his hat and leaning forward, presenting his neck as a target. "Here, chop my head off. I would rather lie here dead than tote your kettle."

The warrior backed away and lowered his tomahawk. The warrior probably calculated that the British would pay more for Goodman as a live prisoner than for his scalp.

When we left the campsite, two Indians and Goodman took a different trail that led to the west. I found out later that the Indians had left some of their gear at another location and were going to retrieve it before heading back to their village across the Ohio.

We marched northward, chasing our shadows, as the sun beat upon our backs—and a north wind whipped against our faces. About the noon hour, we stopped to rest. I fell to the ground in exhaustion and hunger. There was no food, or at least, not enough for 147 of us.

Boone explained to several of us, "You can eat bark. Cut a piece of bark from this elm tree and eat the soft stringy innerds. That's gonna give you loose bowels, but you can reduce those effects by eating oak bark, like this one here," and pointed to a large oak tree. "It ain't your mother's roast beef, but it'll keep you alive."

They had taken our guns but not our knives. So we cut off some bark. I cleared the snow from a rock, sat down, and held my pathetic meal. Buddy pranced up with a mouse struggling to get free. He sat in the snow beside me and we ate together. It was awful. Probably the worst "food" I had ever eaten, but gulped it down with the hope that it would keep me alive. I placed my arm around Buddy's neck. That lasted but a moment as Crooked Eyes came from behind, kicked my arm away from Buddy and yelled in Shawnee. Buddy turned on Crooked Eyes, barking and showing his teeth. Buddy fixed his teeth around his ankle. I rushed over, pulled Buddy away, and told him, "No." Crooked Eyes turned away.

We continued our march as the temperature dropped, the sun hidden by clouds, and the north wind continued to blow. Our moccasins were a poor fit for a march in the snow. My feet became wet, cold, and numb. Buddy frequently walked by my side, which made me smile despite the circumstances.

I awoke to a snowflake landing on my cheek on the morning of the third day after our capture. I lay there weak, my belly aching for sustenance. From where would the energy come for the day's grind through the snow? Bam. Crooked Eyes stomped on my stomach and shouted at me. I did not need a translator.

The snow fell soundlessly on Crooked Eyes' hat and the pack on his back as I followed him in our line of Shawnees and patriots, trudging and slipping in the snow. As I focused on his pack, an observation hit me like a hammer: he carried no rifle. All the Indians possessed rifles supplied by the British. Some also carried bows, but all lugged a rifle. Crooked Eyes' bow was long, stout, and polished. He carried two quivers of arrows.

By noon, the snowfall grew so thick that I could not see beyond six feet in front of me. The north wind pierced our deer hide pants and coats, threatening to freeze our feet and hands. We stopped to rest and eat tree bark. After eating some bitter bark, I wandered farther off the trail and knelt in over a foot of snow. I scooped up several handfuls and ate, holding it in my mouth letting it melt, then swallowing my drink.

Travel was slow as the snow deepened and the cold taxed our

strength. We stopped for the night next to a large rock with a wide flat face. The Shawnee warriors built a fire next to the rock face, kindling my hopes that a cooked meal would soon follow. I sat down on a rock and warmed my feet between my hands.

A gunshot sounded, followed by the yelp of a dog. Had the Shawnee killed one of their dogs? Then I heard another yelp but no gunshot. Crooked Eyes soon appeared, with his eyes focused on me and his mouth in a grim smile. He held his bow and a bloody arrow. I scanned our group for a sign of Buddy, but only found another dog. Only one of the three dogs was visible, and it was not Buddy. As the aroma of the fire and a meal drifted toward me, a sickening realization struck me like a punch to my gut. As I caught the aroma of fire and meat, I felt nauseous. I wanted to fall to the ground and weep. I wanted to go over to the man that shot Buddy and whack him in the head with the butt of a gun. I knew it was Crooked Eyes. But his vigilant stare tied me in place.

Soon Crooked Eyes walked up to me with a nice portion of meat and said, with a wicked grin. "Eat."

I took it from him, knowing a refusal would be met with a thrashing. I sat down on my pack and held it, thinking of Buddy and how much enjoyment his company had given me. I could not eat my friend. Buddy had defended me from Crooked Eyes. However, in a sense, he sacrificed his life so I could live. So, I ate meditating on Buddy's loyalty. The tears pricked behind my eyes, but I did not let them fall.

The sixth day brought sunshine and a southwesterly breeze. The promise of the sunshine was soon dampened by Crooked Eyes kicking me in the rear. After a three-hour march, we entered a clearing, and all the Indians put down their packs. Just beyond, I could see a large body of water: the Ohio. We were at the mouth of Limestone Creek as it entered the Ohio. I strode up to the muddy shore, smelled the air, and sensed the cool breeze in my face. The wind blew against the current of the mighty Ohio, giving rise to waves and white caps. The Ohio was larger than the James, the New, and the Kentucky Rivers, maybe greater than all three combined.

The Indians shot a large buck, one of the heftiest I had ever seen. Crooked Eyes hit him first with an arrow. They launched into skinning, slicing, and cooking. They separated out the intestines and boiled them into a jelly.

Crooked Eyes took some of the boiled jelly and offered some to Boone, with a smile and a motion of taking his hand to his mouth. Then he spoke in Shawnee.

"He says you must eat the jelly before you eat the meat," Pompey explained. "He says it will kill you if you do not eat the jelly first."

Boone took the jelly from Crooked Eyes and gulped it down, immediately spewing it out, to the laughter of all the Shawnee.

Crooked Eyes brought Boone some more jelly, again with a hand-to-mouth motion.

They offered it to all of us captives, with the same hurling result. They would not give us any venison until we kept the jelly down. With distorted faces and repeated retches, we managed to keep some down and eat our meager share of venison. Within an hour, that great buck was a skeleton. Split one hundred and fifty ways, my portion was not sizable, but it was more than I had eaten the previous five days.

While some Shawnee hunted and cooked, others prepared our transportation across the river. They uncovered a large canoe frame and stretched four large buffalo hides to cover its hull.

Twenty men with their packs caused the canoe to float low in the water. The wind was brisk against the current, resulting in white caps and a spray of river water into our faces. As the warriors paddled us toward the center of the river, a large wave splashed bitter cold water into my face. I gripped the canoe's gunwales as if that would help keep the canoe afloat. Crooked

Eyes poked me with his paddle and then motioned for me to cup my hands and scoop water from the canoe. All the non-paddlers bailed water as wave after wave splashed into the canoe. The cold water numbed my hands. We reached the north side of the Ohio and scurried out of the canoe so two Indians could return for the next load of passengers.

The Indians with us hunted and built a fire. The last load crossed as the sun set. We all had a bite to eat from the success of the hunters' efforts. We sat around the fire in silence until Ben asked, "Captain, do Indians really burn people at the stake?"

Boone thought for a moment. "Yes. But usually as an act of revenge. Don't worry, Chief Blackfish appears to be on our side, and I'll argue against it if it comes up."

With the moon and stars shining in the dark sky, we began our nighttime and sleeping ritual. Lying on the cold hard ground, I thought of Buddy. I was powerless to save him, yet his sacrifice kept me alive. Buddy had befriended me during this dark time, but I was powerless to save him. Would I survive this gauntlet of the ordeal of captivity? Would I be burned at the stake, or sold to the British and imprisoned? Would I ever see my family again or taste my mother's chicken stew? After hours, I fell into a restless sleep.

On the fourth day after crossing the Ohio, we arrived at Chillicothe, a Shawnee town located on the Little Miami River. I was weak from the lack of food and the arduous trek through bitter winter weather. Chillicothe offered the promise of rest and food, but it could not remove the dark clouds of captivity.

Time in Captivity: 10 Days

CHAPTER SEVEN

AN OLD INDIAN CHIEF AND HIS WIFE

MID-FEBRUARY 1778

The Shawnee of Chillicothe welcomed their returning victorious warriors. They came out in large numbers, about two hundred, from their corn fields, from their campfires and wigwams, and from their washing in the river. Not one of them was lost and when they saw us captives, they smiled and raised their hands in celebration. Chillicothe greeted both warriors and captives with food—hominy, corn cakes, and boiled venison. After traveling ten days through snow with little sustenance, this was a scrumptious banquet.

Our first night in Chillicothe, I was shocked that we could sleep untethered. They gave us freedom to roam through town or walk to the river. No longer did guards watch us constantly. Boone explained that they thought we would get lost if we tried to escape. Though some things improved, Crooked Eyes still guarded me from a distance with his suspicious glances, and a dark clouded future still haunted my thoughts.

The wigwams were huts built of small logs and bark, each with a chimney and a door. There was a large rectangular council house where they held frequent village meetings. An enormous maple tree stood near the council house with its barren branches coated with snow.

On the morning of the third day, Boone gathered us together. "The people here at Chillicothe met last night to determine who'd be adopted and who would be sold to the British."

"Sold to the British?" shouted Humphries. "I'd much rather live with the Indians. The British are brutal toward their prisoners."

"We should all be adopted by the Shawnee," Johnson said.

"They don't give us a vote," Boone answered. He then read off the seventeen names of those being adopted, which included me, Ben Kelly, Ansel Goodman, Andrew Johnson, Arabia Brown, and himself. Those to be sold included John Brown, Richard Wade, William Humphries, James Morton, and Samuel English.

"No!" shouted John Brown.

Wade spat on the ground but said nothing.

English said nothing, but smiled.

"Those going to the British will travel to Detroit in a couple of weeks," Boone continued. "For those adopted, a necessary part of the custom is to run the gauntlet. Even though they promised me you wouldn't have to, the village people are insistin' on it. Since I ran it back on the trail, I don't have to. Steel your nerves for it. After that, you'll meet your new parents."

I sought solitude. I followed a trail to the river, sat on a flat rock, and leaned against a maple tree. Memories of my family filled my thoughts—Ma, Pa, Elizabeth, Molly, Patsy, Genny, Sally, Nancy, George, and James. Would I ever see them again? That question came to me like the sound of a galloping horse in the distance that grew louder and louder as the horse approached. The pain of that question started small, scarcely perceptible, but grew as I remembered Ma's daily prayers for me, Pa saving me from the mama bear, Elizabeth cutting my hair with such care, and laughing and playing with my sisters and brothers. Tears flowed down my cheeks. I cupped my hand over my mouth to muffle my bawling.

I must have cried for half an hour when Captain Boone came up beside me and put his arm around my shoulders, "Do you miss your family, son?"

I nodded.

"Me too," he continued. "What's happened is dang dreadful. But you may still see them again. Keep your head up. My advice to all of us who're being adopted is to fully embrace the life we've been given. Win the trust of your families and the entire tribe. Give 'em no reason to be suspicious. Enjoy your life among the Shawnee. It's better than a British prison, and it's better than death. Do that, and you can walk out of here whenever you want. Keep your head up and your eyes open. When you find the right opportunity, pounce on it, and never look back. I promise you . . . " Boone waited for me to look him in the eye, then said, "The day for your escape *will* come."

The pain in my chest eased ever so slightly, and the tears stopped flowing. I swallowed. "Thank you, sir." I met his gaze and gave him a half-smile.

"Let's go back and meet your new family," he instructed. We rose and walked back. My attention shifted toward the challenge of the gauntlet and who my new family would be.

The whole town—men, women, and children—gathered in a large field, lined up in two rows about six feet apart with their clubs and tomahawks ready. Ben was the first to run. He got about a third of the way down the line, then ran toward the right line and knocked down two Indians, who then tumbled down a bank. The Shawnee laughed and cheered that he completed his run and suffered only minor injuries. Five others took their turns at the gauntlet, receiving serious blows and even broke bones, but they completed their runs.

My turn came next. I readied myself, stomach tight and palms sweaty. I peered straight down the gauntlet to the finish. Someone smacked me on my behind, and I launched my race. A boy, maybe ten years old, took the first swing and struck me in the belly, but I stayed on my feet. Next, a large, middle-aged woman whacked me in the legs and knocked me down. Two girls pounced on me and pulled my hair, to the amusement of all. I emerged from the pile and dragged one of the girls as she clung to my leg. I charged forward, shaking her loose. I aimed for the finish. Crooked Eyes was up ahead, clutching his tomahawk in striking position, prepared to wallop me. I raced on, though slowed by the blows of sticks and clubs. I calculated my strategy and moved over to Crooked Eyes' side of the line. Before I reached him, and well out of range of his tomahawk, I halted long enough for Crooked Eyes to swing and miss. I accelerated again and pulled even with him as he finished his swing, and pushed him, knocking him off balance, causing him to fall to the ground. This made everyone—except Crooked Eyes—laugh heartily. Just a few more whacks and I finished the gauntlet. As I caught my breath, I felt the sting of the blows and limped slightly, but was grateful to finish.

After the gauntlet, those of us being adopted gathered under a great oak tree. The village people surrounded us. Blackfish gave a speech for all to hear, though there was no interpreter for the captives. After the speech, two or three Indians gathered around each adoptee. An Indian and his wife approached me. The man was large, over six feet tall, and the woman was short, less than five feet tall. They were older than most Indians, perhaps in their mid-sixties. Their faces wore many wrinkles and folds in their rough skin, perhaps a reflection of years of hardship, suffering, and pain. Both had beautiful gray hair. The manner and tone of their voices were gentle, in contrast to Crooked Eyes. There was kindness in their eyes.

The man's name was *Wyapeteet*, or Kicking Elk, and the woman's was *Metsemeewaapanwi*, or Morning Moon. I introduced myself, but after they struggled to pronounce "Daniel," they pointed to me and said in turn, "*Nahashamo*." That was the name they had given me.

"*Nahashamo*." I repeated. "*Nahashamo*." I soon learned my new name meant "White Chief."

They nodded their heads several times, smiling back at me.

Now that we had met our adoptive families, other Indians made us sit on the ground. One warrior held me; another warrior dipped his fingers in ash on a piece to bark. He grabbed a small lock of my hair and yanked.

"Owwww," I screamed, while the other warrior continued to hold me.

He yanked again until he pulled it out. I winced and grunted. This continued and eventually my scalp went numb and he left only a lock of hair on the crown of my head. This, he braided and stuck silver jewelry in. Then he took a large needle like instrument and moved his hands toward my face. I jerked back and held up my arms in front of my face. Then the women intervened by motioning with hands to assure me it was what was expected and I should let the warrior proceed. They bored through my nose and ears and placed earrings and nose jewelry on me. I preferred not to wear nose and earrings but my goal was to win their trust so I let them proceed. Then the young women of the tribe motioned us down to the river. They reached for my shirt and removed it. Then they took hold of my breeches and I again I jumped back, not understanding their intentions. The women were all smiles and were determined to have their way. I looked at the other captives and they were being stripped too. I bit my lip and allowed them to proceed. Stripped, the women led us down to the river until we were waist deep. Though the weather was warm for late February, the water was frigid. They scrubbed me with European soap, then plunged me under water to rinse, and scrubbed and rinsed again. I was never so clean.

My new mother met me on the riverbank with new clothes. Kicking Elk and Morning Moon lead me to their home: a domed wigwam constructed with a dozen wooden poles and tree bark. There was a fire in the center and an opening in the roof to let the smoke escape. We had a tasty meal of stew cooked over the outdoor firepit.

My adopted parents dressed me in the finest of Shawnee clothing, decorated with red beads and silver buckles. They gave me a breechcloth, a buckskin shirt that extended below my waist, and buckskin gaiters reaching above the knee. Morning Moon draped a red and black blanket over my shoulders, then secured it with a belt made of tree bark. She placed new moccasins on my feet. Kicking Elk placed on my head a small round grey hat with a red feather stuck in it. Lastly, they painted my face with red and black paint. I did not know how to respond. I was surprised at their generosity.

The town of Chillicothe filled the council house, everyone dressed in their finest clothes. As we sat down on bearskins, they handed each adoptee a tomahawk, a pipe, and a small pouch containing flint, steel, and some tobacco. Everyone was silent as we smoked our pipes. I sat in this silence, impressed by the unity of the solemn faces around me, all embracing the significance of adding new members to their community. I felt important and valued and momentarily forgot my harsh reality. Following everyone else's example, I stuffed some tobacco in the pipe and lit it. I watched Captain Boone to see how he smoked, then gently brought the pipe to my lips and inhaled. I stifled choking coughs as the smoke hit the back of my throat and tried again. After a couple of tries, I managed to inhale without coughing.

Chief Blackfish rose and spoke, with bold and dramatic movements. He often pointed to us. He seemed to be telling the story of our capture. The Chillicothe villagers already knew the story, but they responded with jubilant applause and triumphant gestures. Boone was smiling politely, so I did the same. Some of the other captives did not smile.

Blackfish spoke to the adoptees, with Pompey interpreting. "My brothers, today you are adopted into our family. We are of the same flesh, the same blood, and the same bones. Through this ceremony, all the white blood has been washed from your bodies. We receive you into the Shawnee nation." Blackfish spoke with his arms held high and wide. His voice rose and fell, and the sweat on his cheeks glistened in the firelight. He walked from one area to another as he examined the eyes of each adoptee. "You are adopted into our family, a great family, and we receive you with great soberness to be one with us, according to our law and customs. Do not be afraid. The Great Spirit requires us to love and fight for you as we love and fight for one another. We regard you as one of us, and you are to regard yourselves as one of our people."

Our circumstances of being taken under threat of death and held against our wills made this speech hard to accept. I thought of the many warriors that made passionate speeches in favor of killing us, and of Crooked Eyes rough treatment.

After the ceremony, I returned to my new home with my new parents. Kicking Elk pointed toward a bearskin on the ground, which I understood to mean this was my bed and a second bearskin served as my cover. Kicking Elk and Morning Moon lay on another bearskin on the other side of the fire.

I crawled under my bearskin, lay on my back with my hands behind my head, and gazed into the darkness. I exhaled as though I had held my breath all day. It was not so bad. No one threatened my life, my new parents provided for me, and I had a strategy to return to my family. My day began in tears but ended with a slight smile.

The familiar sound of a rooster crowing woke me. Daylight revealed ears of corn hanging above me on strings. Wooden bowls and spoons were set out by the fire, which heated iron kettles hung from a pole.

After offering me some cornbread, Kicking Elk motioned for me to follow him. He showed me the fields where the women planted corn, beans, and squash, and he introduced me to some young men, some about my age, some middle aged. A friendly dog, with light brown and white fur, pranced up to us. Kicking Elk knelt to receive her welcome with a smile and a hug.

Kicking Elk turned to me and acted out shooting a rifle, then put his hands on his head like antlers, yelled "pow," and fell over. I laughed despite myself, as did Kicking Elk. I nodded, hoping I had not misinterpreted his invitation to hunt.

Two of the men approached me. One of them, pointed to himself, said, "*Waneskahalawi.*" meaning Bold Hunter. The other pointed to himself and said, "*Cawwimeysa,*" which means Ran in Thorns. I recognized Ran in Thorns as Ben's guard, kinder and more reasonable than Crooked Eyes.

Then Bold Hunter called out, "*Wiikanwi,*" which means Honey. The dog scampered to him. Bold Hunter stooped down, wrapped his arm around her. I reached down, let her smell my hand, gave her a pat on her side.

Hopping to their feet, the men showed me things like a rifle, a powder horn, a bow, and an arrow and taught me their words for them. They patiently corrected my pronunciation until it was to their satisfaction. With that brief lesson, we headed out of town, everyone carrying a rifle except me. Kicking Elk stayed behind.

We hiked a trail for several miles through the forest. We crossed creeks and climbed hills. Bold Hunter pulled a deer hide from his pack and had Honey smell it. Honey trotted ahead, leading us off the trodden path through thick undergrowth. She stopped, frozen, and gazed straight ahead. Following Bold Hunter's lead, we knelt low in the briars while Bold Hunter and one other crept forward. The doe meandered into view. They raised their rifles and shot. The deer bolted through the forest, trailing blood. Honey took off after her, barking as she dashed around trees and leaped over rocks. We sprinted after them for a quarter of a mile. The deer paused by a large tree, and as she turned to run again, Bold Hunter fired another shot that dropped her.

The hunters jumped and whooped. They drew knives for field dressing and quartering the deer. Bold Hunter assigned portions for each of us to carry back to Chillicothe.

Upon our return laughter caught our attention. A group of Shawnee men and Americans had gathered around Andrew Johnson, who was called "Pecula," or "Little Duck." Pompey translated for the captives.

"Pecula, hit this target," said a Shawnee who hung a hat on a tree branch and mimicked a rifle shot.

Another handed Johnson a rifle, and he propped it on his arm, took a half-hearted aim, and pulled the trigger, missing not only the hat but the whole tree. The Shawnee roared with laughter.

"Which way is Kentucky?" Pompey translated a question.

Andrew walked in circles as he pondered the question, then pointed north. Again, they roared with laughter. "Little Duck" fooled them into believing he was a naïve and childlike fellow.

Boone, whose Shawnee name was *Sheltowee*, or "Big Turtle,"

stood in the crowd and spoke to further promote Johnson's ruse as Pompey translated, "Andrew Johnson is slightly crazy, but we like him and make sure he doesn't get himself lost or into situations that he'll hurt himself."

Andrew entertained his captors with his simpleton behavior and fooled them. However, sustaining that behavior in every circumstance over time is not something I could have succeeded at.

Johnson's entertainment was interrupted by the arrival of two Shawnee and Ansel Goodman, who was naked, loaded with bear meat, and singing. The two Indians with Goodman pushed him from behind as they laughed and yelled the Indian word for "Gauntlet." The villagers rushed to the field with their clubs and formed two lines. One kicked Goodman in the rear, and he fell and lay still. The two Shawnees picked him up and shouted at him. Goodman stumbled as he ran, weak and weighed down. Some strikes knocked him to the ground amid laughter and celebration. At the end, a blow on the head knocked him down. Then he rose, staggered to the end, and tumbled to the cold earth. Women of the village picked pieces of bear meat off him until he was left sprawled on the ground, naked. Then, to my wonder, an elderly Shawnee couple approached Goodman and spoke with him. They helped him sit up, wrapped him in a blanket and gave him a drink of water. After a few minutes, they helped him up and walked him to their house.

That night, there was another village meeting in the council house. I sat with my new father and mother on bearskins as we smoked our pipes. Then Blackfish spoke, though there was no interpreter. During his speech, he pointed to Boone and the captives that were not adopted. I learned later that Blackfish told the village that the ten captives who had not been adopted would be taken to the British up north. Boone was to travel with them.

After Blackfish, Bold Hunter spoke. He pointed to those of us that had gone hunting. The villagers laughed at his story. With his hands, Bold Hunter made the motion of shooting a rifle and killing a deer. He picked up Honey and cheered.

After the meeting, a family—father, mother, their adult daughter, and her infant son—chatted with Kicking Elk and Morning Moon. Kicking Elk ushered them toward me and smiled. The father was above average in height and a man of middle age. The man pointed to himself and said, "*Pemoutee*" (Long Stepper). The mother was shorter than the other women, with some gray in her hair. She pointed to herself and said, "*Wiilatomahawk*," (Uses Her Ax).

Their daughter's long, black hair partially concealed her face, but revealed a pleasant smile. She pointed to herself and said "*Wawpatheea*" (Gliding Swan), and then to her son, and said "*Ala-aqua*" (Rising Star).

Gliding Swan handed Rising Star to her mother and spoke with her hands, pointing toward the river, motioning washing herself and pointed at me. She pointed to herself. I took that to mean that she was one of the young women who had washed me before the adoption ceremony.

I chuckled nervously and tried to say, "*neawai*," which Boone had mentioned meant "thank you."

She moved a half step closer and pulled back her hair. There was kindness and sincerity in her voice, "I teach . . . speak . . . Shawnee."

I responded with a smile and full-sized nod and said, "Thank you. I would like that." I did not know if she understood.

Then, something jolted me. My heart beat increased. The dim firelight had not allowed me to detect it earlier. I suppose when she was washing the white off me, I was too preoccupied with the adoption rituals to notice it. Gliding Swan was a fine-looking young woman, with long black hair, smooth complexion, and a sparkle in her eyes. She smiled and turned to take back her son. As she walked away with her parents, my eyes lingered on her swishing hair.

Time in Captivity: 20 Days

CHAPTER EIGHT

AN ENCOUNTER WITH WOLVES

MARCH 1778

During the winter many Shawnee leave the village by family units to spend the cold months dispersed throughout their hunting grounds. As the first signs of spring appeared in March, those dispersed began to return to Chillicothe. Amidst the influx of people, ten salt-maker captives, Boone, Chief Blackfish, and an additional twenty Shawnee warriors gathered at the council house before they departed on their journey to the British town of Detroit. To my dark amusement, Crooked Eyes was assigned to Samuel English—a fitting arrangement for two ornery creatures. The Shawnee sold many of their captives to the British for a couple of blankets or silver trinkets for trading. The British also bought white scalps for half the price.

As the Shawnee and their captives receded into the forest, Bold Hunter greeted me. Through hand motions he invited me to go hunting. I nodded my head in agreement and then motioned that we needed to tell Kicking Elk and Morning Moon. He nodded as we both turned toward their house.

We gathered up some dried deer meat, blankets, two guns,

with powder and ammunition and tomahawks. I placed my Shawnee knife in its sheath and strapped it to my belt.

This was to be an overnight venture. Bold Hunter looked me in the eye and, with a pleasant smile, handed me a gun. I received the gun and returned his gaze with my own smile. "*Neawai*," I said, and knew I must prove myself trustworthy.

We hiked westward, Honey by our side, following a trail Bold Hunter knew well. We ascended hills and traversed streams, stopped for a moment for a drink and to eat some deer meat. Honey detected a scent and deviated from the trail. We followed her with our rifles loaded. Honey halted. There in the glade, two hundred elk grazed in the grass. We laid down our supplies, cocked our rifles, and walked toward them, avoiding the slightest disturbance of the underbrush around our legs. Bold Hunter pointed to the elk nearest to us, and I nodded. We raised our rifles. I aimed at the head. Bang! Bang! The herd darted, but our target only took a few steps before collapsing. We raised our rifles and shouted in triumph.

Without delay, we set aside our rifles and packs and pulled out our knives and tomahawks to skin and butcher the elk. After about forty minutes, Bold Hunter pointed at my knife and spoke Shawnee.

He recognized the knife. He must have known the Indian whom I killed on the Wilderness Road before we reached Boonesborough. I shrugged, feeling uncomfortable, and hoping it had not been anyone close to him.

A nearby ominous howl interrupted Bold Hunter. Honey barked and scampered toward the howl. Bold Hunter grabbed his rifle, powder horn, and lead balls, then bolted after Honey. In haste, I hacked the carcass with my tomahawk and slashed the meat with my knife. A multitude of howling wolves soon surrounded us. Bold Hunter fired. I gathered up the meat in the elk hide and threw my pack over my shoulders. Abandoning what remained of the carcass, I dragged the full elk skin over to

Bold Hunter and Honey. Honey barked, snarled, and growled, warding off the wolves.

Half of the pack tore into the carcass while the other half lunged at the hide full of meat. Honey barked, making them back off long enough for me to drop my bundle beside Bold Hunter, but the wolves kept their eyes on us. Bold Hunter shouted at me, but I did not understand. He made a motion of striking flint. I bolted into the woods and gathered an armful of small sticks and leaves from the ground, all of it still wet. I struck the flint and steel, showering the soggy pile with sparks repeatedly to no effect. Daylight was waning quickly now. Bold Hunter shot another wolf.

The wolves' snarls and the scrape of teeth on bone assaulted my ears as I kept striking. I looked over my shoulder and saw the last of twilight reflect in their eyes as they turned to us. I remembered the moment the mother bear charged me and wondered if this time, I would lose my life. I struck the flint again and the sparks held. I gently blew on it, a small puff of smoke rising from the tinder. I blew again, and a couple small tongues of flame appeared. My heart pounding, I tried to remain calm as I gently placed small twigs over the fledgling fire. At last, the flames grew to about ten inches high. It was not enough to keep the wolves away but gave us hope that the fire would soon blaze. The wet wood took an excruciatingly long time to catch, and the wolves seemed bigger and hungrier every minute. Finally, I placed some choice dry wood on the fire and blew hard at the flames. My blaze grew to about half my height. The wolves backed away, but the howls were unceasing.

We quickly exhausted all the dry wood nearby and only had a small amount of gunpowder and five lead balls remaining. I grabbed the end of a modest-sized burning pine log and my tomahawk. I motioned to Bold Hunter that I would venture out for wood. He nodded and cocked his rifle. Two wolves came close to me, and I shoved the firebrand toward them. Honey came to my side to threaten them with her barks and the display of her teeth. As they backed off, I chopped up a fallen tree and drug a portion of the tree back to the fire, stopping now and then to brandish the burning log. Back in the safety of the fire, I cut the branch into smaller pieces, but it would only feed the fire for another hour.

We did not sleep that night. The constant need to feed the fire and stand watch with guns loaded and half-cocked demanded our attention. Our ventures beyond the campfire required that we take turns carrying firebrands into the darkness, while the other kept his gun poised to shoot any wolves that threatened us. I cooked some elk meat on a rock near the fire. We grabbed morsels to eat whenever the wolves backed away.

Finally, at dawn, the howls ceased. The wolves departed. One lead ball remained in our arsenal. I walked to the elk carcass to find a small skinny wolf searching for the last morsel, but only a skeleton remained. I wished him good hunting as he skulked away.

Exhausted, we killed the fire, loaded up our gear and spoils, and began the slow hike back to Chillicothe. On the trail, I thought back to Bold Hunter pointing at my knife. He did not seem upset, but someone else might. I could not let anyone else see it. I would find another knife to use among my Shawnee friends.

My thoughts were interrupted when Bold Hunter pointed out things and taught me the Shawnee words for them. He pointed to a tree and said, "*teequee,*" then to a bird and said, "*wiskeloutha.*" He corrected how I spoke them until I got it right.

When we arrived at Chillicothe Bold Hunter and I parted to get some sleep before the evening meeting at the council house. I showed the elk meat to Kicking Elk and Morning Moon. They received my offering with wide smiles. I presented the hide to Kicking Elk, who proceeded to lay it on the ground and salt it for tanning. Morning Moon took a portion of the meat and motioned with her arm for me to follow.

She led me to the wigwam of Long Stepper's family, who greeted us with smiles and open arms. Morning Moon presented Uses Her Ax with the bundle of elk meat and extended her hand toward me while she talked. Uses Her Ax turned toward me, put her hand to her heart, and said, "*Neawai*," the word for "thank you" which I had now perfected.

"It's my pleasure," I said with slight bow.

Gliding Swan approached me. "I teach you speak."

I could not wipe the smile from my face. "Yes!"

She pointed to the elk meat and then placed her fists with her pointing forefingers on her head, imitating the elk's antlers, and said, "*waapiti*." (elk)

I nodded and said "*waapiti*."

We sat down, and Gliding Swan taught me other common Shawnee words and phrases. Sometimes my pronunciation made her giggle, but she patiently corrected me until I got each one right. After almost half an hour, she had to go, so I said, "Goodbye" in Shawnee as she had taught me.

On the way back to our house, I picked up a turkey feather from the ground. I could make a writing quill from this feather. From our fireplace, I retrieved several pieces of coal, ground it up, and added a small amount of water to make ink. Crooked Eyes had only taken my quill pen and ink. I still had my paper. I wrote down all the words that Gliding Swan and Bold Hunter had taught me, spelling them as best I could by how English words sound and are spelled. Then, I lay down for a nap.

That evening, the council house swarmed with anticipation as folks gathered for their first meeting after returning from a cold, isolated winter. Many people stood and told stories, generating much laughter. Though I did not understand their words, their actions conveyed meaning clearly. I was very proud when I caught a few words that Bold Hunter or Gliding Swan had taught me.

Bold Hunter told the story of our night with the wolves. He pointed to me and then to Honey. He aimed his imaginary rifle, said, "Pow." Then he fell over, producing cheers and laughter. Then he placed his hands and fingers on his head depicting an elk. I yelled out, "*waapiti,*" to everyone's approval. He howled like a wolf to the laughter of the crowd. Everyone seemed to enjoy the story and after the meeting many approached me speaking Shawnee. I determined that one day I would learn the Shawnee language, and one day I would tell a story that would make them all laugh.

Time in Captivity: 30 Days

CHAPTER NINE

A FLOCK OF TURKEYS

APRIL 1778

"Tonight's the night I escape," whispered Andrew Johnson as we walked together to the river on a brisk April morning.

"What?" I asked.

"SSSSHHH! You're the only person I'm telling, 'cause I need your help. Today and tonight is the Bread Dance celebration. While all their attention is on the dance tonight, I'm just gonna walk out. They won't know I've gone until tomorrow."

"I'd like to help if I could, but my aim is to win their trust, so that they aren't suspicious of me leavin'. That was Captain's idea for the best way to escape. I don't want to give them reason to distrust me."

"Oh, I know that's what Cap'n Boone has been doin', walkin' around smilin' and whistlin' like he enjoys being here," Andrew replied. "I won't ask you to do anything that'd make them suspicious of you. All I want you to do is this: after I dance tonight, you get up and dance, draw attention to yourself. Imitate the Shawnee, but do it crazy-like so they all look at you and laugh and have fun watchin' you. Then, I'll slip away into the night and run as fast as I can to Kentucky."

I thought for a moment, then nodded. "I'll do it. I think I can dance crazy and make everyone laugh, but I shouldn't be seen with you today, or they may suspect me. Good luck."

The rest of the day, I thought of this dance—how I could copy the Indians' dance yet display my awkward version to entertain and amuse them.

That afternoon, Bold Hunter entered our wigwam, "White Chief, today is the Bread Festival. The ball game is about to begin. It's the men against the women. Let's go play."

"I would like," I said.

"I will play also," Gliding Swan hollered from the wigwam next door. "The women will win today." She triumphantly raised both arms in the air.

Uses Her Ax also joined us. Pompey met us at the field. The ball consisted of two round pieces of buckskin, sewn together, and stuffed with deer hair. The game was played on a field with two posts set up as goals on opposite ends of the field. Men could only kick the ball, while women could pick it up, run with it, and throw it. The objective was to be the first team to score eight points by getting the ball between the posts, tracked by a scorekeeper on the side of the field, who placed a peg in the ground for each goal.

All ages of Shawnee played the game, from young teenagers to those in their fifties. Uses Her Ax started the game by tossing the ball up. Bold Hunter kicked to me, and I kicked it toward our goal. My kick went right into the hands of a woman, who ran down the field toward her goal. One of the men tackled her and took the ball, with everyone laughing. It was not long before the women had the ball and threw the ball to Gliding Swan who caught it and passed it to another, who ran across the goal line. The women cheered. In the next sequence, Uses Her Ax threw the ball to Gliding Swan who ran down the field. I stood between she and the goal and tackled her. We both tumbled to the ground. Another man took the ball from her. As we rose, she smiled, spoke Shawnee, and threw a clump of grass at me. I laughed and smiled back. The man who took the ball from Gliding Swan kicked it to another who kicked it across the goal. The game went back and forth, and each team scored several times. At the end, the men won eight pegs to six.

As the game concluded, Uses Her Ax took the ball to the center of the field and spoke a prayer, with the rest of us gathered around. Pompey translated for me, "Grandmother, our Creator, thank you for bringing us through the cold winter and bringing us back together as a people. We ask for rain to make our corn and squash grow in abundance." Uses Her Ax slit the ball open, raised it above her head, and let the deer hair filling flutter away in the wind.

The Shawnee enjoyed other games like foot races, and rifle and archery shooting contests. After the football match, we witnessed the final shots of the archery contest between Ran in Thorns and Crooked Eyes. Ran in Thorns made a good shot but it was off the mark by a foot. Crooked Eyes then let his arrow fly, hitting the bullseye dead on. Crooked Eyes jumped and hollered.

"Crooked Eyes wins every year," Pompey explained. "He does not shoot rifles. He learned to aim an arrow when he was a small child and became the best shot in the village. When the British gave us rifles, he still preferred the bow. When you walk by his wigwam, you will see him making arrows or stringing bows."

We went to our wigwams to eat before the dance. I worried about Johnson. He was smart and skilled, but so were the Indians. I wondered what it would be like, traveling alone in the wilderness with little supplies. Winter had passed but there were dangers everywhere. Though I was determined to escape I was not ready. Still, I felt a little envious.

Men and women prepared for the dance in the orange twilight, gathering logs for the fire, dressing in their fine

Shawnee regalia, and painting their faces and bodies. They brought pipes for smoking, liquor for drinking, and drums for music. I asked Kicking Elk to paint me, and he painted three black marks on each of my cheeks, forehead, and chin.

Kicking Elk and Morning Moon led the way from our house and we found a place to sit beside Long Stepper and his family. The fire blazed taller than a man, lighting the area, as the sun set below the hilltops. The village gathered, smoking and chatting as they sat on logs or the ground. Everyone smoked and chatted. Then, about twenty men come out of the forest with whoops and gunfire, carrying game—squirrels, racoons, rabbits, and a beaver. As the men walked into the circle, the drummer began with a steady slow beat. They left their game in a pile near the fire before taking their seats. When the drummer increased the tempo and sang, the hunters rose from their seats and began their dance. It was like a rhythmic march, circling the fire single file. They stepped toe to heel in unison. After several minutes, the drummer stopped and switched to a new beat. Some women joined, forming another circle outside the men's, and they danced around for several more minutes, chanting and singing. When the music ended, the men sat on a log, and the women brought them food for which they cheered and thanked the women.

Blackfish walked to the center of the circle and he lifted his hands and face to the sky. I sought out Pompey to translate as the chief spoke. "Our Grandmother, the Creator, we ask that you prosper our corn, squash, and bean crops this growing season, that you would provide food for our people. We thank you for the animals of the forest, for the deer, elk, bear, beavers, buffaloes, and wolves, which you put on earth to help us. Thunderbirds, we ask that you send rain, but make the lightning go around us. Our Creator, we pray that sickness go around us and not harm the people."

When Blackfish sat down, the drummer resumed, joined by

two men with cow horns and gourd rattlers, all singing. Several women danced, including Gliding Swan. I watched her elegant movements so closely that I did not notice when Andrew began his dance. He danced with big clumsy gestures, spinning around but always keeping an eye on the spectators. His dance was more reminiscent of a dying animal than any steps I had seen, either from white men or Indians. I could not stop myself from laughing along with everyone else. He entertained the crowd for several minutes, then sat down behind his family.

I hopped to my feet and joined the dancers. I tried to respectfully imitate the others, moving slowly and carefully. I caught Gliding Swan's eye and she smiled. My cheeks got hot as I became even more aware of my sloppy dance. But I then realized: the sloppier, the better. I shoved my inhibitions down and danced with as much energy as I could muster. I displayed the paint on my chest and face. The Shawnee laughed and cheered. I could not tell if it was for me, but I kept going. Kicking Elk and Morning Moon smiled but Crooked Eyes scowled. At the end I crashed beside Kicking Elk and Morning Moon. I glanced over to an empty spot where Andrew had sat.

Chillicothe was quiet the next morning. I walked through village to the river. Upon my return there was quite a stir at Andrew's house. His father searched the whole village for Andrew, and some warriors departed on horseback to hunt for him. I was tense all day, though I did my best not to show it. At the end of the day the searchers returned with heads drooped.

The leaves of the oak, poplar, and maple, and the flowers of the redbud, crab apple, and dogwood displayed color and promise for our life in the woodlands of Ohio. The songs of the cardinal and blue jay permeated the air as the villagers went about their work—the women in their planting and cooking, and the men in their hunting. My ability with the language had improved, as I reviewed my list of Shawnee words daily. I practiced often with my family, Bold Hunter, and Gliding Swan.

One evening, as I sat around the fire with Kicking Elk and Morning Moon smoking our pipes, Kicking Elk spoke. "White Chief, you are a worthy son for us. We are glad you have come.

"You know that I was once chief of our people. We had a son. His name was Swift Wolf." Kicking Elk paused. His chin quivered. A tear rolled down his cheek. He gathered himself again. "He was a great warrior and hunter. He died several moons ago, before you came. The Great Spirit has sent you to take his place. You have demonstrated bravery and skill as a hunter."

"I can never replace Swift Wolf but will try to be a worthy son. It is an honor to be in your family," I humbly replied in even humbler Shawnee.

Kicking Elk's words revealed a father grieving for his lost son. Swift Wolf embodied hope for Kicking Elk and Morning Moon, hope for the future. That hope had vanished. I could not look them in the eye. I could not be who they wanted, but I could help them until I found my opportunity to leave. I was not in a big hurry about it. The only thing that really upset me was imagining that my family might think I was dead. I hated the idea of Ma and the kids crying, of Pa's sad face. But I had to wait for the right moment to steal away.

One spring morning, as Bold Hunter reviewed my pronunciation of Shawnee words, the spectacle of many people heading toward the Council House interrupted us.

"The traders have brought items to trade," Bold Hunter explained. "Let us go see what they have to sell." I was pleased that I understood exactly what he said. I was also pleased that this was an opportunity to trade my elk hide for a knife.

We joined in with those headed for the maple tree at the Council House. The traders were Louis Lorimier, a French Canadian, and James Girty. Girty was captured as a teenager and had lived among the Shawnee for the previous twenty years. They often traveled with the Shawnee in their raids against settlers and fought for their cause. Lorimier and Girty displayed their goods on buffalo hides that lay on the ground. Daniel Boone, who had recently returned with Blackfish and the other warriors, stood among the people, surveying the goods for sale.

As Bold Hunter and I arrived, Boone greeted me with a smile, "Hey, Daniel."

I waved and welcomed him back from Detroit, showing off the Shawnee I had learned.

"You've learned to speak Shawnee very well."

"Thank you," I replied in English. "Good to see you again, sir. How was your journey to Detroit?"

"The weather was favorable and the captives were delivered to Detroit," Boone said. "The conditions here are better than in Detroit, and the Shawnee are more agreeable to live with than the British." He lowered his voice, "I hear that Johnson left us for Kentucky."

I nodded and quickly recounted the tale.

Boone nodded but frowned. "I wish he had waited. Blackfish is gathering warriors here for an attack on Boonesborough. We must get word to them so they can be prepared."

My stomach sank. "What can I do, sir?"

"Nothing," Boone said, shaking his head. "But I believe I've won their trust. I'll keep an eye out for an opportunity and leave as soon as I can. Best keep this conversation to ourselves."

I nodded, and Boone walked away. I watched as he bought a few blocks of maple sugar and gave some to his two small Shawnee sisters. They jumped up and down and laughed as they ate them.

I looked over some of the items, finding an inconspicuous

bone knife. I traded my elk hide for the knife and five maple sugar blocks, to share with my family, plus one for me.

I placed my block of sugar in my mouth, kept it there without swallowing, treasuring the sweet maple flavor. It was a small oasis of enjoyment amidst the constant peril of captivity.

I proceeded to our wigwam and presented Kicking Elk, Morning Moon, Gliding Swan, and Rising Star with their gift. All received the maple sugar with smiles and squeals of delight.

As spring turned into summer, the dark clouds of battle grew over Chillicothe. The number of warriors increased to about four hundred. Despite the gloom these warriors brought the salt-maker captives, Boone continued to walk around the village with a smile, appearing to enjoy himself. I had no doubt his plan of escape formed below his cheerful exterior. He waited for the moment, even while he whistled.

In mid-June, Boone and I joined a hunting party that included Crooked Eyes and Blackfish. We trekked far into the woods with no game. As the sun dipped behind the trees, Boone was left in charge of the horses on the trail while the rest of us moved into the underbrush. Suddenly, a flock of turkeys took off, and we ran after them, shooting a few down. When we returned, Boone was gone, along with one of the horses.

"Boone is gone," Crooked Eyes yelled.

Everyone turned around to find no one with the horses. Boone had galloped away on one of them.

"Go after Boone," Blackfish ordered, as three men rode off in different directions.

An hour later they returned, without Boone.

"He'll get lost," one of them declared to the approval of the others.

I was certain that Boone would soon be back in Boonesborough to warn them of a Shawnee attack.

Crooked Eyes stepped up to me, so close I could smell his foul breath. He pointed his knife at my face. "If you attempt to escape, you will not get lost. You will die. I will scalp you."

Time in Captivity: 118 Days

CHAPTER TEN
THE PANTHER
JULY 1778

Sparks rained on the damp tinder. Starting the fire was a trial, but the sporadic rains made finding dry wood an even greater task. For the rains came, first in downpours, then in light drizzles, then short periods of no rain. I split open logs, piled them near the fire, and covered them with deer hide. Seeing some blue sky beyond the clouds as a sign that I had seen the last downpour, I built the fire into a blaze to leave some hot coals for Morning Moon to cook.

I helped Morning Moon hang a pot of venison stew over the fire, and she complimented me on my fire making skills. She left me in charge of the stew as she went down to the river.

As Morning Moon departed, Gliding Swan approached with a smile, carrying her own pot. Rising Star toddled behind. "May I use your fire to cook my stew? I will help you keep it burning."

"Yes, there is room for two," I said with a smile. I took the pot from her and hung it next to the other. We sat on a log.

"You speak Shawnee well," Gliding Swan said, leaning in a little closer.

I faced her directly. "Thank you! You have been a great teacher," I stammered, slightly.

"I saw you make marks on your paper after our lessons. What do they mean?"

"In English, the words we speak can go on paper. The marks are called letters, and they represent different sounds. I take Shawnee words and spell them out with English letters. Then, I write down what those words mean in English," I explained.

"This has helped you learn to speak," she observed. "Show me the marks and what they mean."

I nodded in agreement and went inside the house to get my Shawnee language papers, and then returned to the fire and our conversation. I pointed out some of the words and my attempt to write them with English letters.

"Make the marks for Rising Star," she requested.

I dipped the quill in my charcoal ink and spelled out Rising Star as it sounded.

"See, Gliding Swan? Each mark or letter has a sound. Even if you do not know the name, you can sound it out from the marks."

Gliding Swan pointed to the letters for Rising Star and spoke his name, "Rising Star," with a smile.

"Writing the Shawnee words has helped me learn to speak Shawnee," I said.

"I want to write his name. How do you hold the feather?"

I passed her the quill and adjusted it in her hand.

After I guided her through writing each letter, she smiled and said, "*Ala-aqua* (Rising Star)."

There were a few moments of silence, then Gliding Swan changed the subject. "I understand Big Turtle has left Chillicothe."

I nodded.

Gliding Swan became solemn. "Will you also leave Chillicothe?"

Though my one goal was to escape and return to my family in Virginia, I dared not ever reveal it. "Oh no. I like it here," I said. "I admire and respect Kicking Elk and Morning Moon. They are kind. You and Long Stepper and Uses Her Ax are kind too."

Gliding Swan brightened up. "I am glad. Kicking Elk and Morning Moon need someone who can provide for them."

I stared into the fire, unsure how to continue the conversation.

"Do you know why Crooked Eyes is so cruel to me?"

"He is cruel to everyone. His parents died when he was young, and he moved from family to family until he was grown. No woman would marry him because he was so cruel." Gliding Swan turned to me. "I think he is lonely."

I nodded. She watched her son play with a stick in the dirt.

"I want to ask you something," I said. "Don't answer if you don't want to."

"You may ask," she said.

"How did your husband die?"

Gliding Swan gazed at the ground and I immediately regretted asking.

She lifted her head. "His name was Swift Wolf. White settlers in Kentucky shot and killed him last autumn. Ten of our Shawnee men left Chillicothe, but only seven returned."

"I am so sorry to hear that. It must be hard to lose your husband."

Gliding Swan nodded. "He was a good husband and father. Rising Star misses him a lot. And I'm sure Kicking Elk and Morning Moon do too. He was their son." She glanced at Rising Star again. "Tell me, did you have a family in Virginia? Do you have a wife?"

"I have my parents, six sisters, and two brothers. But I don't have a wife. I'm only sixteen."

"That is young, but not too young in Chillicothe. I was sixteen when I married."

Unsure what to say next, I suggested we get more firewood.

That night, as I lay in my bed, I could not sleep, as I reflected on Gliding Swan's story and her husband, Swift Wolf. Could Swift Wolf have been among those we shot and killed when we marched to Boonesborough? Could he be the man I killed? Was I the source of Kicking Elk's, Morning Moon's, and Gliding Swan's greatest pain? I could never let them see the knife.

"I killed a large buffalo," shouted Kicking Elk. "I need help to carry it." He walked from wigwam-to-wigwam recruiting laborers for the task.

"I will help," I said.

Kicking Elk enlisted me and six other men to carry the load. We traveled a trail northwest of the village and arrived at the clearing where two other men had just cut up the beast. It was a bull of the largest kind of buffalo.

Kicking Elk assigned parts of the buffalo for each of us to carry. He stood beside me.

"You will carry the head," Kicking Elk said, pointing to it.

I gazed at my assignment. The head was about four feet tall and three feet wide. How could I carry it? I grabbed it, but could barely move it.

"We must go before the sun sets. We have our load to carry. Now you carry yours," Kicking Elk said.

"That is a heavy load you have to carry," another said as he slapped my back.

I turned around. They all stared at me and my buffalo head. Then they all erupted in laughter. Kicking Elk laughed the loudest. We cut out the horns and teeth and left the head for the wolves.

That evening, Kicking Elk, Morning Moon, and I sat on logs around the fire outside our wigwam and feasted on the buffalo meat. Content and filled with his supper, Kicking Elk found his pipe, filled it with tobacco, and lit it. He smoked his pipe as if every breath had its own purpose.

"White Chief, I have seen Crooked Eyes look at you with hatred in his eyes and speak harshly to you. Has he hurt you?"

"Crooked Eyes was my guard when we marched from Kentucky to Chillicothe. He still believes it is his job to guard me."

"I will speak with Crooked Eyes. He is no longer your guard." Kicking Elk sat in silence as he smoked, then spoke again. "White Chief, you are a fine warrior and son. You have learned our ways and our tongue like a swift horse bringing good news. You have been good news for Morning Moon and me." Kicking Elk paused and took a couple of puffs.

"Thank you," I said. I inhaled smoke from my own pipe. "You have been generous to me, and have provided me with shelter, food, and clothes."

"We are pleased with you," Kicking said. "I am old. One day I will be too feeble to hunt and Morning Moon will be too old to plant and to cook. Our son has died and cannot take care of us. The Great Spirit has sent you to take his place, to care for us in our old age."

"You have honored me by taking me into your house and family. I will do my best to care for you as you grow older. But that day has not yet come since you are both strong and healthy."

That night as I lay in my bed, this conversation haunted me. I had tried to speak with sincerity, and a part of me did desire to take care of Kicking Elk and Morning Moon. They were so kind to me and always made sure I was comfortable and had food to eat. They had a wonderful sense of humor. But I was beyond someone they liked. I was their hope for the future, someone who would take care of them in their old age. Yet one day, I was not sure when, it would be time for me to leave. I both longed for and despised the day. I would not have the opportunity to say goodbye. My escape would sadden them, distress them, and thwart their efforts to provide for their later years. I hated for that day to come, but come it would, and it motivated me to treat them with kindness and respect.

The morning sun lit our way along the forest trail as Kicking Elk, Long Stepper, Crooked Eyes, Ben Kelly (Fighting Fish), Ran in Thorns, Bold Hunter, and I trekked to our hunting grounds. We followed a creek until it widened out into a small pond created by a beaver dam, where animals would come. Above the creek and pond, there was a wigwam, which we used for overnight hunts.

As we gathered at the wigwam to discuss where we each would hunt, Crooked Eyes moved close to me. Crooked Eyes turned and faced me, then reached for his knife but did not pull it from its sheath. "I must keep an eye on our prisoners to make sure they do not escape."

Kicking Elk marched over to Crooked Eyes, stood close to him, and examined his face. Crooked Eyes stepped back.

"You threaten my son, White Chief," Kicking Elk said. "You are no longer White Chief's guard. These threats must cease."

"The whites all want to escape. I will do my part to keep them here."

"Your job is complete, do not threaten White Chief."

Crooked Eyes grunted and moved away from me. We spread out around the pond, and I sat on a rock beside a bush with my gun half-cocked. We waited. Birds sang in the trees and a breeze whispered through the branches. I attempted a deer call every fifteen minutes or so. A bush rustled near me. I could not see the deer, so I made the call again, and the bush rustled again. Raising my rifle, I repeated the call. The deer rustled leaves closer and closer, but still I could not see it. Puzzled by the unusual movement of this deer, I stood up to see it. Instead, a huge panther filled my vision, its tail beating and shaking the bush. I screamed and stumbled back. I forgot to shoot my gun. The panther leapt away, twenty feet in its first bound, perhaps as flabbergasted as I was. I suppose if I had stayed down another minute, the panther would have caught his prey.

The others rushed toward me laughing.

Bold Hunter reached me first. "I saw you, but I never saw the panther. I screamed too when it leaped."

"You need to change your deer call," shouted Long Stepper. "We do not need any large cats coming when we hunt for deer."

"You all right, Son?" Kicking Elk asked.

"Yes, I was lucky,"

Ben came up to me, slapped me on the back, and said in English, "You have a terrifying scream. I think you scared that panther more than he scared you."

"Well, I don't know that I've ever been so scared. But that was one time when being terrified probably saved my life," I replied in Shawnee, so as not to arouse suspicion since Crooked Eyes stood nearby.

"I have seen many panthers run as they chase their prey," Ran in Thorns said. "None have run faster than that panther."

I tried not to look at Crooked Eyes, though I could tell he was staring at me.

As the sun set, a couple hundred Shawnee gathered in the Chillicothe council house. I sat between Bold Hunter and Ben. After a couple of villagers shared their stories, Bold Hunter put an elbow in my side and said with a smile, "Tell your panther story."

I had never spoken before a crowd, but I sometimes imagined myself doing so, and making people laugh. This was my opportunity. Bold Hunter's elbow gave me the confidence. I rose from my seat, lifted my hands as I examined the faces of the people seated in the council house, and waited until there was silence again, and I had everyone's attention. The first words were hard to find. My armpits were wet. "A panther has given me the greatest fright I have encountered in the forest." Someone in the crowd said "OH!" I told the story of my deer calls and blew through my closed lips and teeth, "buzz!" to everyone's delight. My confidence grew. I repeated my startled scream when I realized my "deer" was a panther. They roared with laughter and smiles. I continued, "My scream terrified the panther. He was more scared than me!" I spread my arms, pointing to opposite walls of the room, "He leapt the width of the Council house to get away from me." Everyone clapped and laughed. I smiled and sat down.

Then, it was Bold Hunter's turn. He told the story from his viewpoint from behind the tree and said, "We were all amazed by how White Chief conquered the panther with his scream."

Then Kicking Elk rose and told his version of the story and concluded with, "White Chief made the panther run with his voice."

Everyone clapped, and shouted, "White Chief!"

After a couple more stories, Chief Blackfish stood up, raised his arms above his head, walked to both sides of the fire, and said, "Many settlers come over the mountains and down the Ohio into Kentucky. The white men are stealing our land! They are killing our deer, bear, and buffalo. The land and the animals rightfully belong to us. How much more will they take before they are satisfied? Will you let them take any more from you? We must rise up, stand our ground, and say 'No more!' We must teach the settlers not to come to Kentucky. Over 400 warriors have gathered here in Chillicothe. We will attack Boonesborough in one week and burn it down. Then the settlers will not have a fort to hide in."

Many shook their fists and shouted, "Burn Boonesborough!"

Ben and I and the other captives were quiet. The thought of marching on Boonesborough made me want to vomit.

Blackfish returned to his seat.

After the meeting, many people greeted me and said they liked my story. Gliding Swan approached with a smile, holding Rising Star, and placed her hand on my arm, smiling, and said, "I am glad that panther did not attack you, White Chief."

I thanked her and nodded in agreement.

"You have learned much in a short time," Gliding Swan responded. With that she turned and followed the others out of the council house.

Ben Kelly walked up next and spoke in English, "You're entirely accepted in Chillicothe. I bet you could walk out whenever you wanted."

"Sh! Someone might know English." I glanced at Crooked Eyes who left the council house with a final glare at me. "One Shawnee is always suspicious," I replied.

I began to imagine all the ways I could escape, now very possible, and I talked about it with Ben whenever I could.

Time in Captivity: 163 Days

CHAPTER ELEVEN

THE KNIFE

SEPTEMBER 1778

The time had come to unleash the assault on Boonesborough. The whole town gathered at the Council House, including the warriors with bodies and faces painted for war.

"Many whites come from across the mountains and steal our hunting grounds, but Kentucky belongs to Shawnee," Blackfish said. "We must send the whites back to where they came from. Their blood will be on their own heads, for they have not listened to our warnings. Chief Cornstalk sought peace with the Americans, but they murdered him. The whites do not want peace; they want war. They will get war, and they will suffer for their crimes. Tomorrow, we leave for battle and we will burn Boonesborough down to the dirt it stands on"

Several of the warriors shouted in agreement, with raised fists in the air, "Burn Boonesborough."

"Kill the white man."

"Send them back."

As Blackfish spoke, my stomach churned and tightened to the point of vomit. The notion of war against my fellow soldiers at the fort produced a pain in my chest.

Blackfish began again, "We leave for battle, but the whites who have made their home with us will not go with us. They will not fight against their own. They will stay here and take care of our women and children." Blackfish stared each captive in the eye.

To this, I nodded in agreement. These words provided a little relief. I was still afraid, but at least I would not have to fight my friends.

The war dance began. An elderly Indian sang and beat his drum. The painted warriors moved into a circle around the fire, holding their spears or tomahawks. They stepped toward the south. They stretched their tomahawks toward Boonesborough and delivered repulsive shrieks. They spun and danced back toward the fire. One at a time they sang as they moved around the fire while the others chanted "He-uh, he-uh." I did not sleep that night.

The war party departed the next morning.

The time was not right for me to escape. Kicking Elk spoke of spending the approaching winter at a camp away from Chillicothe. My adopted family would need my assistance with hunting and other chores.

The war party returned after a month. I expected to see the warriors return in jubilant celebration, with many scalps and captives. But there were no scalps and no captives. The warriors trudged into town; heads hung low.

I ran up to Bold Hunter, "What happened?"

"It was a long battle of many days. But their fort was strong, and they fought hard. We could not get close, for their rifles killed many of us. We tried to dig a tunnel and come up into the fort, but the rains came and collapsed the tunnel. After many days of rain, we decided to return.

My heart leapt at this news. I forced my best somber face until I found a private place to celebrate.

After the first frost, Kicking Elk said to me, "White Chief, winter comes, and we must prepare to leave Chillicothe. We need tomahawks, rifles, powder, lead balls, kettles, and other cooking wares, blankets, and hides. We will find a place with water to stay the winter, and where we can find game to eat. Long Stepper, Uses Her Ax, Gliding Swan, and Rising Star will come with us, as they will need our help. We will build a wigwam large enough for all of us."

"Do you know a suitable place for us to go?" I asked.

"We will go to a place farther downriver. A nice stream flows into the river there and is not far from the beaver pond, where you scared the panther. There is a decent amount of game there," Kicking Elk answered. "We will pack up our things today and leave early in the morning."

We took one of the horses that belonged to another family. I packed my things and helped load the horse with the cooking gear, blankets, skins, rifles, and tomahawks.

We walked along a trail that took us to Beaver Pond. Below the pond, we picked up the trail that followed the stream, toward our proposed winter camp. As we approached our destination, Kicking Elk stopped and pointed to a large rock in a clearing with some nearby pine trees. "Look. When you see that rock and those nearby trees, you are close."

We arrived at our destination in early afternoon and located a level area for the wigwam on a hill above the river. A short distance away, above the smaller stream, was a spring to provide water to drink and cook with. Without delay, the women began construction of our wigwam, and the men headed south to hunt.

I stayed behind to assist the women before embarking on my hunt.

I put the sun at my back and found a trail that headed north. I sat on a rock and leaned against an oak tree near a clearing. I listened to the sounds of the forest, cardinals, robins, and blue jays, and the breeze that blew through the tree limbs as I reflected on my circumstances. Though a captive, I was safe, loved, and needed by my adopted family. I would get to spend the winter with Gliding Swan. I would not see Crooked Eyes for months. In many ways I liked my life with the Indians—the strong bond among their people, the love they expressed for one another, their recognition and acceptance of me as a member of their community, and the adventure of living in the beautiful and bountiful wilderness. Life with the Indians was certainly more exhilarating than on my parents' farm. And the hair on my once-shaven head had grown out four inches. I was relieved that no one required that I shave my head again. Despite my agreeable circumstances, each day among the Shawnee brought reminders that I was a foreigner among these lovely yet still strange people. My yearning for my family and my desire to escape deepened with each day. But the day of my escape had not yet come, for winter approached, with no way to cross the cold Ohio River. Furthermore, I desired to see my adopted family safely through the winter.

I waited an hour, making occasional deer calls, before a buck appeared across the glade. I sounded another call. He moved closer. I cocked my rifle and took aim. He moved still closer. I aimed for his head and pulled the trigger. He flinched and fell where he stood. Delighted with my success, I rushed over to him and waited while he made his final kicks. I cut him open and cleaned out all his entrails. I removed the hide from the legs and discarded the bones. I tied the foreleg hides to the hindleg hides, forming two shoulder straps. With the deer slung over my shoulders, I trekked back to our winter home.

Kicking Elk and Long Stepper welcomed me back with smiles as they surveyed my prize. Kicking Elk said, "This buck will provide food for many days. I picked an excellent place for our winter."

Morning Moon cooked the venison in a stew of which we all ate our fill. The late fall afternoon sun dipped behind the nearby hills and left us in darkness, save for our campfire and the crescent moon rising in the sky. We relaxed around the fire with our pipes.

Kicking Elk broke the silence. "White Chief, you have done well. You killed this buck so that we can start this winter season with full stomachs."

I replied, "Thank you. I was fortunate to find this deer."

Kicking Elk wiped a tear from his eye. "You remind me so much of Swift Wolf. It was around this time last year he died. I'm grateful for you, and proud of how you have learned our ways so quickly."

I nodded but was unsure of what to say.

"He was a good hunter," Kicking Elk said, staring into the fire. "He always made sure we had enough to eat. Until . . . " His brows drew together and his lips turned to a scowl. "Those white men must pay with their lives. Only then will I be satisfied."

I swallowed.

"Swift Wolf died fighting for what is rightfully ours," Long Stepper said. "Our land, our hunting grounds, he died for our freedom. He died to protect Rising Star."

Part of me wanted to argue, but something deep down understood Long Stepper.

Kicking Elk looked up with a softened expression. "Yes, I see so much of Swift Wolf in Rising Star."

Morning Moon put her hand on my leg. "White Chief, will you help us protect Rising Star?"

I nodded. "Of course. I will do all I can." This was the best response I could muster. My stomach churned as the image of the Indian I killed flooded my mind.

Morning Moon added, “Rising Star looks just like Swift Wolf did when he was a boy. Swift Wolf lives on through Rising Star.”

As the last puffs of smoke rose from our pipes and the last flames of our campfire were but a flicker, Kicking Elk pronounced, “We are weary from our journey and the work of building our home. Let us rest now. Tomorrow, we will build a canoe so we can hunt on both sides of the river.”

We all retreated into our new winter house, located our beds, and descended into sleep.

The next day, Kicking Elk, Long Stepper, and I rose with the first light of day. We dug up roots from spruce trees to serve as rope to fasten the pieces of the canoe together. We collected sap from spruce trees, usually found around the wounds on the tree. The sap was heated in a pot with fat from an opossum, used to seal the seams. Kicking Elk located birch trees and removed the bark for the hull. Long Stepper split cedar logs to make the gunwales, ribs, sheathing, and paddles. By mid-afternoon, we applied the sealant and set the canoe in the water to test for leaks. We applied additional sealant over several leaks. After numerous tests and sealant applications we had a water-tight canoe. We used this canoe every day to cross the river. I became an adept canoeist, with skillful and efficient paddle strokes.

As the last of the brown oak leaves still clung to their trees, the first snow came, and then melted away. One afternoon in mid-winter, the sun dipped below the hills that surrounded us, and hastened the darkness. We sat around the fire and told stories of the endeavors of the day.

Kicking Elk told his story. “I shot a beaver today. He must have been the grandfather beaver, for he was the hardiest I have ever seen. This beaver will provide us with food for many days. While I cut into the beaver to skin him, my knife slipped from my hand and fell into the water. I was not able to retrieve my knife. I think the Great Spirit sent the beaver so I could find another knife."

The next morning, as I warmed myself by the fire, I observed Kicking Elk inside our wigwam as he searched through my bed and other things. Then he emerged from the wigwam and joined Long Stepper. The two walked down the trail with rifles in hand for a day of hunting. They climbed into the canoe and paddled across the river. Curious as to whether Kicking Elk removed any of my things, I promptly searched my bed. I discovered my knife, the one I traded the elk skin for, was not in its place. I missed this knife, like the loss of a dear friend I had long depended upon. It had become such a useful item to always have nearby. I used it to skin and gut animals, and other daily chores, and for protection from wild animals. My time among the Shawnee had taught me that to borrow without permission was common. I did not consider that Kicking Elk had betrayed me in any way. I had the knife and sheath I had retrieved from the warrior on the road to Boonesborough, and it was still hidden.

Morning Moon, Uses Her Ax, and Gliding Swan worked to prepare food for later in the day. Rising Star played with some sticks as he hit small rocks to see how far he could knock them.

"Would you go with me to the spring and help me put water in this pot and carry it back to the fire?" Gliding Swan asked.

"Yes," I responded, jumping up. To leave the camp without my knife did not feel safe, but the peril of revealing the one I had hidden put a rock in my stomach. I concluded that I could hide it under my clothes and only bring it out to use if required to protect us. "Just a moment. I will be right back," I said. I retrieved the knife, strapped the belt with the sheath around my waist, and covered it with my shirt.

Gliding Swan called Rising Star to come with us. Rising Star ran ahead of us. Gliding Swan and I filled the pot using gourds that we dipped into the spring, while Rising Star stayed on the trail above the stream.

We both grabbed the handle of the full pot to carry it up the hill, but as we turned my eyes beheld a sight that caused my heart to leap out of my chest. On the path above us, a panther crept stealthily, his eyes focused on Rising Star. I touched Gliding Swan's arm, put my finger to my lips, then pointed at the panther. Her face turned sickly, her chin trembled, her eyes filled with tears, but she remained silent. We lowered the pot. I grabbed the knife and crept toward the cat. Rising Star played unaware. The panther took another step, then crouched, ready to strike. I yelled and rushed toward the cat. He leapt onto Rising Star. I sprang forward and stabbed him in the neck. He turned to me with his mouth wide open as we crashed to the ground. I threw my left arm up in defense. He sank those four dagger-like fangs into my forearm, sending burning pain through my arm. I jabbed his neck repeatedly, blood spewing, until his body went limp, but his jaw still clamped on my arm.

The sound of Rising Star's cries elicited a smile. He was still alive. As Gliding Swan rushed to Rising Star, I labored to pry my arm from the cat's jaws. At length, I freed my arm and pushed him off. His blood covered my clothes. I lay on my back, my left arm throbbing in agony, clutched close to my chest. My right arm lay on the ground, as I released the bloody grip on the knife. It fell away from my hand. Gliding Swan embraced Rising Star, cuddled him close to her and whispered, "You are safe, Rising Star. You are safe." After a long embrace, Gliding Swan released her hold on Rising Star and examined him. She removed his clothes, checked his arms, legs, and body, then dressed him again.

I lay there, not able to move, not from the pain in my arm, though that was abundant, but from the awareness that I had just clashed with a panther. It could have killed me; it could have killed Gliding Swan and Rising Star. But I killed it. I survived. We survived.

Gliding Swan came over, still holding Rising Star, and examined my face and my arm. "How badly are you hurt?"

"I cannot move my arm,"

"Let me see. Are you in a lot of pain?"

"Yes. The throbbing and tenderness worsen when I try to move it," I said.

"Keep it still," she responded. Her eyes moved toward my other arm and . . . the knife. I wanted to clutch the knife, to hide it, but could not move that fast. Her eyes focused on the knife and stayed there for an eternity.

She picked it up and placed it in my hand. She avoided eye contact as she said, "Here. Here is your knife. It saved Rising Star's life. You saved Rising Star's life. Put this knife away, under your clothes as before."

Gliding Swan helped me sit up and get to my knees. I lifted my shirt and placed the knife in its sheath.

"How is Rising Star? Was he bitten?" I asked.

"Rising Star is safe. No injuries," she replied.

She would not look at me, so I could not read her face. She was shaken, and obviously grateful, but maybe she also wished the panther had killed me.

"I am so glad," I said. "I was so afraid the panther had mauled him."

"Come over here and sit down again while I wash your arm," Gliding Swan pointed to a log. I took off my shirt, placing the knife under my buckskin leggings, while Gliding Swan retrieved the pot of water. She poured water over my arm and washed off the blood. "Let us go back to our wigwam and find something to wrap around your arm," she said.

Morning Moon and Uses Her Ax were both placing logs on the fire as we arrived.

"White Chief is hurt. He was bitten by a panther," Gliding Swan shouted.

Morning Moon hurried to my side, placing her arm around my waist. I stretched out my arm for her to see and displayed the four blood-filled fang punctures as my blood dripped to the ground.

"I know you are suffering." Her face expressed pain as though she could feel mine.

"It is like my arm was shot with arrows, and then a horse stomped on it," I said.

She helped me find a seat by the fire. She washed my arm, then retrieved a deer hide from the wigwam and cut it into strips which she wrapped around my wounds.

"Keep your arm still and get as much sleep as you can," Morning Moon said.

"Thank you," I said, as I put my shirt back on.

After Morning Moon finished treating my injuries, Gliding Swan recounted the harrowing event. Rising Star toddled over to Uses Her Ax and crawled into her lap.

When Kicking Elk and Long Stepper returned, Gliding Swan told the story again.

"White Chief, I had your knife. Where did you get the knife?" Kicking Elk asked.

Gliding Swan responded before I could speak, "I gave him a cooking knife. He thought there might be danger."

I did not look at her, but my shoulders immediately relaxed.

"And he was right," Kicking Elk stated. "I will go see the carcass of this panther. Its skin is valuable and its meat can go in our stew."

About an hour later, Kicking Elk returned with meat wrapped up in the skin. "Morning Moon, put this in our stew. White Chief, this skin belongs to you, but we will give it to you later. You earned it. I kept the teeth. I buried the remains to keep the wolves away."

That night, after eating, we sat around the fire and smoked our pipes.

"White Chief, you have acted bravely today. You saved Rising Star's life, risking your own. This is an act that deserves honor and recognition. This is the second time you have gotten the best of a panther. You shall no longer be called White Chief. Your new name is *Tunimanhconicheice* (Stalking Panther)."

"Stalking Panther suits you," Long Stepper said. "The panther is a noble and fierce animal, with stealth, cunning, and skill. Stalking Panther is your name."

Later, as I lay on my bed, I could not sleep. My mind kept replaying the panther encounter. It could have turned out much differently. Though my arm still throbbed with pain, I was fortunate to be alive and Rising Star was unharmed. Kicking Elk gave me a new name, Stalking Panther. I liked it. What an honor to receive this name. I was not tall, but this new name made me feel eminent and important. This name made me feel a part of the Shawnee people, rather than a prisoner. Maybe one day, after I escape, I can come back and visit my friends in Chillicothe. I was one of them for all except Crooked Eyes. It seemed Crooked Eyes' mission was to frequently remind me of my captive status.

In the weeks that followed, Morning Moon and Kicking Elk cared for me and my injured arm with great tenderness and personal sacrifice, not allowing me to do any work until my arm healed. There was never a hint that they were annoyed or resented the extra burden my injury caused them. My left arm began to heal, though it remained tender.

"I need your help to fill this kettle and carry it back from the spring," Gliding Swan said one morning. "Can you use your right arm to help carry the kettle? Rising Star is going to stay with Uses Her Ax here at our wigwam."

"Yes. I can help you with my right arm. It is still strong, but my left arm cannot lift much," I replied, stepping into the house to secure the knife under my shirt.

As we filled the kettle, Gliding Swan asked, "Your knife, may I see it again?"

My breath caught. I had dreaded this moment, but there was no use hiding it from her. I handed her the knife.

She examined the knife, felt the sharp blade and point, and caressed the bone handle.

"Do you know it?" I asked without making eye contact.

A tear formed in her eye as she examined it. "It is my husband's knife. There is no other knife like it. How did you get it?"

I heard my own heartbeat. I debated how to answer her and how much detail to provide.

"As we marched to Kentucky, ten or so Shawnee attacked us. Two of our men died, and three Shawnee. I found this knife on one of them. I admired its strength and beauty, so I kept it."

"Do you know who killed Swift Wolf? Was it one of the white men we adopted?"

I tried to remain calm. "Often in battle, we never know whose bullet kills who. Many men shot their guns."

She closed her eyes and pressed her lips together then looked away into the distance and I had a sudden feeling of inadequacy, not able to imagine how it felt to lose a spouse. She was not much older than I, but she was a grown woman. I was still trying to become a man.

"This knife belongs to you. Give it to Rising Star when he becomes a man. He will be a great warrior like his father, Swift Wolf. I cannot keep it. You must take it. Swift Wolf saved Rising Star's life through his knife. This knife also saved my life. This knife is superior to my knife. It cut the panther much deeper than my knife could have."

"Yes, I will keep it for Rising Star when he grows up. He

should have it. I will not tell my parents, or Kicking Elk or Morning Moon, about this knife yet, and you should not either."

"Stalking Panther, will you check your traps today?" Gliding Swan asked one sunny morning.

"Yes, I will leave soon." I replied.

"I will go with you and help you carry all those animals you have caught," she said with a twinkle in her eye and a slight smile on her face.

"Yes. I will need your help."

Gliding Swan and I walked along the trail that led to the beaver pond, checking our traps for beavers or raccoons. We came upon the first one, and there was a hefty beaver caught in the trap, still kicking to free itself. Using a six-foot stick, with a fork on one end, I jammed the beaver's head against the ground, just as Kicking Elk had taught me, and then slit his throat with a cooking knife. We left that trap and started toward the next trap.

"Do you miss your family across the mountains?" Gliding Swan asked.

I slowed down. "Considerably," I said, then resumed my pace, attempting to conceal my determination to escape.

"I can see that you are not content here. You laugh, but not freely. I see sorrow in your eyes."

Gliding Swan took a deep breath. "The canoe we have at our camp. It can carry you back to your family." I froze. "Sometime, when you are on a hunt in the area, you can slip away and take the canoe down this river until it flows to the Ohio, where you can cross over to Kentucky."

Gliding Swan looked at me as tears rolled down my cheeks and my chin quivered. I fought to master my composure.

"Why do you help me?" I asked. "Do you not want to kill

me? I was among the soldiers that killed your husband, that took him from you and Rising Star."

"If the other Shawnee knew, they would want to kill you. It is our way. But you saved the life of my son. You do not belong here. You belong with your people across the mountains."

"Thank you for understanding and for your help. One day, I will need to go, but that time has not yet come," I replied.

We completed the inspection of our traps, but the beaver was our lone prize. When we arrived back at camp, Gliding Swan prepared the beaver meat for our evening meal.

That night, as I lay in my bed, a multitude of thoughts competed for my reflection. Gliding Swan had handed me a shocking gift. My heart beat at a faster pace. My goal was within my grasp. Yet death lay close at hand, revenge for the life of Swift Wolf. It could mean being burned at the stake or a knife in the stomach. I grappled with this into the night, but grew weary and slid into sleep.

On a quiet, mild morning with no breeze, I sat by the fire outside our wigwam, my arm healed. Kicking Elk emerged from his night's sleep to the chirps of a nearby bird and a chorus of other forest songs in the distance. He stretched his arms toward the sky, and said, "Look." He pointed to a small tree about six feet tall with the first sign of green and then to a dogwood tree with its display of pink flowers. "The green leaves and the flowers have returned to the forest. It is time for our return to Chillicothe."

We began packing for our return. Gliding Swan and I carried our canoe up the riverbank, near our wigwam and placed a large hollow log over the canoe and its paddles.

"When the time is right, this canoe is your passage back to

your family," Gliding Swan said. "No one knows this but you and I."

"Thanks for your help. I will always remember your kindness."

"And I will always remember how you saved Rising Star's life."

"May he grow to become a great chief," I said.

We were among the first to arrive in Chillicothe as spring unfurled. Each day, Shawnee streamed into the village until Chillicothe was again full of energy and excitement. The women planted in the fields, and the men departed on hunting treks.

We attended the first town meeting where many shared their stories of winter camp.

"Share your second panther story," Kicking Elk said during a pause after a speaker finished.

I took a breath and rose. This would be a different speech than when I scared the panther. This was not to make the people laugh. And it was also not to tout my bravery, for I felt very fortunate to be alive. It was to tout Rising Star's bright future. The people were silent, waiting for my story. I raised my left arm to display the four scars from the panther's fangs.

"These are the marks from the teeth of a panther. I am most fortunate to be alive to tell this story." I recounted the panther's stealth, his focus on Rising Star, and the fight with the knife. I praised my Shawnee family for their care for me while my wounds healed. I ended with, "The Great Spirit wanted to save Rising Star, for he will grow to become a great warrior for the Shawnee people." The people clapped and cheered as I sat down.

Gliding Swan immediately rose, holding Rising Star, "See

Rising Star lives. He is healthy and strong. I thank White Chief for his bravery in saving Rising Star's life."

Kicking Elk rose. "For White Chief's bravery we have changed his name to Stalking Panther. The panther is a noble and fierce animal. White Chief conquered the panther with his bravery. White Chief will be called Stalking Panther. Morning Moon has made a cloak from the panther's skin." He held the cloak up for all to see then draped it over my shoulders. "Wear this cloak as a reminder of your bravery."

Everyone clapped and shouted, "Stalking Panther," and repeated it several times in agreement. After the meeting many addressed me as Stalking Panther and reached up and felt the panther cloak, and said, "Nice cloak."

The next day the traders Louis Lorimier and James Girty vigorously bartered with the villagers for the skins and furs that the Shawnee brought them. I was determined to find another knife for a deerskin I had acquired during the winter. As I approached the traders, Bold Hunter walked toward me.

"Bold Hunter, how was your winter?"

"Cold, wet, and poor hunting. We are glad to be back in Chillicothe."

"Ours was cold also. I am here to trade this buckskin for a knife."

"What about that knife you had when we killed the elk?"

"I gave that knife to the family," I replied, hoping that would end the conversation.

Bold Hunter changed the subject. "Oh. I have news about Honey. She will have pups. I want you to have one of them."

"Honey is a fine dog. I am sure her pups will be excellent hunting dogs also. I would love one of her pups."

James Girty interrupted our conversation. "Hello Stalking Panther, Bold Hunter. What is it you need today? If you need it, I have it."

"I need a hunting knife," I replied.

"I have three fine hunting knives for you to choose from," replied Girty as he displayed the knives.

I picked up the longest and sharpest. "I will trade you this fine buckskin for this knife."

"Well, now, that is my best knife. You will need more than that skin for that knife."

Bold Hunter intervened, "That is a fine skin. Worth more than the knife."

"I will find someone else to trade with for the skin," I added.

"Let me see that skin," Girty replied.

Girty examined the skin, then said, "Deal. Take your knife."

As we walked away, Bold Hunter spoke, "Come with us hunting. Blackfish is gathering a group of ten or so to hunt as far as the Ohio."

"I will go. When do you plan to leave?" I replied.

"By midday. Meet at the council house."

"I will be there."

At midday, our group of hunters set out along a trail heading south toward the Ohio River. Our group of nine, led by Blackfish, included James Girty, as well as my friends Bold Hunter and Ben Kelly (Fighting Fish). Also among the hunters was Crooked Eyes with his bow.

Time in Captivity: 1 year 60 days

CHAPTER TWELVE

THE STAKE

APRIL 1779

On the third day of our camp by the Ohio, the hunters painted their faces and bodies—a preparation for battle. Blackfish posted scouts on a hill to survey upriver for boats floating down the Ohio. We were not hunting game anymore. We were hunting men—white men. This was about war, not food.

"Striking Snake (James Girty), Fighting Fish (Benjamin Kelly) and Stalking Panther, come here," Blackfish called. "I want you to put on these white men's clothes. When a boat comes down river, call for help and wave the boat over to the shore. Tell them you were captured but have escaped and need their help." Blackfish peered at Ben and me. "Striking Snake has done this before so follow his example. The rest of us will hide behind the trees near the river and wait for the boat to come near, and then we will fire. You must do this, or we will fire on you."

Blackfish's words punched me in the stomach. I knew it was wrong. For over a year, I had striven to win the Shawnees' trust. Now, they were asking something I should not give. I desperately did not want to do it. Yet I did not possess the courage to risk my own life and freedom.

Blackfish walked away.

"I don't like this," I said to Ben.

"Me either."

We followed Striking Snake to the river. The others silently found their places in the trees. Seconds felt like hours as we waited.

"A boat comes," shouted the watch on the hill. "Four men and five horses."

Ben's eyes darted from me to Blackfish, and I knew what he was thinking.

The boat emerged from behind a bend in the river. I glanced behind me into the trees. Crooked Eyes' bow was loaded with an arrow and pointed at the river. James Girty, his long-established loyalty to the Shawnee on full display, waved his arms above his head and yelled, "Help. Help."

I followed his example half-heartedly but tried to be convincing enough for Crooked Eyes. As the boat came closer, the occupants waved back.

"Help us. The Indians captured us, but we escaped. Please let us join you," called Girty.

The helmsman steered the boat toward our shore but did not stop. We ran along the shore, as did the Indians behind the trees. Girty pleaded again, "Please. We're starving and cold. If you leave us, we'll be captured again and killed for sure."

They looked away and seemed to be passing us by. I glanced over my shoulder at Crooked Eyes, who had shifted his bow toward me. My heartbeat pounded in my chest. I wanted to run, but there was nowhere to go. "Stop," I screamed. "Please, I miss my family! I don't want to die here."

The helmsman looked at me and steered the boat closer to shore. They did not get very close but beckoned, "Swim over and get in our boat."

As they motioned for us to come, their boat jammed on a sandbar. Frantically, they pushed on the sandbar with oars to free the boat. Bullets and arrows flew. The two with oars fell. The other two grabbed their rifles and fired back. Then Girty rushed in and Indians swarmed from the trees. They screamed their war whoops, and Crooked Eyes led the attackers. Ben and I turned away. His face was down and his shoulders slumped. I felt a deep pit in my stomach. The warriors captured the two remaining travelers while Girty and Crooked Eyes scalped the dead men.

All the Indians celebrated their victory, raising their arms and rifles in the air with shouts of their conquest. Several Indians boarded the boat, bound the two travelers, and directed them onto the shore. Two Indians pushed the bodies of the two dead men into the river. They placed halters on the horses and led them off.

That night, around the campfire, Crooked Eyes displayed the scalp of his victim with a grin and a gleam in his eyes. He glanced at me as he held the scalp. He stretched the scalp of his victim onto sticks, bent into a circle, and placed it near the fire to dry. Crooked Eyes sat near me as we ate our meal.

"Crooked Eyes, do you wish you could scalp me?" I said.

"You try and escape, and I cut off the top of your head," Crooked Eyes responded with a sly smile.

"I will outrun you."

"Your scalp will be my prize." With that pronouncement, Crooked Eyes rose and left.

"Let's go talk to the prisoners," I said to Ben. "Who are they and where are they headed?"

"Yeah. Let's go."

Each man was tied to a tree, with arms and legs bound. They sat in silence, heads bowed.

"We are so sorry they used us to lure you into that trap," Ben said. "We hoped you wouldn't fall for it, but they were going to shoot us if we didn't help."

"I'm so sorry you're in this quagmire," I added. "We'll do all we can to help you escape."

"Escape?" one of them asked. "You'll help us get out of here? What'll happen if we don't escape? Will they burn us at the stake? Will they scalp us? I don't want to die here!"

""We don't know," Ben answered. "Perhaps they will adopt you like they did us or take you to Detroit to sell you to the British. They have not burned anyone since we have been with them, though they talk about it sometimes."

"As I said, we'll help you escape," I said. "We must plan it. They are vigilant with their captives. They still watch us."

"Wait," one of the men said as we rose to leave. "My name's Edward, and this is Joshua. Thanks for speaking with us."

We both nodded and slipped away quietly.

I could not sleep that night. I had acted like a coward. We hoodwinked those men, lured them into a snare. My actions dashed all the pride I felt for saving Rising Star's life. My injured arm was my badge of courage. Now, I wanted to throw the last remnants of that injury away, for I was not worthy to wear the badge. I resolved to make it right, to help those men escape.

As we hiked back to Chillicothe over the next few days, I devised plan after plan to help the prisoners escape. However, every plan fell apart in my head. I never had a moment alone with Ben to discuss, so I kept my thoughts to myself and always spoke in Shawnee. When we arrived at Chillicothe, Blackfish called a village meeting that evening.

Blackfish stood up, raised his arms high with his palms open and faced the villagers, signaling silence and order. Everyone hushed.

"This week, the Shawnee were victorious against the aggression and corruption of the whites coming from the east."

Blackfish recounted the story of our "great victory." "When their boat caught the sand, we opened fire from behind the trees, killing two and capturing two. Here are their scalps," holding up the two scalps for all to see. The Shawnee cheered with approval while I felt sick. "The other two await their fate."

Blackfish reminded the village of the murder of Chief Cornstalk and his son. "Someone must be held accountable and pay for this injustice," he shouted. He bared his teeth and shook his fists with both arms raised high.

"I say we burn these two Virginians at the stake." Walking around the fire, he looked into the eyes of all his villagers. They hollered their approval.

"Burn the Virginians."

"Death for the white men."

"They must pay for their crime."

We captives were silent and kept our heads down. Kicking Elk, Morning Moon, and Gliding Swan shouted with clenched fists. I stared at the ground and held my arms against my stomach. I could not believe my Shawnee family's actions toward the innocent captives. Yes, the white man had wronged them—I understood that much better now than I did before. But why kill these two young men?

I turned to Bold Hunter. "When will the prisoners be burned?"

"It starts tomorrow morning and lasts all day," he replied.

As we left the council house, I turned to Ben and whispered, "Walk with me for a while. We need to discuss plans to help Edward and Joshua." We walked in the direction of Ben's house away from others.

"Yeah," Ben said. "They're guarded really well. There aren't many opportunities. We only have a few hours before the whole town will be watching them."

"Once everyone's asleep, we can meet up at the large maple

tree beside the council house, go to where they're tied up, and cut them free. Then slip back into our wigwams without being seen."

"That's about our only option. But it might work. Let's do it." Ben replied.

"Good plan. See you in a couple of hours." Then we parted.

I joined Kicking Elk and Morning Moon at our wigwam. As we laid down for the night, I placed my moccasins and knife near the foot of my bed so I could slip out of our wigwam with minimal disturbance. I lay in silence, my mind wrestling with vain attempts to control the outcome of our rescue plan. There was one requirement—that our involvement be undetected—or there might be four prisoners burned at the stake.

I waited until the sounds of methodical breathing, snores, and the lack of movement told me that Kicking Elk and Morning Moon slept. I removed my bearskin cover, slipped on my moccasins, clutched my knife, and stole out of our wigwam.

I approached the maple tree and could discern a silhouette.

"Ben?" I whispered.

Ben turned in my direction and responded with an exaggerated nod.

"Where are the prisoners?" I said.

"Over by that fire yonder."

We hid among some undergrowth and near a tree in the forest, about fifty feet from the fire. Four Shawnee men, including Crooked Eyes, guarded Joshua and Edward. We waited an hour. Three of the guards lay down and appeared to go to sleep. Only Crooked Eyes remained awake. He put a log on the fire and sat down.

He remained motionless for half an hour. I wondered if he had fallen asleep. Was this our chance to cut the prisoners free?

Ben and I pointed at which prisoner we would cut loose before approaching. As we crept closer, we kept a close eye on Crooked Eyes. About twenty feet from the prisoners, we paused.

Crooked Eyes still had not moved. He must be asleep. We snuck closer, our knives ready. At ten feet, one of the Indians lying on the ground stirred. We froze. Then, a second Indian stirred. Then Crooked Eyes stood up. His movements awakened the fourth Indian, who also stood up. Still hidden by the darkness, we retreated in unison, concealing ourselves again in the cover of the forest. We remained undetected by the guards. Hidden in the underbrush, we waited for another opportunity. As the eastern sky became purple and orange with dawn, the four guards badgered and poked the prisoners.

"We missed our chance," Ben whispered. "If we don't go back now, our families will miss us."

I closed my eyes and took a deep breath and nodded.

We turned in retreat. I wanted to say something else, but there was nothing to say. We headed for our respective wigwams and without a sound, I slipped into my bed. I lay there blaming myself for the dreadful fate of those two men. Soon, the birds began their chorus, and Kicking Elk and Morning Moon began to stir. I lay silent.

I finally rose to the scent of fish and greeted my adoptive parents.

"When you've finished eating, we'll go to the burning," Kicking Elk said. "This is an important day! It will not make up for Cornstalk's murder, but it will be a portion of justice. They will suffer for their crimes against the Shawnee. We will go together."

I would witness the torture and execution of two men that I helped capture. My stomach turned inside out. I vomited my fish on the ground.

"Are you sick?" Morning Moon said as she rushed to my side.

"I will recover," I said. "I will go with you and Kicking Elk."

A large group of men, women, and children gathered around a large campfire just outside the village. They stripped Joshua naked and painted him black. They bound his hands behind his back and led him to a fifteen-foot small oak tree stripped of its branches and buried in the ground near the fire. At the top of this post was a grape vine to which they tied Joshua's bound hands. He had just enough slack to walk around the post.

Edward, hands and feet still bound, sat on the ground, forced to witness Joshua's execution. Crooked Eyes and the other guards taunted him, "You next." Edward was to be taken to another village for his execution.

Chief Blackfish stood close to the fire, raised his arms high, and shouted for the attention of the villagers. "Today, we punish the white Virginians for their crimes. White men killed the peaceful Chief Cornstalk though he was innocent, so the white men must pay! Today, this Virginian will be burned to *death*." Blackfish pointed to Joshua, raised his right fist in the air, and shouted "death!"

The crowd cheered and shouted. They took long poles that had burned in two and pressed the burning ends into Joshua's naked body. Then they took guns, filled them with powder and shot at him. Children picked up burning sticks and stuck them in his side. He screamed. I felt as if the fire was searing my own flesh. Though I was not actively torturing him, I was just as guilty.

Joshua stumbled away from one Indian, only to be met by another. Many red-hot coals fell on the ground where he staggered, forcing him to tread on hot embers. After two hours of this torture Joshua called out, "God have mercy on my soul!"

I stood and walked away, Joshua's cries echoing in my head. My deception had disgraced, beat, scorched, and killed this man. I could not escape the weight of my cowardice. The memory of my deceptive pleas to the men in the boat mocked me.

Back at our wigwam, I did not know where to go to find peace. With no sleep the night before, I lay on my bed but still could not sleep. After a restless hour, I rose from my bed, walked down by the river, and sat on the same rock where I had grieved over my capture and separation from my family. I could not bear the thought that Blackfish would command me to participate in another death. The time had come to leave.

Time in Captivity: 1 year 90 days

CHAPTER THIRTEEN

THE TERRIFYING SHADOW

MAY 1779

Five hungry puppies climbed over each other as they stretched their necks for food from their mother's teats. Honey lay on a buffalo hide like a queen surrounded by her attendants. Bold Hunter smiled and laughed as he played with the puppies.

Bold Hunter welcomed me and invited me to choose a puppy to take. I selected one that reminded me of Rex when he was a pup.

"What will you name him?" Bold Hunter asked.

"Kicking Elk will name him," I said. "He has always wanted a hunting dog, and this pup will be helpful as he gets older."

Bold Hunter nodded and invited me to return in a couple of weeks to take the puppy.

I departed and then ambled through the streets of Chillicothe to the wigwam where Ben lived. Ben tended a fire outside.

"Hey Ben. I need to talk to you. Let's walk toward the river together. There's no one over there now."

"I have a plan for escape," I said, as we walked. "I have a canoe hidden near the Beaver Pond area. The next time we go hunting over there, I will steal away, paddle down the Little Miami, and across the Ohio. Will you join me?"

Ben frowned. "Daniel, you know I want to get back to Virginia, but we are leaving in a couple days for Salt Creek. We'll be gone a month or more. Besides, these escapes work better one at a time. You go if you have the opportunity."

I nodded. "The time has come for me to go. I can't bear another attack on a river boat."

"I'll see you back in New London. We'll go hunting together and talk about the fun time we had here."

We grabbed each other's forearm, not knowing when, or if, we would see each other again.

Two weeks later, I took Honey's puppy to Kicking Elk, sitting outside our wigwam. Gliding Swan was tending a fire outside her wigwam.

"Kicking Elk, meet your new hunting partner," I said. "This is one of Honey's pups. He is yours."

"It is with much gratitude that I accept this gift," Kicking Elk replied. "What is his name?"

"You will name him since he is yours."

"Set him on the ground and let me see him walk."

I set the pup on the ground. He darted straight to Kicking Elk, his fur streaming behind him.

"Look how fast he is," Kicking Elk observed with a smile. "I will name him Swift Runner."

He played with Swift Runner for a few moments, tossing and tugging with a stick. He turned to Gliding Swan.

"We are leaving for a hunting trip tomorrow and will be gone for a few days. Will you watch over Swift Runner, and keep him fed?"

"Yes, I will watch him and introduce him to Rising Star."

"We will hunt near Beaver Pond," I added. "Long Stepper, Bold Hunter, and Ran in Thorns will hunt with us."

Gliding Swan examined my face. She held her gaze longer than usual. "May you have great success on the hunt. And may your journey be safe."

At that moment, Crooked Eyes passed by our wigwam, and stood beside me. "I will join you on your hunt tomorrow. I want to hunt the beaver pond area again."

We will leave at sunrise tomorrow morning," Kicking Elk said.

Water dripped and fell into a puddle, forming ripples on the floor of the wigwam. The sound of the drops as they hit the water broke the silence as six of us huddled inside the wigwam near Beaver Pond. Outside, the rain descended in torrents. Streams gushed where there had never been streams before. Water poured over the beaver dam. Below the dam the creek became a raging river. This was the second day of our hunting venture, and all we could do was wait, without much to talk about. My escape dominated my thoughts. However, it could not be rushed. It had to be the right moment. Did the canoe still wait for me? Or had the flooded river washed it away?

On the third day, the rain slowed, then stopped and yielded to the sun. Breezes out of the west blew clouds across the sky. The patches of blue sky brought promise that we could hunt again. It was afternoon and too late to dare my escape. I wanted as much daylight for travel as possible, and as much time as possible before I would be missed. One more day, then I would bolt for freedom.

That afternoon, I traveled with Bold Hunter north to some tree-covered hills that would be among the first areas to drain after the recent rains. Near the crest of a hill, we parted, each to find a place to hide and wait for a deer. I started my deer calls. Within fifteen minutes, five deer appeared. Bold Hunter motioned that he also saw them. I raised my rifle, aimed for the head of the largest and closest deer. My shot was on target, and the deer collapsed. Bold Hunter's shot sounded immediately afterward and struck its target. We both raised our rifles, hollered at our conquest, and rushed to our prey.

That night we ate venison, told our hunting stories, and planned our hunts for the following day. I had to influence the hunting plans of our group so that I would hunt the area south of camp, the direction where my canoe lay hidden, without appearing odd and without Crooked Eyes anywhere near me.

"Today, I hunted in the north," I said. "Tomorrow, I will hunt in the south."

"We had such success in the north," Bold Hunter said. "I want to go back there."

"We hunted the south today and did not even see deer tracks," Long Stepper said. "I want to go with Kicking Elk to the north."

"I still want to go south," I said. "The deer like my call . . . mmmuuuu." They all laughed. "If there is a deer near there, they will come when I call."

"Either a deer or a panther will come." Long Stepper laughed, joined by the others.

"The deer certainly came when Stalking Panther hollered today," Bold Hunter said.

"I will hunt to the west," Ran in Thorns said. "We shot a deer there today."

All had spoken except Crooked Eyes. I held my breath.

"I will go to the west with Ran in Thorns," Crooked Eyes said.

I let out my breath and felt my heart pound with anticipation. This time tomorrow, I would be in Kentucky.

The north wind blew against my back as wet leaves splashed against my face. I raced along the trail, south of camp. My heart hammered against my chest. Though it was morning, the sky was still dark with rain clouds and the storm that loomed on the northeast horizon. A few patches of blue between the clouds propelled me forward. I slipped frequently in muddy patches and occasionally landed on a sharp rock, but I was oblivious to pain. The trail was narrow, but I sensed the door to my freedom expanding wide before me. Everything seemed right. It was early in the morning, and no one suspected my escape. Crooked Eyes was far to the west. I pictured the canoe waiting for me, that would carry me down a swift moving river. I hauled my rifle, powder, balls, knife, and tomahawk. I also carried a pouch of roasted venison, left over from the night before. After an hour of jogging, I paused to rest and drink from a stream. Then, my vision of freedom spurred me to resume my flight.

Within a minute, I encountered an obstacle on the path that reduced my run to a halt. My head jerked back. I calmed my trembling hands. My urge was to run, but that would be a mistake. Fifty feet in front of me stood Crooked Eyes with his bow, and Ran in Thorns.

I recovered enough to say, "Crooked Eyes, Ran in Thornes, your plan was to hunt to the west."

"We will hunt with you," Crooked Eyes said. "You need our help."

I battled to master my composure. "Yeah. Yeah. Good. Come with me. I know a good place."

I knew a place to hunt from our winter in the area. I led them there.

"Let us spread out. You go over by yonder tree, and I will hunt from this rock," I instructed Crooked Eyes.

"Ran in Thorns can hunt there. I will hunt near you."

"We will have better success if we spread out," I insisted.

"No good. I will hunt with you." Crooked Eyes' wicked sneer sent a chill down my spine.

We sat down by a tree. After about thirty minutes, three deer appeared. Crooked Eyes let his arrow fly. Ran in Thorns shot his rifle. The deer ran.

Crooked Eyes and Ran in Thorns chased after the deer, but I stayed still. They were soon out of sight. I bolted the other way, toward my canoe. Even if Crooked Eyes and Ran in Thorns ran after me, I could outrun them. I would be out of Crooked Eyes' range. If Ran in Thorns stopped to re-load, I would be out of sight. I never looked back.

I paused to catch my breath and walk. Then, I heard the voice of Crooked Eyes, "I catch you, Stalking Panther, and then I kill you." An arrow landed near my feet.

I broke into a sprint, faster than I have ever run. When I felt my legs were about to give out, I spotted a large hollow tree on the ground near the trail. I crawled in to be out of sight from either end.

I waited and tried to get my breath under control.

The sound of two runners grew louder. The footsteps slowed and stopped right by me.

"I must rest. I must sit." Two light thumps rocked my log. I held my breath and I heard my heart thunder in my ears.

"He cannot be far," Ran in Thorns said.

"When I catch him, I will shoot him through the heart and scalp him," Crooked Eyes said.

"No. He must face Blackfish and Kicking Elk for his betrayal."

Crooked Eyes stood, jostling the log. "We must keep up our pursuit, or we will not catch him."

The two men continued down the trail. Now they were between me and my canoe. I crawled out of the log and left the trail. I followed the trail, but from a distance, through thick undergrowth and rocky terrain. My progress was laborious, but I reasoned that they did not know where I was headed, and, with no sign of me, they would grow weary of their chase.

At last, I viewed the large rock and pine trees. I halted to detect any sign of Crooked Eyes in the area. Seeing no sign of people and hearing no voices, I proceeded with caution.

I lifted the hollow tree to find the canoe and paddles still there. I threw my pack and rifle in and pushed off into the river. Soon, I floated in the full current, careful to keep the bow headed downstream. The rain-swollen river propelled me toward freedom though I wished I could travel faster. I had left the pain of captivity behind and my mind raced with thoughts of Fort Boonesborough, New London, and Ma's chicken stew. I could not really be free until I arrived there.

The Ohio River was twenty miles away, but with just an hour of daylight left, I needed to find a place to camp for the night. Just as the light in the western sky dimmed, I found a suitable level place on the shore. I ate some of the roasted venison from the night before and then rested, though sleep was scarce.

At the first sign of light in the east, I again pushed my transport into the river. After about an hour, the current slowed as the river widened and flowed over its normal banks. The water was like a lake, and the direction of the river current no longer apparent. I floated to a tree and climbed it, scanning the water's surface. There was discernable current to the west. I headed in that direction and the Little Miami soon propelled me toward the Ohio River and Kentucky.

By that afternoon I reached the Ohio. Pausing at the mouth of the Little Miami I scouted the river from a higher elevation. I ate half of the venison that was left and launched my canoe, aiming it downstream at an angle toward Kentucky. The flow of the river carried me downstream, but if I made progress toward Kentucky, I was satisfied. I soon reached the other side and pulled my canoe up on shore. I was well pleased with my journey so far.

My immediate destination was Limestone Creek, a long two days of travel. I stayed behind the row of trees along the shore, out of sight of any Indians on the river. From Limestone Creek I would find the buffalo trace that would take me to Blue Licks, where we were captured, and then on to Boonesborough.

I made generous progress toward my destination until the morning of the second day. With each step Chillicothe became more a memory and freedom moved closer to reality. It was almost assured now. Though the rain had ceased, there were still many dark thunderclouds threatening to veil the sun. Distant rumbles of thunder spurred me on. Hunger led me to veer off my course farther into the forest in search of game. I spied a flock of turkeys within range. My bullet was on target. A big bearded gobbler was down. Finding a small clearing, I built a fire to cook my meal. As I took my first bite, thunder cracked nearby, hastening me to finish my meal. Roasted turkey tasted so enjoyable and was all I would need to eat until I reached Limestone Creek. As a light rain fell, my escape to safety was a certainty. After smothering the fire, I gathered my pack and loaded my rifle. Then, the sound of raindrops was trumped by thunder. No, it was a gunshot! The sound sent a shock through my whole body. My heart beat against my chest. Sweat ran down my arms. That shot meant there were other humans nearby. Were they allies? Or enemies? They could either usher me toward safety or be the last obstacle between me and freedom.

As the rain began to pour, I hid in a thicket of cane. After a minute, six Indians stopped at my campfire coals. They pointed to my tracks and seemed to stare right at me. I darted through the thicket and sought cover. I found a large poplar tree with a hollow area at its base. I slithered inside the nook and held my breath. Three of them rushed by me on both sides without observing me. I hoped they would keep marching. When they were about to move on, one of them turned around. He pointed at me and shouted, and they all charged.

I darted back through the cane thicket and found a large tree beyond the thicket to hide behind. However, the mud signaled my trail. They pointed right toward me, so I raced down a hill, endeavoring to keep trees and rocks between me and my pursuers. The large rocks at the top of the next hill promised a hiding place. I wedged myself between the rocks and stayed motionless. One of them darted right in front of me but did not see me. They spoke a language like Shawnee, for I recognized many of their words. Between hand gestures, the expressions on their faces, and the similar language, I could understand what they said.

Thunder boomed as the clouds parted to reveal the sun. Then, a horrifying sight appeared. On the ground before me was the shadow of a man who stood behind me, with his tomahawk raised, poised for a strike. *Would that shadow be the last sight my eyes would ever see?* I held my breath. *Would that breath be the last air I would ever breathe?* I screamed. Then another man knocked down my would-be executioner. At this, I bolted, but two men caught me and shoved me to the ground.

"You cannot kill him," one of them yelled at the other. He had a long, deep scar across his left cheek. "We must find out who he is. He is worth more alive than dead."

I pushed myself to my feet. "I am Stalking Panther from Chillicothe."

"You are a white man dressed like a Shawnee, with your buckskin shirt and gaiters. Why do you travel alone?"

As I scrambled for an answer another Indian spoke up, "You are a captured white man who has escaped."

"He is our enemy," said the Indian with the scarred face. "We scalp our enemies. The British pay for prisoners, and for scalps. They will pay us double for this one."

At that, he placed his leg in front of my legs and his hand on my back, pushed me forward, and knocked me to the ground face down. He stood over me with his scalping knife in hand, stomped his foot on my back near my shoulders, and forced my chest to the ground. With his knee on my back, he grabbed my hair, jabbed the point of his knife into my head. A hot, sharp pain cut across and all around my head. Then, he wrenched my hair off my head and screamed a roar of triumph. I responded with my own scream and doubted I would live to see the next day.

Blood flowed from the top of my head down, covered my forehead, ran into my eyes, around my nose, and into my mouth. It streamed around my ears and down my back and dripped into pools on the ground where I lay. The top of my head was on fire. I reached up with a trembling hand and touched where my hair once lay, which sent streams of blood into my eyes and seemed to add fuel to that fire. I lost consciousness.

I awoke sometime later, still lying in my blood. I opened my eyes. The Indian with the scar examined my scalp, his prize. He seemed to cherish it as he cleaned it with his knife and scraped off the blood. I could not pull my eyes away, though the sight made me want to vomit. That was *my* scalp. Cutting off a small foot-long branch from a nearby tree and fastening the ends together, he stretched my scalp over it like a tambourine. He walked away, carrying a long stick with five other scalps. No doubt my scalp would be added to his collection after it dried.

"You will be fine," said the Indian who scalped me. "You just will not have long hair." He paused, then added, " . . . or even short hair." They all roared with laughter.

My losses overwhelmed me. I lost my hope of seeing Boonesborough, Virginia, and my family. I lost my freedom. I lost my scalp. I lay there wanting to cry but held it in until darkness took me again.

I opened my eyes as one of the Indians took a deer hide,

placed it on my head, and secured it with a buffalo tug tied around my head.

"What tribe are you?" I asked.

"Miami," he replied. "We live to the north."

"What is your name?"

"My name is Red Hawk."

We camped there that night but packed up the next morning. Red Hawk took my rifle, tomahawk, and knife and motioned with his hand for me to follow the other Indians in their march. Red Hawk marched behind me. We marched north toward the Ohio, away from Boonesborough. As we marched, I wept inwardly, more from the idea of losing my hair and blood, and my freedom, than from the pain. When we reached the Ohio, he helped me take off my deer hide cap and washed my head in the river, then placed it back on my head.

Though it was kind of him to help me, I could not muster a thank you.

Two of the Indians brought out a small canoe hidden in the bush. All six loaded their guns and packs in it. They pushed it into the water ahead of them as they waded in to swim. I waded into the water. My heartbeat accelerated. I hesitated.

"I cannot swim," I shouted to Red Hawk.

"You must learn fast," he replied. "Find a log."

I found a log and I pushed it ahead of me until I was waist deep. I lay on the log and it sank below the surface. I could not keep my head above the surface. Arms flailing, I fought for the surface and air. I lunged for Red Hawk but could not reach him. I fought for a breath but sank again. Red Hawk pulled me up, and I lunged for him. He threw me off, and I sank again. I managed to break the surface and grabbed a breath before going back down. I kicked and flailed but remained under the water now. My heart pounded. Something poked my side, and I grabbed it. I was then pulled up out of the water to the south bank by Red Hawk, holding a branch. I climbed onto land and breathed heavily.

Red Hawk had the others bring the canoe back, and I sat in it as he pushed it across. I took several deep breaths and calmed down. I repositioned my buckskin cap on my wounded head.

After we crossed the river, we marched north. North was away from Boonesborough, away from freedom. North was toward captivity and the unknown.

We journeyed through the summer and into the fall. My new band of Indians treated me with respect and kindness, though they were vigilant to ensure that I did not escape, tying my arms and legs to two of them at night. The top of my head remained tender and susceptible to bleeding. I always kept my deer hide "cap" on to protect my head from the sun, flies, and the assault of tree branches. I washed it in river water whenever I had the opportunity. We traveled into Canada and on occasion visited other Indian villages.

The midday sun was bright, set against a cloudless blue sky. The tree leaves dazzled with yellow, orange, and red colors. My six captors and I entered Detroit, our destination and my next home, a British prison and dungeon for captured American soldiers. We marched into Fort Lernoult. A British soldier met us at the door. He was the first Redcoat I had seen since I joined the militia. He eyed the ropes that bound my hands and examined my face.

He led us to a room with a desk and chair. Seated at the desk was the fort commander. A guard stood nearby.

One of the Miami captors spoke first in broken English, "We have come to sell you prisoner and scalps. How much you pay?"

"We pay you five blankets and two rifles for this prisoner and these scalps," the commander replied.

"We want five blankets and four rifles."

"We will give you five blankets and three rifles. That is all we can spare."

"We accept. Here is your prisoner," my captor said as he pushed me toward the commander.

They left with the soldier who had brought us in, and the commander looked me over.

"What's your name, age, and rank?" the commander asked.

"Daniel Asbury. Age seventeen, private."

"Asbury, I am Colonel Arent Schuyler de Peyster, I make this offer to you once. You can have your freedom if you agree to fight in King George's army."

"I don't have to think about that," I replied. "I'd take a rifle shot to my head, a knife through my side, a rope around my neck, or a prison cell to rot in before I'd fight for your king."

De Peyster glared at me for about ten seconds. "That's rash and arrogant talk for someone so young. You shall have your wish. That's a fine buckskin shirt. Take it off."

I complied but slowly. The guard whacked my back with the butt of his gun. I removed my shirt.

"This'll trade well with the Indians," de Peyster said. "You best spend your time tonight preparin' to meet your God. Tomorrow you'll hang." He turned to the soldier, "Take this traitor to his cell."

Time in Captivity: 1 year 240 days

CHAPTER FOURTEEN
THE PRISON
OCTOBER 1779

The passageway was dark, lit only by a few rays of sun entering windows in nearby jail cells. The smell was raunchy and musty, the putrid odor of rotten food with whiffs of urine and feces. The chain that connected the irons around my ankles clanged on the floor as I walked toward my prison chambers. Wearing only my loincloth, gaiters, and my deer hide cap covering my scalp wound, I shivered. At the end of the hallway, the guard opened a cell door for me.

"Step inside your new home," he said.

"Do you have any clothes for me?" I asked.

"We ain't got no extra clothes," he responded. "Besides, you ain't goin' to live long enough to need clothes. You need to prepare to die. You best spend tonight makin' your peace with God, for tomorrow you'll hang. There will be no meal for you tonight, but we'll feed ya before ya hang tomorrow."

"You can't hang me without a trial. That's a crime."

"We don't follow those rules out here." He closed the door.

My room was a dungeon—dark, damp, and dirty, with only a small window high up letting in a bit of light. The whiffs of putrid and rotten odors detected in the hallway were suffocating inside the room. The room was empty, save for some straw for a bed on the floor and one metal tub in a corner. I walked over to inspect it, but before I reached it, the stink made me puke. It was half full of excrement.

I pondered my state and the words spoken to me: "Make peace with your God, for tomorrow you'll hang." My captivity had reached an end, with no hope for escape. Although I had faced death many times since joining the militia, this was the first time I had been told I would die by those who held me captive. Crooked Eyes vowed many times that he would kill me. But those seemed to be empty threats. This promise had a certainty about it, and I had no power to alter my circumstances. And was this promise of death a just and fitting end for me? For I still loathed the day that I betrayed those four travelers. I thought back to the day I had decided to join the militia. What else could I have done? Yes, I wanted to see the world, but I also had protected my family, left them Pa who was much better able to care for them. I thought of my Shawnee family, now without a son. I wondered if things could have turned out any differently but could not see how.

As the morning light shone through the window, I wondered about whether this was my last morning and how it would feel to be dead. I knew how it felt to be alive—scared, hungry, cold, in pain, but glad for the sunlight. What was death?

The quietness of the morning was interrupted when the guard opened the door and yelled, "Here's yer food!" He tossed in a piece of bread that just missed the excrement tub. I rose and picked it up. Half of it was covered in mold. My stomach growled. I tore off the moldy part, gobbled down my last "meal" and waited.

A couple of hours later the guard returned. "Today is not your hangin' day after all. You're bein' moved to the jail with the others. Follow me."

I could hardly believe it. All I could do was follow, my chains clanging on the floor.

Down several dark hallways, we passed rooms full of prisoners. I reckoned there were several hundred. He opened the door to a crowded room and motioned me in. I entered, shuffling my chained feet, and beheld misery. The foul odor made my stomach turn over. I clenched my teeth, tightened my stomach, and clamped my hands to my mouth to suppress my vomit. The room held about sixty prisoners. Some stood, some sat, and some lay in the dirt and straw. None had bathed for months. Some in chains and some not. They all had long hair and long beards. Three chamber pots were in one corner. I sat in another corner beside three others in silence.

After a while, I asked the one closest to me, "How long you been here?"

He shrugged. "Year and a half or so. I've lost track of time."

Though I did not recognize him in the dim light, his voice seemed familiar. "William Humphries! It's me, Daniel Asbury."

"Daniel! It's nice to hear a familiar voice. James Morton is here, too." He gestured to the man next to him.

"Hey there, James. If I must sit in a dungeon, it might as well be with friends."

"Daniel, they left you in Chillicothe," Morton said. "How did you get here?"

"I escaped a year later but got captured by some Miamis when I was a half-day's walk from Limestone."

"Well, you've gone from bushes and jumped into the briars," Humphries said. "The Indians treated us and fed us much better than the Redcoats. These Brits are the real savages. They're tryin' to kill us by starvation and sickness. They see us as traitors who deserve to die. Every day, someone in this room dies. We're fortunate to be alive."

"How's the food?"

Morton pursed his lips and shook his head. "If I wasn't weak and nearly starved, I'd laugh. 'Bout every three days they bring us food, which is less food than you'd eat for one meal. They're supposed to give us some today."

"Are the other Boonesborough soldiers here?" I asked.

"Yeah," Humpries said. "Wade and Brown escaped but were re-captured. Brought 'em here, then shipped 'em back east, to Montreal. Samuel English volunteered to serve in the British army. But you might have guessed that."

"I'm sure English is happy now that he's back with the British," I said.

"I'm glad Wade and Brown tried an escape," said Morton. "But these Redcoats make it extremely hard with these chains and dungeon walls."

"William, your wife and boys must be mighty worried," I said. "I hope you can git back to them soon."

Humphries gazed across the room then back at me, as he twisted a lock of his hair. "Yeah, that's all I think about. They need me to take care of 'em. They probably think I died. But I am too weak to try to escape."

"That's brutal," I said. "My Ma and Pa probably think I died. I want to get back to them somethin' fierce."

About an hour later, the door opened, and the prisoners moved toward the door. The guards brought in three baskets of food and a tub of water. I followed Humphries and Morton toward the food. We walked by a basket and grabbed a piece. It was a piece of spoiled raw pork. Back at our spot against the wall, we gnawed on our meal, our great hunger overcoming the repulsiveness of our food. The first urge from my stomach was to throw it out of my mouth, but I would get nothing better for nourishment. I used all my concentration to keep it down. The others were concerned of dying from hunger, but I wondered if the food would be just as fatal. Three cups hung from the rim of the water tub. The water was gray and smelled foul, but it was all we had. I dared not drink as much as my body craved for fear that the illness that appeared to afflict half of the people in the room would soon fall upon me. I drank what I could to stay alive. The meal did not cheer the prisoners, for the food was only an instrument of death, slower and more torturous than hanging. A silent cloud of doom filled the room.

That night, I gathered as much straw as I could find scattered on the floor for my bed and lay down. Something crawled up my leg, wiggled across my waist, and slithered up my chest. I jumped up and brushed my entire body several times, not convinced I had removed all the creatures. In the dim moonlight that shone through the prison window, I discovered several large roaches, ants, and all sorts of vermin I could not name. I pushed away the straw and settled for the hard rock floor, placing my arm under my head for a pillow. As I did, my deerskin "hat" fell off. I caressed the top of my head to remove whatever might have crawled there. Five months after my scalping, the scab fell off and left tender skin, still vulnerable to further injury. Confident the intruders were gone, I placed my hat back on top and resecured it with a rope around my forehead, then laid my head back down on my arm. Shivering in the cold and pondering my plight, I tried to sleep. How far away from home I was. How far I had fallen from the delightful times with my family in the hills of Virginia, imprisoned in a dark dungeon, as death stood right in front of me.

The next morning, a rush of prisoners scrambling for biscuits awakened me. Half a biscuit landed near my feet. I grabbed it and embraced it. Not everyone got even that much. The stale bread grew green mold on one side. I broke it open and removed a worm. Driven by great hunger, I tossed the wiggler into some straw, brushed off the mold, and ate the biscuit.

I sat against the wall in the cold room, contemplating my hunger and lack of clothes. I examined my wrists and ankles—red, raw, and bleeding from the rusty irons that bound them. A loud, relentless cough from the man who sat beside me pleaded for my attention. His cough lingered for several minutes.

I fetched a cup of the murky water for him. "Drink. Maybe this will help."

The man took a sip, and after another minute of struggling to stop, his cough quieted.

The man was perhaps fifty years old, but a few months in a British prison can add years to one's appearance. "That's a dreadful cough you have."

"Yeah. I'm afraid it's goin' to get the best of me," he replied. "I have been sick for three or four weeks, and it is not gettin' any better since they won't let any doctors help us.

"What's your name, sir? And where you from?" I asked.

"Thomas Jones, from Philadelphia. I'm a tailor with a wife and three daughters," he said.

"My name is Daniel Asbury from Virginia. I joined the militia so my father wouldn't have to leave our family. We supported the settlers in Kentucky in their fight against the Indians and British."

"I hear it's beautiful in Kentucky."

"Yes, sir. Beautiful indeed. But ya couldn't enjoy it for all the fightin'. Then me and some others got ourselves captured. Now, here we are."

"So sorry for your tribulation. I can't think of a worse place to be than here. The war won't last forever. Maybe we can hang on long enough to return to our families."

"I certainly hope so, sir."

After that, we both leaned back against the wall in silence.

About the middle of the day, the guards identified twenty prisoners and led them out of the room. They soon appeared in the courtyard, which we could see through the window.

Meanwhile, as many as possible crowded around the windows and narrow openings in the walls to get as much fresh air as possible. I was in the third group of prisoners to go outside. I helped Mr. Jones walk with our group. Once outside, I took deep breaths of the fall air and lifted up my head so the sun could shine on my face. I longed for those brief respites from the dungeon filth, despite the chilly air and my inadequate clothing. Hundreds of faces peered through the windows and small openings in the prison walls, heads stacked on top of heads.

One night Mr. Jones said to me, "I'd like to ask a favor from you. I may not make it out of here alive. If you are ever in Philadelphia, would you visit my wife and daughters and tell them I love them?"

"Yes, I will. It'd be an honor."

"Thanks. Now . . . " Mr. Jones was interrupted by a coughing fit. When he got control, he continued, "If I die, take my clothes. They can't do a dead man any good and they may save your life, with winter comin'."

"Don't say that. You're goin' to make it out of here alive. You'll get to tell your wife and daughters you love them yourself."

"I am bona fide sick. And once you get this kind of sick in this place, there's no way to get well again."

He gave me a sad smile before lying down. I lay down beside him and closed my eyes, falling asleep as he coughed every few minutes.

I opened my eyes just as the morning light entered the prison cell. Mr. Jones lay motionless and peaceful, his eyes still closed, without a cough or any sign of suffering. That notion startled me. He was not suffering. Was he still alive? I touched his hand. It was cold. I shook him, but he could not be roused. I woke Humphries and pointed at Mr. Jones.

"I think Mr. Jones may have . . . ." I stopped, realizing I had never said this about someone.

Humphries examined him and shook him. Then, Humphries put his hand to his neck and his finger under his nose. "He's gone. Thomas Jones is at peace."

"He asked me to tell his wife and daughters that he loved them." I hesitated. "He also wanted me to have his clothes. Said they can't do a dead man any good but may save my life with winter comin'."

"Here, take 'em before someone else does," Humphries replied, as he unbuttoned his shirt.

I removed his trousers and took the shirt from Humphries. I appealed to a guard to remove my chains long enough to don my new shirt and trousers. The relief of my shivers was immediate. In that moment of thankfulness, I knew I had to visit Mrs. Jones and her daughters, should I have the opportunity.

As the guards removed Mr. Jones' body, other guards threw food into the room. During the scramble, I obtained a small piece. After the food, we crowded near the windows to get a few breaths of outside air, when we heard shouts in the courtyard.

"God save the king," yelled a British soldier. Additional voices joined in. Several of us rose to look out the window to observe the spectacle. We saw six Redcoats surrounding a new prisoner.

"Say it, traitor," hollered one Redcoat, then hit him in the face and knocked him to the ground.

He rose, and another punched him in the belly. "Say the words. You rebel. 'God save the king.'"

The man, in his mid-forties, with his palms up to stop the abuse, stood up straight, removed his hat in respect, and said, "God save us all."

At this, another Redcoat pulled out his sword and ran him through, first through the arm and then through his belly. The man received these wounds in silence, without a word of protest. Two guards picked up the wounded man, assisted him to walk, and delivered him to our prison room.

I hurried as fast as my weakened legs would carry me to the prison door and yelled for a guard's help, "Guard. We need a doctor."

There was no immediate response, so I yelled again, "Guard, come."

I took a metal cup from the water bucket and banged it against the metal bars and moved it across the bars to increase the racket. "Guard, we need a doctor."

As the guard approached the room, I backed away from the door and replaced the cup at the bucket of water.

When the guard arrived, I explained, "This man needs a doctor. He'll die if he's not treated."

The guard came into the room, bashed me across the head with a stout rod, knocked me to the floor, and said, "There's no doctor for prisoners. Traitors don't get doctors. Treat him yourselves."

Humphries, two other prisoners, and I gathered around him. "We need to wash his wounds," Humphries said. "Then, he needs a bandage to stop his bleedin'."

I fetched a cup of water from the bucket but hesitated as I handed it to Humphries. The water was dirtier than the soldier's blade.

"It's all we have," he said, as if reading my mind, and took the cup and poured it over the wounds. "There's a clean spot on his shirt. Tear it off for a bandage."

I did as Humphries instructed and handed it to him. Humphries wrapped it around his wound.

The man raised his head. "Thank you, lads. Your kindness will be rewarded from Heaven."

"What's your name, sir?" I asked.

"Captain Charles Woodhull. I have a farm in western Pennsylvania. Redcoats captured my men and I north of Fort Pitt. What's your name, son?"

"Daniel Asbury, from Virginia," I replied.

"Well, Daniel Asbury from Virginia, thank you for helpin' me. I hope you get out of this hell hole soon."

"Thank you. I hope so too. But they're doin' their best to kill us.

We were powerless to help him except to sit with him and get him some food and water, filthy as it was. After a few days, the wounds turned yellow-green and began to ooze pus. The bandages were soaked through, his blood dripping on the floor. Charles' pain grew each day.

"I'm going to sing you boys a song from Psalms," Charles said one night, his voice steady despite his pain. The room was quiet.

Attend unto my cry;
For I am brought very low:
Deliver me from my persecutors;
For they are stronger than I.
Bring my soul out of prison,
That I may praise Thy Name.

Silent appreciation filled the room. Morton cried out, "Sing it again."

Charles sang it again.

Attend unto my cry;

A couple men joined in.

For I am brought very low:

A few more joined as best they could.

Deliver me from my persecutors;

Now most of the men were singing.

For they are stronger than I.

Then, I joined along with everyone else.

Bring my soul out of prison,
That I may praise Thy Name.

For the first time in my life, I prayed. I sang that prayer to God. I did not know if He was listening, but I had nothing else to lose.

Charles' wounds grew darker and swollen over the next few days. He was in agony, and I remembered Joshua, burning alive. Yes, I missed the comfort of my Shawnee life, but the Indians were cruel as well. It seemed to be a common failing of men.

"Ask the guard for a pen and paper," Charles told Humphries. "I must write my wife."

Humphries called for the guard. "Captain Woodhull is near death. He's requested a pen and paper to write his wife. We ask for your merciful consideration of his request."

The guard examined Charles from the doorway and then frowned. To my surprise, he said, "I'll grant his request."

We gathered around Charles as he wrote. When he finished, he said, "I have asked my dear Jane to come. And to bring a wagon load of food from our farm.

After he gave the letter to the guard, he turned to me. "I don't have long to live. When I'm gone, I want you to have my hat. Your hat can scarcely be called a hat and keeps fallin' off."

"Thank you. You are very generous."

One morning, after a couple of weeks, I stood by the window getting some fresh air with about twenty other prisoners. Jane Woodhull rolled into the courtyard on a wagon. She wore a blue dress and a white bonnet—a pleasant sight, for we prisoners rarely laid our eyes on a woman. Charles still clung to his life. Two guards carried him out to meet her. The guards raised Charles up to the seat in the wagon as Jane received him and placed his head in her lap. As they conversed, she caressed his hair. Tears streamed down her cheeks. Eventually, his head fell to one side, and Jane buried her face in his chest. After a few minutes, she rose and spoke to the guards. The guards unloaded the wagon and brought us bread, ham, butter, and corn. We all ate, thankful for every morsel and the uplifting memories of Charles Woodhull. After we finished, James Morton began to sing the song Charles taught us, and we all joined in,

"Attend unto my cry;
for I am brought very low:
deliver me from my persecutors;
for they are stronger than I.
Bring my soul out of prison,
that I may praise Thy Name."

I felt something then—I think we all did—that united us and made the prison a little less like hell on earth.

After the song finished, the guard came to the door and called out, "Daniel Asbury."

"Here," I responded and walked to the door.

"Mrs. Woodhull requested that you be given Mr. Woodhull's hat. She also brought an extra coat from their home," the guard said as he handed me the coat and hat.

This event of Charles' visit with his wife before he died, the delivery of the food to the prisoners, and the gift of the clothes to me was the one incident in prison where the guards treated us like human beings.

"Thank you," I replied and received the bundle. The hat was made of sturdy material, dark green, with a black band around it and a wide brim, curled up on one side. I was proud and grateful to wear it. Charles Woodhull was a generous soul. I have never forgotten him.

The cold of the winter came, but I was spared much suffering. The clothes, coat, and hat from Woodhull kept me warm enough to survive. The memory of the meal supplied by Jane Woodhull did me as much benefit as the meal itself and preserved my life in that dungeon.

Time in Captivity: 1 year 300 days

CHAPTER FIFTEEN

THE PRISON GUARD

JANUARY 1780

Many prisoners died from starvation and disease. I spent hours lost in the memory of past meals—ma's chicken stew, and meals with the Shawnee, eating a fresh-killed beaver with corn and beans from the fields. I did not do it to torture myself; the memories pushed in and would not leave. I envisioned a hunk of fire-roasted buffalo just out of my reach, or one of Ma's pies, and began to salivate. The hunger was like a second person in my body, someone I had to appease with pathetic promises that were never fulfilled.

If it were not for the kind ladies from the town of Detroit, who would, on occasion, bring food for us, many more would have died. They brought cured hams and sometimes kettles of soup with vegetables and beef. That soup! I do not suppose it was the best soup in the world, with the freshest vegetables and chunks of savory meat, but we all declared it was the best soup. When those ladies brought soup, we were all reduced to children, with tears in our eyes for the gift we were given.

One cold winter day, two guards opened the chamber door and placed a kettle of soup on the floor. They distributed tin cups to the prisoners as we stood in line for a bit of this soup. I reached the head of the line and extended my cup to be filled—my saliva running down my chin—when a guard put his boot on the edge of the kettle, pushed it over, and spilled the precious soup on the floor.

"Virginians get no soup," the guard proclaimed.

That voice was familiar. My body froze. My fingers trembled. My heart raced. I wanted to run and hide, but had nowhere to go. Samuel English stood over me, his cane held high. Then he struck me on the head and knocked my hat off, drawing blood from my tender scalp.

"Whoa. That's quite a sight, young Daniel. I see someone's taken more than just a smidgen of blood from the top of your head," shouted English with a smirk. "You'll be delighted to hear I've been promoted to head guard, and now you rebel prisoners are mine to punish."

I scrambled for my hat, dragging my chains, and retreated to my place against the wall. The other prisoners swarmed the floor to recover and devour what food they could from the spilled soup, now fouled with the dirt of that hellish place.

How would English gain the revenge he had promised me two years earlier? I could think of nothing else for the rest of that day.

Our group of about twenty lined up at the door of our chambers, waiting for our turn to go outside. We marched into the courtyard on a windy day, and there stood English by the fire, holding an iron rod in the flames. I hid behind some larger men, away from the fire.

"Come here, you rebels, and warm yourselves. It's cold out here," English shouted and motioned us to come to the fire.

The prisoners moved closer, but I kept as far away as

possible from English. Then English took the rod with both hands and whacked a prisoner, bashing him to the ground.

"You're a stinkin' traitor, and the penalty for betrayin' your country is death. All of you should be beaten; you deserve to die. Who's next?" English shouted as he glared at each of us.

I pretended not to see English's abuse. Then he shouted, "Asbury. Your day of punishment is comin'."

I moved farther away and looked at the ground. As we ambled back in, he shouted at me again, "Asbury. Come here." I hesitated, but moved closer. "That's a nice coat and hat you have there. Where'd you get those?"

"Another prisoner gave them to me as he died," I replied.

"Well, take 'em off. Somebody in town'll pay me a lot of money for these."

I made no effort to take them off, cherishing them now that winter had arrived. He pulled the iron rod back, ready to strike. I threw off my hat. He smiled as I removed my coat and handed it to him. There was no way to defend myself or my rights to the coat and hat.

"You're not goin' to be needin' these. You'll not live long enough to see the spring."

Once inside our crowded prison chambers, I found my place against the wall beside Humphries and Morton and wrapped my arms around my body to stay warm. I fell asleep, only to be awakened around midnight by guards shouting at the prisoners.

English read five names from a piece of paper. "You five are to be hanged."

I was amazed I was not on the list. I figured someone higher up than English decided who would be hanged. The guards dragged the five out of the room, tied their hands behind their backs, and tied a handkerchief between their teeth.

"Prepare to die," English said. "Make your peace with God. For I will surely fix your body between heaven and earth, and all the traitors in this room will soon follow you."

"You can't hang us. There's been no trial," one of the prisoners shouted.

"For what crime are you hangin' them?" another shouted.

English did not answer as he marched the five souls into the courtyard. We gathered around the windows of our prison chambers to witness. When the first man stepped up on the gallows, they removed his handkerchief from his mouth and placed the rope around his neck.

"Don't do this heinous crime," the man cried. "I beg you. The Lord Almighty will judge you for this." He bowed his head. "God, have mercy on my soul, for I am a sinner."

English nodded to the executioner, who pulled the lever. The prisoner fell. The rope tightened. The man kicked until he could no longer.

The scene was repeated four times, but I could not watch. I dragged my chains to my place against the wall and wondered when English would call my name for my turn at the gallows. I raised my knees, placed my arms on them, and then rested my head on my arms. How did I get so far away from home and family to be in this dungeon of death?

Prisoners died, or were murdered, and new prisoners arrived every day. They came in strong and healthy, full of fervor for the American cause. After a few months, their strength was gone. Everyone suffered from starvation, fever, dysentery, or various ailments of the lungs.

Samuel English called out, "Anyone can end their sufferin' by announcin' your allegiance to the king and enlisting in his army. Is anyone ready to end their sufferin'?"

"I'll take starvation or the black plague before I would serve the king," shouted a prisoner.

"Give me freedom, or give me a rope around my neck," shouted another.

"Death and sufferin' ye shall have," returned English.

Later that day, I joined Humphries as he conversed with two

brothers, Peter and David Hawkins, from Pennsylvania. They had been in prison for two years and were both near death.

"I'm not sure I agree with the harsh stance we're takin'," Humphries whispered. "Peter and David, you have a duty to the cause of freedom, but you also have a duty to stay alive for yourself and your families. Why don't you enlist in the British army and then desert? Go home to your families. Do it before you both die."

"We took an oath of allegiance to serve Pennsylvania, and I will be loyal to that oath if I have but one more breath to breathe," responded Peter.

"Hear, hear. I ag . . . " David agreed, but he could not speak the last word, for he burst into a coughing fit that lasted about two minutes and cost him precious strength.

I dragged my chains over to the water bucket and fetched a cup of water for David.

"Here. Drink this, it will help your cough," I suggested.

David took the drink, and it eased his cough. When our food was thrown in, Humphries and I scrambled for all we could muster, not only to feed us but Peter and David also. Over the next three days, David grew frailer and his illness ghastlier.

"David, you've got to join the British army to save your life," Humphries pleaded. "To stay here is a death sentence."

The next morning, Peter awoke to find his brother had passed. Peter's condition was not much better: he had the same dreadful cough and the appearance of a walking skeleton.

"I'll help you take David's body to the door," Humphries whispered to Peter. "First chance you get, volunteer for the British army, then after you have gained some strength, escape."

That night, around midnight, the prison guards awakened us, and Samuel English again read from his paper and called in his Scottish accent for five prisoners to march to the gallows. They took two from our room and three from the room next door. The guards gagged the prisoners and bound their hands behind their backs.

English stood at the door and shouted so all could hear, but he glared right at me, or so it seemed. "Tonight, you can listen to the cries of your fellow prisoners. Your day will come soon. Until then, make your peace with God."

"Your actions are criminal," one prisoner yelled. "One day, there will be a reckonin'. You'll have to stand before God and give account for your actions." English walked away before he finished.

I stood by the prison window and witnessed the prisoners stagger to the gallows. In his twisted sense of justice, English smiled as each prisoner uttered their shrieks of terror and their pleas to God. I saw myself in each man. What I would say, I did not know, but that terror would be mine. I saw no hope of escaping what seemed certain death.

As was his habit, the morning after a hanging, English came into the middle of our room to make his appeal for prisoners to turn. Peter knelt at his feet.

"Anyone can end their sufferin' by announcin' your allegiance to the king and enlisting in his army," English shouted. "Who will come over to fight for the king? Is anyone ready to end their sufferin'?"

"I will," Peter muttered.

"What's that? I can't hear you. Speak up."

"I will fight for the king," Peter spoke louder.

We could all hear him, but English shouted again. "Speak up so I can hear you."

Hawkins yelled as loud as his frail body would allow. "I will fight for the king."

"That's what I wanted to hear," English replied. "Guards, help this man to his new quarters."

With that, Peter Hawkins left the prison chambers to receive a tolerable meal and attention from a physician.

I reflected on my life two and a half years earlier. I had longed to be on my own, make my own decisions and fortune, and see the world. I had seen the world all right, and discovered it to be a cruel and dangerous place. I was a worn-out thread's width away from death. I wondered if my brother George made it home alive. Or was he killed in battle, or imprisoned in another dreadful British dungeon? My mother was right to oppose my going to fight in the war. Now, all I wanted was to get back to my family in Virginia.

The snowflakes descended from the gray-white sky. Some, caught by the occasional gust and carried through the bars of our prison window, landed on the faces of the weary prisoners, desperate to get a breath of fresh, even icy air. My coat lost to the dreadful Samuel English, I stood about ten feet from the window, strained for a few breaths of outside air, and hugged myself in my shirt and trousers.

"Here's your food," Samuel English broke the silence with his surly voice as he threw a few buckets of uncooked spoiled pork into the room.

"To ease our crowded conditions, some of the benevolent people of the town of Detroit have volunteered to house some of you," English continued. "The followin' prisoners will come forward to be escorted to their new quarters." He unfurled a scroll and called out seven names, including Humphries, Morton, and me. He glared at me as he called my name.

I said farewell to Humphries and Morton and walked toward the door. English stood in my path and said, "Stayin' in town doesn't mean you rebels won't hang."

I responded with silence, changed my course away from English, and focused my eyes on the other prisoners lined up at the door. I shuffled my feet, bound by my irons and chains, and marveled at my great fortune as I departed that place of disease and death.

The brisk wind in my face made me work so much harder as I dragged the chains that connected my ankles through ten inches of snow. I followed the guards as they led us prisoners to our new homes. My bare head stung in the icy wind. I did not mind these hardships, since I had left the dungeon and advanced toward a new home, with real food and shelter.

The guard knocked on the door of a modest home, and it was answered by an elderly couple. He had a gray beard and mustache, trimmed and combed. The man exhibited a twinkle in his eye and a smile on his face. The woman wore a bonnet that covered her gray hair and a white apron over her dress. She beamed with a welcoming face. They both opened their arms with a hearty reception for me. An extraordinary aroma from inside the house also welcomed me. It was an aroma that aroused memories of my home in Virginia. It was the fragrance of chicken stew. I strained to conceal the tear that rolled down my cheek and the smile that tried to form around my mouth.

"Come right in," the man said. "We believe you have brought our new house guest."

The guard motioned for me to step forward. "State your name, age, and where you're from."

"My name's Daniel Asbury. Age eighteen. From Bedford County, Virginia," I responded.

"We're Mary and John Justice," the man said. "Daniel, we welcome you into our home and hope you'll be comfortable here."

"We'll post guards throughout the city," the guard said. "We take off the chains around your wrists, but you'll keep your chains and irons on your legs, so ya' can't run away."

I waved goodbye to my fellow prisoners, then turned back to Mary and John.

I must have been a ghastly sight: covered in five months of

grime. My beard and the hair growing at the back of my head were long and greasy. My clothes were dark with dirt and had a stench that would make a skunk jealous. Due to the starvation conditions in the prison, I was like a skeleton.

"Oh, Daniel! Aren't you a sight to behold," Mrs. Justice exclaimed. "Let's get you cleaned up, and then we'll get you some food."

"I'd appreciate that," I said. "You're very kind."

Mr. Justice stared at the top of my head. "Oh my!"

"Oh, my poor boy. What have they done to you?" asked Mrs. Justice.

"That's a bit of a long story," I said.

"Here," Mr. Justice said, "eat this bread and drink some tea while we heat the water for your bath, and you can tell us all about it."

The bread and tea were heavenly. I spun my tale of capture, escape, and capture again. I made sure to tell the Justices how well the Natives treated me despite the scalping. I almost contrasted the bearable treatment of the Natives to the torturous conditions of the British prison, but thought better of it.

Mr. Justice poured the hot water into the tub in the back room and said, "When you finish your bath, put on these clean clothes as best you can with your chains. Mrs. Justice will sew up some pants special for chains around the ankles. When you're dressed, we'll have some chicken stew ready for you."

At the mention of chicken stew, a smile formed across my face. "Thank you, Mr. Justice. I owe my life to your kindness."

I stepped, chains and all, into the bath and let the warm, sudsy water wash against my body, a feeling I had not experienced for over two years. After two years of cold river baths, or none at all, this bath warmed my very bones. If my stomach had been full, I would have stayed in the tub all afternoon, but the aroma from the hearth, where Mrs. Justice cooked, reached the back room, and my hunger overruled my desire to soak in the bath water.

As I dressed, a mirror in the corner of the room caught my attention. My curiosity drew me to it. I had not gazed into one in over two years. Hesitant, trembling, I peered into the mirror, and winced. I did not believe it was me. The scalp, the starvation, and the illness had all changed my face. The skin of my cheeks drooped down, with no skin on my scalp to hold it up. Lack of food had caused my cheekbones to protrude. My bare scalp was bumpy, and my beard was scraggly.

I examined my old clothes. In addition to the filth, they were worn thin, with several holes. I carried them to Mr. Justice for disposal.

The three of us sat down at their table. Mr. Justice offered a prayer, "We thank Thee, Lord, for your bountiful supply of our needs. We thank Thee that Daniel can share this meal with us. Amen."

The meal, a bowl of chicken stew, was so delicious that I wanted to devour it all, but my manners restrained me.

"Daniel, I know you could eat a houseful of food, but it's best you start out small, then work your way to larger meals," Mr. Justice said.

"Thank you," I repeated between mouthfuls. "Thank you for your kindness." I swallowed and took a breath. "I've heard nothing about the war for two years. Do you get any news here?"

"News about the war is scarce, and not recent. I do hear that the British are fighting in the south. They captured Savannah, and the whole state of Georgia, and all the rice, corn, cattle, and horses in Georgia."

This was not good news for the patriot cause. I remained quiet.

Mr. and Mrs. Justice exchanged a look.

"We're disheartened, too," Mr. Justice said.

I perked up.

"We're patriots," Mrs. Justice whispered, "but everyone here thinks we're Tories."

"Oh, I won't tell anyone. I am so grateful for your kindness."

They smiled at me. "Of course," Mrs. Justice said. "When you finish your food, why don't you go lie down for the afternoon, and we'll have another meal for you tonight."

I lay in my warm bed all afternoon and contemplated my auspicious circumstances and the newfound hope that I could survive the disease, the starvation, the beatings, and the hangings. The recovery of my health and strength progressed in the weeks that followed. The Justices were so kind and fed me well. Mrs. Justice made me a pair of pants that were open along the inseams of the pant legs. I could button them closed once they were on, and they did not interfere with my chains. I could tuck the pants legs inside the irons around my ankles to protect them from constant contact with the iron. They gave me another coat and hat. The coat was equal in quality to that given to me by Woodhull. The hat was not as fine but suited my purposes. It was a red knit hat that fit snuggly on my scalp. In the months that followed I cherished both. Their presence and warmth kindled pleasant memories of the Justices' generosity—their warm bed, delicious meals, and kind words. They gave to me with no thought of the burden that I was to them, which was a lesson and an example to me. Would I ever be able to serve others like that . . . if I was ever free again?

Guards were always present along the street, to prevent prisoners from escaping. Once a month Samuel English stopped in to see me and threaten me with a hanging. Then, early in the summer, English knocked on the Justices' door.

"Daniel Asbury. Come out immediately."

Time in Captivity: 2 years 107 days

CHAPTER SIXTEEN

A LEAKY CANOE

JUNE 1780

"Daniel Asbury, you're bein' transferred to the Fort Chambly prison in Montreal. Step out of the house and follow the guards."

I stood there. Tears formed in my eyes and streamed down my cheeks.

Mrs. Justice appeared at the door behind me and handed me my hat, coat, and a piece of buttered bread. "You take care of yourself, Daniel, and may the Lord protect you. We were blessed to have you these last few months."

After a hard swallow, I held out my shaking arms to the Justices. "Thank you. You've both been kind and your generosity saved my life. I'll always remember you with fond and thankful memories." I hugged them both.

As I followed the line of the six other prisoners led by the guards, I turned around to get one last view of the Justices. The Justices waved at me, and I waved back. I felt stronger and healthier than I had in months, but now faced the prospect of additional harsh treatment by the British. Among the prisoners were William Humphries and James Morton. I caught their eye, and we each exchanged smiles and nods. We marched toward the docks, where a sailboat with two masts was berthed, the heftiest boat I had ever seen. The name on the back of the ship was *Huron*. English watched while we filed across the gangplank.

"Asbury," English yelled. "Don't think that you've escaped your fate. You'll hang yet. You'll hang by the neck and your feet will dangle in the air until there's no kick left in 'em."

I was silent.

"Rebels," said one of the men on the ship. "My name be Captain Morris, and I am in command of the *Huron*. This ship'll be your prison for the next few days. You're bein' transferred to Fort Chambly in Montreal. The *Huron* will take you part of the way, to Fort Niagara. Transportation of prisoners is not our sole mission. The *Huron*'s loaded with beaver, mink, raccoon, deer, buffalo, and bear furs and hides. You'll haul those furs fifteen miles from Lake Erie to Fort Niagara, where you'll board another ship bound for Ft Chambly. You'll spend your time below deck, but you'll be allowed to come on deck twice a day, once in the mornin' and once in the evenin', weather permittin'. You'll be fed two meals a day." Captain Morris introduced the crew members and instructed one of them to take us below deck.

Below deck, the six of us prisoners each found a hammock and introduced ourselves to each other. Besides Humphries and Morton there were three prisoners from Pennsylvania. We traded stories of where we were from and how we were captured.

"Cap'n wants everyone on deck as we shove off," called a voice from on deck. We scrambled on deck, and the voice continued. "If you can see the land from on deck, it helps you get accustomed to the waves of the sea and the roll of the ship. Some people get mighty sick on board a ship for several days."

The sun was high in the sky and drew sweat on our faces and arms, but the stiff breeze offered some relief. The baggy white shirts and long hair of the crew flapped in the wind as they went about their duties. The crewmen untied the boat and allowed it to drift away from the dock. Then they raised the sails. The southwest wind filled the sails and pushed the boat into the river.

There was silence for several minutes, except for the slosh of water against the hull and the calling of distant birds. The Detroit harbor, and Samuel English still standing at the dock, faded into the distance. His parting words that I would hang by the neck did not fade. I wondered why English had not had me hung when he had the chance. Maybe he did not have the authority. He always read the names for hanging from the piece of paper written by his superiors. Or maybe English was not as heartless as his brutal words indicated. Nevertheless, English's prediction continued to haunt me in the days and months that followed.

Detroit dwindled out of sight as the expanse of Lake Erie emerged before us. "You prisoners have had enough time on deck," said the captain. "You have been able to see the shore while your legs learn the familiarity of the sea. All prisoners below."

All six of us shuffled our feet, dragged our chains, and climbed down the ladder below deck to our quarters. Below deck, we rested and had occasional conversations. We listened to the captain bark orders to the helmsman against the constant background sound of the water against the hull of the ship. We had fair weather and a fortuitous breeze, and they fed us tolerable meals. In the evenings, we made another trip on deck and enjoyed the cool night air and dazzling displays of stars in the night sky. I could feel the hopelessness of the British prison begin to dissolve. The stars reminded me of the world beyond men, the world that was neither kind nor cruel but a mystery.

After three days, we sailed down another river on the other end of Lake Erie and anchored by an island in the river as the sun receded below the horizon.

"This is as far as the *Huron* will take you," Captain Morris said, after we assembled on deck. "You'll sleep on board tonight, then, at sunrise tomorrow, you'll take the ship's cargo to shore in our long boat. Then you'll each carry a load to Fort Niagara. We'll take your chains off for this part of the journey. You'll get your chains back at Fort Chambly."

As the first light appeared in the eastern sky, the crew lowered the long boat into the water, and the guards removed our chains. We passed bundles of furs and hides from the *Huron* to the long boat. Three prisoners, one guard, one crew and three bundles of furs took their places in the boat.

I sat in the bow as the captain yelled instructions. "Each of you take an oar. Now listen to the sounds in the distance." He paused for us all to listen. "Do you hear that roar? Now look to the east. Do you see the mist risin' in those two places? That's the roar and the mist from two towering and massive waterfalls. The largest you'll ever see in your life. All this water around you is flowin' toward those falls. If you're not careful, you'll be swept along with the current over the falls to crash on the rocks below. You must row like your lives depend on it. For indeed, your lives do depend on it. Now shove off."

Off we floated into the river. Each man, motivated by Captain's words, rowed with vigor. While the current of the river was obvious, we moved across the river with efficiency and soon landed on the other side. After all the prisoners, guards, and cargo were across, the prisoners each took a load of furs, tied with buffalo tugs, slung it over his back, and began the trek along Niagara River. I made slow progress under the hefty load and trailed behind the others. My legs buckled and I tumbled.

"Pick yourself up and keep going," yelled one of the guards.

I hobbled to my feet and swung my load over my back.

The distant roar of the waterfalls intensified. As we trekked along the rim of the gorge the falls came into view. We stood still. We gazed at the massive white sheets of water that crashed on the rocks below. We marveled at the rainbows that the sun lit up in the mist.

In that moment, the lead guard seemed to forget the mission of transporting hides and furs. "Let's climb down those rocks yonder and git a view from inside the canyon. We'll leave our loads over there. We've got to get a closer view."

We approached the falls from the bottom of the gorge, our faces and clothes wet from the heavy mist. The sight was a spectacle to ponder. Amidst the thunder that engulfed us, I marveled at the immense power of the water as it crashed on the rocks and the pool below. The display was mesmerizing, and I felt like I could gaze at the falls all day. We witnessed the scene for only a moment, but in that moment, we were all equal, guards and prisoners, all human together.

The guard cleared his throat. "We best get back to our loads. We have several miles to go before we can rest for the night."

We traveled along the rim of the gorge for several miles then descended toward flatter terrain. I labored under my load and fell behind. The guard kicked me in my rear. "Keep up."

After another hundred yards, I tripped on a rock and fell face down.

Humphries laid his pack down and came to me. He helped me back on my feet, and then examined my pack. "Daniel, you've got the heaviest load. Take mine. It's much lighter."

"Thanks, William. I'd appreciate it."

I picked up Humphries lighter pack. We proceeded on our journey along the Niagara River and made camp as the sun set.

That night as I lay down to sleep, I thought of Humphries's kindness to carry my load. He did not have to take the heavier load. Had our loads been reversed, I would not have volunteered to take the heavier pack. This reminded me of the kindness of the men in prison, Thomas Jones and Charles Woodhull. They suffered illness from diseased lungs and infected wounds, yet thought of me and my need for clothes. I thought of the generosity of John and Mary Justice and their selfless care for me while I recovered from my ordeal in the dungeon. Would I ever be able to serve others in such a selfless manner?

About noon the following day, Fort Niagara appeared on an impressive distant hill that overlooked the mouth of the great river as it emptied into Lake Ontario. We unloaded our burdens in a storeroom, then enjoyed one of the benefits of being forced to carry heavy loads—a fine meal. We savored some outstanding chicken, potatoes, and green beans that night.

On the third day at Fort Niagara, one of our guards shouted into our prison cell, "Your time of leisure's come to an end. Our ship's arrived and you must carry your loads down to the dock."

We followed him to the storeroom and once again seized our weighty bundle of furs and positioned them on our backs. Below the fort, at the docks, was a small town, busy with activity. We marched by stores, taverns, and street vendors on our way to our ship, the *Seneca,* an even larger ship than the *Huron*.

The helmsman focused his eyes on the horizon while the southeast breeze filled the sails and heeled the ship toward the port side. I stood near the bow with the wind in my face and my precious hat in my hands. The ship ascended the gentle swells of the lake and then descended into the troughs that followed. For a moment, I was free. I had been a captive for two-and-a-half years, suffering starvation, illness, being shot at, and the threat of being hanged. But in this moment—the beauty of the water, the wind flapping my clothes, my full stomach—I felt the freedom of life once again.

"All prisoners below deck," barked the captain.

My "moment of freedom" had ended.

We sailed across Lake Ontario and down the St. Lawrence River, arriving in Montreal on the fifth day. After toting our furs to below the Lachine rapids, the guards refastened the irons on our ankles. We marched to Fort Chambly, a stone fort built upon a rock that protrudes into the Richelieu River. The Richelieu empties into the St. Lawrence a few miles to the north. The guards led us inside the courtyard where the commanding officer met us.

"You have arrived at Fort Chambly, your new prison," the officer said. "This is a work prison, and we expect you to work. In exchange, we give you two decent meals a day. You take care of us with your hard work, and we take care of you with wholesome food, and shelter in the winter. But if you try to escape, or help another prisoner escape, you'll be hanged. We have several work projects. Your project is to build a grain mill on Bouchard Island in the St Lawrence River. You will join two other prisoners who are here at Chambly. In the warm months, you'll work and sleep on the island. You'll keep your chains around your legs so you won't swim away. In the winter months, you'll stay here at the fort. Tomorrow, you'll go to the island." The officer paused as he pulled out a piece of paper. "When I call your name, you will answer 'here.'"

He proceeded to call out the names of the six prisoners, all of whom answered, "Here."

"Guard. Take 'em to their cell."

The guard led us down a long dark hallway and opened the door to the cell. Our cell was a converted army barracks with beds, mattresses, and a wash pan. The best part was that it lacked the putrid smell of the Detroit dungeon.

Already in the room were two other prisoners. My eyes widened.

"Richard Wade! John Brown!" I exclaimed.

Brown gave me a confused look as I approached him.

"It's me, Daniel Asbury, from Bedford County. We got captured in Kentucky."

"Daniel, of course!" Brown exclaimed as he shook my hand. "You look . . . different."

"Yeah. The hazards of war can change a man," I replied, taking off my hat to display my scalped head.

"Oh. Look what they've done to you."

"I escaped from Chillicothe, but some Miami captured and scalped me, then sold me to the British in Detroit."

"Well then, you've discovered that the British are harsher than the Indians," Brown said. "The British have nearly murdered Richard. He's sick and close to death," John pointed at Wade, who waved with a weak smile. "I try to keep him comfortable and make sure he gets food and water."

"Sorry to hear that. I came with William Humphries and James Morton."

"We've got ourselves a salt-maker reunion," Brown said. "I have to say they treat us better here than in Detroit. The work isn't dreadful, and they feed ya decent."

Wade sat up on his bed. "Well hey there James, William, and Daniel. It's gratifyin' to see so many friends are still alive."

"John tells us you been ill. Sorry to hear that," Morton said.

"Yeah, I reckon I would've died if John hadn't taken care of me. I'm on the mend now. Should be back helpin' you with the work in a month or so."

Early the next morning, a large canoe carried us down the Richelieu River until we entered the St. Lawrence River, where we turned upriver toward Bouchard Island, our workplace and "home" for the remainder of the summer. The island was large, about a mile across at its widest, and five miles long. It lay in the middle of the river, about a half mile from each shore. There were rapids along the north side of the island near the location where we would build the grain mill.

We gathered around one of the guards for instructions. "While Wade is nursing his illness, Asbury, Morton, and Humphries, you're diggin' the foundation. Brown, you're splittin' lumber into boards. You other three, you're digging up rocks for the foundation. We feed you two meals a day, and you sleep on the island. Everyone keeps their chains so you don't swim away at night. Let's get to work."

"Where do we sleep?" Humphries asked.

"Wherever you can find a level spot. There are some blankets over by that tree yonder."

"What if it rains?" Morton asked.

"Find a big tree to get under. After you finish the roof for the mill there will be some shelter."

The work was brutal and grueling. The ground was tough, with many rocks. But the hard work, fresh air, and the promise of food was a delight compared to the starvation, filth, and stench of the Detroit prison. After a few hours they brought our food. We gathered around Wade.

"Hey Richard, this looks like our salt boilin' crew," Morton said. "Everybody's workin' while Richard's lyin' in the shade."

"You keep lyin' there, Richard," I said before leaning in. I whispered, "And while you're lyin' there, be thinkin' of a way to get us off this island."

"Oh. I got some ideas. We will discuss those another time."

That night, only two guards remained on the island, and they slept away from us. We found a soft place to bunk down and resumed our conversation.

"We've got to find us a boat," Wade said. "Either steal one or build one. There is no way we can swim in these irons."

"The boats are always guarded," Brown said. "We'll have to build one. Daniel, did you learn how to build canoes from the Indians?"

"Yes, but you need the right kind of trees—birch trees. I ain't seen any birch trees on this island yet."

"Well, keep your eyes on the watch for some," Wade said. "This is a considerable island with a heap of trees. I know there's a way we can do it."

The conversation died as Humphries began to snore. I looked up at the stars on that pleasant summer night, thankful I could see the stars. Sleeping outdoors brought hope that I would survive this captivity ordeal, although there was no end in sight. I also thought of Wade's illness. Brown's faithful care and labor kept him alive. Our captivity had become a group effort in survival as we supported and assisted each other. The talk of escape increased my longing to see my family. What were they thinking in my long absence? I could almost sense Ma praying for me, wondering if I had died, and crying. I could even sense a tear fall from Pa's cheek. And what did my brothers and sisters think happened to me? What would Elizabeth think of my scalped head? What would Molly think of my panther bite wound? I wanted to tell Dad and James about hunting with Daniel Boone.

The construction continued all summer. At night, after we were sure the guards still on the island had fallen asleep, two or three of us would slip away, searching for birch trees to construct canoes. On rare occurrences, all the guards left in the canoes, allowing all of us to search the island. By the time our summer and fall on the island ended, we completed the foundation and walls of the mill, but we found no birch trees. When the first snow fell on the island we moved back to Fort Chambly for the winter. Ninety-six other prisoners joined us from other work projects.

Once all the prisoners were inside the fort the commander assembled us in the courtyard. "I have some important news to share with you about the war. The British are going to win the war. One of your generals has decided to fight for the King of

England. American Benedict Arnold has become a general in the British Army. Arnold saw that the American war effort was doomed and came over to the winning side. I give you the same opportunity. Come over to fight for the king and get your chains removed. Will any of you do that now?"

"Never. The king is a tyrant. We fight for our liberty," was our response voiced by multiple prisoners.

We spent the winter in the barracks scheming for our escape. In the spring of the new year, 1781, we returned to Bouchard Island to finish construction of the mill. Richard Wade's health improved, allowing him to fully participate in the work.

One pleasant June evening, we ate our meal and waited for the guards to leave the island. This was an evening in which all the guards left the island. After their boats were out of sight, the eight of us continued our exploration of the island. Morton and I searched an area we had not yet explored.

"Look. What's that?" Morton said, pointing to something buried in a bramble of briars.

We pulled away the branches of briars to reveal a huge canoe. We stared at each other with wide eyes and open mouths. Many of the thwarts and ribs were broken, and the hull, weakened with age, had three large holes. But it was a boat.

"Can it be mended?" Morton asked.

I examined it for a moment. "Some of the wood is rotten and the holes are large. But yes. I reckon it can be made to float again. Let's take this to a place where we can hide it and fix it."

Morton's mouth became a wide grin, and his eyes sparkled. "A place on the other side of the island is well hidden by trees. Let's take it there."

Morton attempted to lift it. "It's too heavy for us two to manage. Let's go get some help."

We located the others. "We found a boat!" Morton said, his face beaming. "It's a big canoe that will hold all of us. It's in need of repair. Daniel thinks we can get it floatin' again."

"We must carry it to another location where we can work on it without bein' seen," I added.

"Let's do it tonight. The moon is bright," Morton said.

With all in agreement, we headed for the boat. Upon our arrival, Morton and I yanked the bushes away from the canoe for all to examine the broken thwarts and large holes in the hull of the canoe.

"You call this a boat!" exclaimed Wade.

"This won't even float, and it sure won't carry eight people with leg irons," someone else said.

"Well now, hold off on your judgments," Brown said. "What'd you expect? A shiny new boat with paddles? It's a start. Let's see what we can do with it."

"Yeah," Humphries said. "This is the first thing we've found that gives us any hope of gettin' back home. Let's give this a try."

"Agreed," Brown said. "Let's fix her up and get off this island."

We carried the canoe over our heads to a flat spot in a stand of trees on the other side of the island.

"We must never give the guards a reason to explore this spot," I said when we had hidden it. "We can never leave tracks or wear a path here."

The others nodded, and we returned to our work camp not long before dawn.

Over the next month, we transformed the dilapidated canoe into a promising boat. We experimented with several kinds of tree bark to patch the holes before finding that spruce worked best. We soaked cedar wood and bent it into ribs, fastening them with spruce and cedar roots. Finally, we sealed the seams with resin from pine and spruce trees. She was not much to look at, but she promised freedom, and for that we named her *Liberty*.

The next day, as the sun set below the horizon, we waited for the guards to quieten and settle into their sleep.

"Let's put *Liberty* in the water tonight and see how she floats," Wade whispered.

We all agreed. After the guards made no further movements, the eight of us snuck away toward our boat. We set *Liberty* in the St. Lawrence River. She floated! We marveled at how our doubts had been transformed into confidence *Liberty* would soon carry us to freedom.

"Now. One of us needs to get in her," Wade said.

Morton stepped in as the rest of us held the boat. It floated, with no sign of water comin' in.

"Someone else get in," instructed Wade.

Brown climbed in. The added strain caused water to seep into the bottom of the canoe.

"There's water comin' in near the stern," I stated.

Wade examined the stern. "Someone else step in."

Humphries got in. This opened a larger leak.

"Whoa," I said. "She's not ready. It'll never carry all of us. We've got to work on that leak."

Over the next three days, we covered the bottom with spruce bark and sealed the seams and joints with pine resin. As the canoe lay on the ground, hull up, we admired our work, and imagined our freedom.

"That boat is sealed as sound as we can get 'er," Wade declared. "I say we leave tomorrow, after it gets dark and the guards fall asleep."

We all agreed.

"We'll have to travel by night," added Brown, "and lay up in the creeks and trees by day. We just follow the Richelieu River back to the colonies. I'm ready to go."

"We should save as much of our food tomorrow as we can," Morton said.

"That food won't last us long. We'll have to catch fish and rabbits the rest of the way," someone else added.

The next day, all I could think about was our escape to liberty until the notion of re-capture and a rope around my neck chased away my dreams of freedom. Also, we would have to traverse the wilderness with no weapons. We would need more than our hands to catch fish and rabbits.

Like runners waiting for the flag to drop, we waited for the last of the guards to leave. We waited for darkness. We waited for the remaining guards to sleep. We waited even longer to ensure they were asleep. Then we slipped away.

We carried *Liberty* to the shore and set her in the river. Wade, Brown, and Morton climbed into the boat. No leaks. Another stepped in and a small puddle appeared. Another followed and water covered the bottom.

"We'll have to use our hats to bail," Wade said.

Then a sixth man joined them, and the seep became a flow. When I followed, the flow became a gush. I stared at the water filling the boat. My heart raced. My hands trembled. I held my breath. My chains would surely carry me to the bottom of the river. I jumped out.

"I can't go," I shouted. "I'll drown with these chains on."

"Come on, we'll bail and keep us afloat," urged Wade.

Humphries sighed. "Daniel's right. The boat can only handle six passengers. You six go, Daniel and I will catch the next boat and meet you in Boston."

"There won't be another boat. Come on," replied Wade.

"Just the same, you guys go," Humphries said. "May God go with you and give you a safe journey home."

"All right then," Wade replied. "Let's go and get as far as we can before daylight."

Humphries and I pushed them off. Two men paddled, and four bailed with their hats. Then *Liberty* faded into the darkness. The two of us walked back to our worksite without a word and lay down. I could not sleep. Freedom was still just a dream.

The next morning, we began our work as though nothing had changed. The two guards on the island said nothing to us about the missing men. But when more guards arrived with our food, they looked around.

"Where are the other prisoners?" shouted one of them.

"We woke up this morning, and they were gone," replied Humphries.

"They must be around here somewhere," I said. "There's no way to get off this island."

Another guard approached, pointing at us. "You two were on their crew. If they escaped, you were in on it. And you'll hang for it."

Time in Captivity: 3 years 150 days

CHAPTER SEVENTEEN
THE EXCHANGE
JULY 1781

"Why would we hang? We didn't escape," protested Humphries. "Keep lookin'. You'll find them. They can't have gone far."

"You two back to work while we sort out what's happened," instructed a guard.

We went back to work, while the guards consulted among themselves. They searched the island all day and came back in the evening.

"It seems we have some missin' prisoners," one guard said. "You two are hereby no longer permitted to leave the work site. We will watch you every night until the mill is complete, at which point you will be court-martialed for helping the other prisoners to escape."

Protesting was pointless. Though they could not prove we had helped, they had made up their minds. The work slowed considerably since we were down to only two of us, and we were in no hurry to get to our court-martial, which would likely end with us hanging. I had not figured I would hang for not escaping. I replayed the scene of the leaky canoe over and over in my mind, and wished I were one of the six. But then one of them would have been stuck here. We all deserved to be free.

We finished the mill as the weather turned cold. As the guards paddled us down the Saint Lawrence I thought of Wade, Brown, Morton, and the others. Had the canoe stayed afloat? Had they reached their homes. I remembered my last escape and what had happened when the Miami caught me. Nothing was certain, I knew. Still, I wished fiercely that the canoe had held us all.

No one spoke as the guards paddled us up the Richelieu River toward Fort Chambly. The last of the red, orange, and yellow leaves clung to their branches. The sky was blue. The river was peaceful. I was not. I fought to relax the tension in my stomach but could not. A tear formed in my right eye and rolled down my cheek. Samuel English's parting words haunted me: "You will hang by the neck and your feet will dangle in the air until there is no kick left in 'em." Did I have only a few days left on this earth?

The next day, we followed two guards to a large room where three officers acting as judges sat behind a table. The guards who had overseen our work sat on the sides of the room. The commander hammered a gavel, "The court martial of Daniel Asbury and William Humphries will come to order." He had us stand and introduce ourselves before calling one of the guards to testify.

"Tell us what you know about the escaped prisoners," the commander said.

"I made frequent checks on the eight prisoners and their work," the guard said. On the morning of July 15, we found only two prisoners on the site and they have not come forward with any information as to how the other six escaped."

The commander peered at Humphries. "Private Humphries step forward."

Humphries rose, stepped toward the table, and faced the officers.

"How did the prisoners escape?"

"The prisoners you speak of were part of our work crew to build the mill. When we awoke on the morning of July 15, they were gone."

"Did you see them escape?"

"I've told you what happened."

The commander paused, then asked, "You know nothin' else?"

"I've told you what I know."

The commander grew increasingly frustrated as he invented creative ways to ask the same questions but received no additional information.

"You may return to your seat. Private Asbury, step forward."

The commander stared at me for several seconds before he spoke. His chin held high; his nostrils flared. "Private Asbury, I hope your testimony will bring this mystery into the daylight. Step forward and face the judges."

I shuffled my feet, dragging my chains, until I stood before the judges.

"Private Asbury, how did the prisoners escape?"

I closed my eyes while I rubbed the sweat off my hands. I took a deep breath, then answered, "We worked with the six prisoners in question all summer long. When we awoke on the morning of July 15, they were gone. The two of us here on trial continued our work as usual. We've done nothing wrong."

"Why didn't you stop them?" the commander asked.

"When we awoke on the morning in question, they were gone."

"We have already established that. Where do you think they are?"

"I reckon they're either back in the colonies, with their

families, or lyin' at the bottom of the St. Lawrence River, still bound by their chains."

"Do you have anything else to say?"

"No, sir."

"You may return to your seat. The judges will confer to determine the verdict."

After several minutes of discussion among the judges, the commander said for all in the courtroom to hear, "Silence and order in this courtroom. The judges have reached their verdict."

He paused for everyone to quiet themselves. "The verdict of the judges is the followin': The two prisoners, William Humphries and Daniel Asbury, have not provided sufficient information to establish their innocence. They were workmates and friends with the escaped prisoners. Without a doubt, they helped the prisoners escape. The penalty for attempted escape, or helpin' a prisoner escape, is hangin' by the neck until dead. Daniel Asbury and William Humphries will hang tomorrow at 10 am. Sergeant, take the prisoners to their new quarters where they will await their execution." The commander pounded the gavel on the table.

I stared at the floor. I could not believe this sentence of death. After all the dangers I had escaped, I'd never see Ma and Pa again. I'd never go home.

They isolated us from the other prisoners in separate quarters and left us alone. The room had two modest chairs and two beds. We sat in silence, contemplating what lay before us. Eventually, there was a knock on the door, and a man in black robes stepped in, introducing himself as a priest.

"I've come to pray for you in this, your darkest hour, to help you make peace with God before you cross into the next life."

"You're an Englishman," Humphries said. "And an Englishman is the last thing I want to see on my last night in this world. The English have inflicted so much pain and sufferin', and injustice on me, and there can be no peace in your presence. Please let us spend our final night alive without havin' to look upon an Englishman."

"My son, don't treat your final night on this earth in a triflin' manner," the reverend replied. "I don't believe you understand the gravity of what you're about to face."

"You'd have us make our peace with God," Humphries said. "I can find no peace if I spend my final hours in the presence of an Englishman. The notion of death does not seem so repulsive compared to the ill treatment and sufferin' I have received at the hands of the English. Please depart from our presence."

The reverend pursed his lips and retreated from our quarters.

"William, you have been a good friend," I said. "You helped me get through the dungeon in Detroit."

"Detroit was a dark place, full of pain. It helps if you can share sufferin' with friends. When you showed up in Detroit, the misery was a little more bearable." Humphries paused, then continued. "My biggest pain . . . " Humphries paused again. His voice quivered and tears flowed as he sobbed. After a while he regained his composure. "My biggest sorrow is that I will never see Mary and the boys again. I can't fathom the anguish my absence has caused them. And them not knowing what has become of me. They must think I'm dead."

"Yeah. It's not just us that suffer. Our families suffer. This war is an awful thing."

We tried to comfort one another, but without much success. The clergyman returned about midnight to a disagreeable reception. "Why don't you go pray for your ownself," Humphries said. "All you English are committin' the gravest sins day and night"—though he did not say it so politely. The man departed again.

I was quiet the rest of the night and did not sleep. I stared out the window into the darkness. The priest had come to talk about God with us. I did not know how to think about God. I only knew the song Charles Woodhull taught us. "Bring my soul out of prison, that I may praise Thy Name." I closed my eyes and prayed that prayer. God seemed so distant from me. Did He hear me?

I thought of my family. Each one's face rose before my eyes, and I remembered how they spoke, what they liked, how different each was from the others. I remembered Elizabeth cutting my hair, Molly warning me about the dangers of panthers, James playing with his bilbo stick, Patsy and I swimming in the James River, Genny and Sally helping gather rocks for the fireplace at the river, and Nancy crawling into my lap. I wondered if George had returned from the war. I recalled Pa saving me from the bear. I wished he could save me from the hangman's noose. I imagined Ma praying on the back porch in the early morning. Was she praying now? I longed to be with them, if only for an hour, but knew I would never see them again.

Before dawn, the drummers beat their drums in the courtyard, and then came the irritating sound of the rusty iron prison door as it turned on its hinges, accompanied by the sight of the guards, who removed our chains. They escorted us to the courtyard, where the gallows stood with two ropes that hung from a horizontal beam. We stood in our appointed places beside the gallows, surrounded by the prison guards. The other prisoners were brought out to witness our punishment. I still found it hard to believe it would happen. Here I was, young and strong, ready to live. I had done some bad things, but for most of it, I had no choice. I thought of Swift Wolf, how it was either him or me. It all seemed very gloomy. I especially did not want to think of the worst thing, of luring the men on the river boat.

While other prisoners found their places, we spoke to one another one last time. Humphries stretched out his long arms. We held each other for a minute then Humphries said, "Daniel you've been the best soldier and fellow prisoner. It has been an honor to know you."

"You too, William," I said. "You've served your country well. Thank you for how you have helped me and carried my load when I was too weak."

"You're welcome, Daniel. I'm sorry this has happened to you at such a young age."

With as much bravery as we could muster, we each stepped back to our places.

All stood at attention as the commander read our sentence. "Prisoners Daniel Asbury and William Humphries have been tried and found guilty of abettin' the escape of fellow prisoners. They shall be hanged from the gallows until dead."

The words "They shall be hanged from the gallows until dead" rang in my ears. My chin trembled. My body shook under my clothes. I could almost hear my heartbeat. Sweat rolled down my forehead and cheeks.

"Lead the prisoners to the gallows," the commander said.

We each took our places under the ropes. The executioner pulled the noose over Humphries head, then mine. The coarse fibers scraped my scalp, every sensation elevated. The knot was heavier than I expected, resting on the back of my neck.

The executioner placed his hand on the lever. Then, a soldier with a bright red coat and shiny black boots ran into the courtyard, carrying an envelope.

"Halt the executions!" he shouted.

He ran up to the commander and handed him the envelope. My heart pounded even faster. I could not breathe.

The commander tore open the envelope, unfolded the paper, and ran his eyes over the message. The whole courtyard was silent as he read it again, his frown deepening. He said something to the messenger, then read it a third time. His arms fell to his sides, and he looked up.

"The war between England and the American colonies is

over," he declared. "Lord Cornwallis has surrendered to General Washington at Yorktown, Virginia. Although the end of the war is not official, the fighting has ended. The conditions for peace will be negotiated in Paris. All executions of prisoners must halt, but all prisoners will remain here. However, as a substitute for execution, prisoners will receive forty lashes each."

This news was so thrilling and astonishing, I could barely take it in. What if the news of the war's end had come one day later! I let my head roll back and gazed up at the sky as the weight of doom lifted from me. Wasn't the sky the most beautiful blue? So lofty and so mild, so sweet; the air tasted like apples. The urge to dance and shout for the canceled execution overshadowed the joyous news that the fighting was over. The colonies had won their freedom from England. All the prisoners, assembled to witness our execution, erupted with shouts of "We won!" and "The war is over!" and with hugs and dances and jumps of joy. We threw our hats into the air.

Some minutes passed before the commander could restore order in the assembly. "Bring the prisoners, Asbury and Humphries, forward to receive their forty lashes," he shouted.

We stepped into the center of a semi-circle of guards that had formed in the courtyard. The other prisoners stood against the building but had full view of the spectacle through the opening in the semi-circle. Humphries received his forty lashes first. He grunted but did not cry out. His back was covered in blood. My punishment came next. I almost did not expect it to hurt, so relieved was I. But it hurt like fire. Still, as the lashes were laid on my back, as the pain made me weak, it helped to remember that I would not hang. I would survive this as I did all the rest. Then, the guards led Humphries and me to the infirmary to heal.

The next year passed at Fort Chambly. We gazed through the prison bars as the snow came and then melted. The anticipation of our eventual release made the days pass like a lame horse in a race. Try as you might, you could not push it any faster. But we knew the day of our freedom was coming. It became the most popular topic of conversation among the prisoners. The guards were less brutal and treated us with more respect.

On a November morning in 1782, a cold breeze awakened me as it rustled my long beard. I adjusted my hat and pulled Mr. Justice's coat over my shoulders as the first light appeared through the window. I arose and stepped over Humphries's sleeping body to peer out. A snowflake landed on my nose. The guards opened the cell door, then deposited our food. I had just finished my biscuit when the guards summoned us to the courtyard.

All of us assembled in the courtyard. We waited as the snow fell in silence. The Richelieu River rapids gurgled in the background.

"For sixty of you, today is a fortunate day," the commander began. "Sixty of you will be moved to Quebec where on November 8, you'll be exchanged for sixty British prisoners. There, you'll board a ship bound for Philadelphia. You'll be free to go back to your homes and families. You'll load onto a ship docked here at Fort Chambly immediately. As I call your name, move toward the north door. Listen, for I will only call your name once."

He looked down at a sheet of paper. "Daniel Asbury," he called.

I blinked. Had I heard right? I waited a second. The commander looked at the silent crowd, then turned back to his sheet. As he opened his mouth to speak, I shouted, "Here!"

He scowled at me and pointed to the north gate.

I hustled to the gate as a jubilant silent cheer rose inside of me. When I arrived, a guard crouched down and removed the irons around my ankles.

I felt like I would float up to the sky without the weight of the shackles. The relief was immeasurable, and memories flashed through my mind of all the terrible things I had endured for almost five years. The realization that the suffering was over fetched tears that trickled down my cheeks. The winter air was cold on my wet cheeks, but I could not detect the cold, for freedom was so close. I could almost stretch out my arms and grasp it.

When all sixty of us were gathered and unchained, the guards opened the gate, and we were led out.

I turned back toward my prison mates and spied Humphries. "William, your turn is comin' soon."

"Take care of yourself, Daniel," he shouted. "If you are in Richmond, tell Mary I love her and that I'm coming soon. Her brother is Martin Overstreet. That's Martin Overstreet. I'll see you in Virginia."

"Martin Overstreet," I repeated. "I'll do that."

We loaded onto a schooner called *Hope*. We were rather crowded on the small ship, but no one complained. We were all filled with the anticipation of freedom and returning home to our families. The excitement of our victory over the British inspired a man to beat the thwarts of the hull like a drum to the tune of "Yankee Doodle." Another hummed the tune through his teeth and pressed lips that sounded like a flute, and we all sang:

Yankee Doodle went to town,
A-riding on a pony,
stuck a feather in his cap
and called it macaroni.

Yankee Doodle keep it up,
Yankee Doodle dandy,
Mind the music and the step,
and with the girls be handy.

Hope sailed all day and through the night down the St. Lawrence River, aided by the downstream flow of the river and a vigorous southwest breeze, which blew puffs of snow below deck. The packed room did not allow for much sleep, though we nodded our heads at times to seize a few moments of slumber. We docked in Quebec, next to a flagpole with a large British flag that flapped in the breeze. We disembarked and awaited further instruction.

I placed one hand on my hat to keep it atop my head and the other arm pressed against Mr. Justice's coat to stay warm. All of us turned toward the sea to examine the horizon for the first hint of an American ship. After an hour or so, we perceived a black dot. After another hour, the dot became a ship. After another hour, we observed its flag.

Then, someone declared, "I see the red and white stripes and the circle of stars."

We all responded with claps and shouts of "Hooray!" "Home, here we come!" and "Freedom at last!"

Our cheers dwindled as we waited. We became silent under the weight of that moment. The moment our liberty had arrived, symbolized in the *USS Hague*. She turned her port side to the wharf, and the ship's crew worked in tandem with the shore crew to fasten the ship to the dock.

The British lieutenant had us line up in single file as he called our names. We witnessed the British prisoners as they walked the gangplank to the shore. Then, the guard led us as we walked on board the *USS Hague*. Our feet now stood on United States property. We were no longer prisoners but free men. We spoke no words, for no words could express what we felt. I attempted to restrain the tears that formed in my eyes, but when I perceived that every eye around me was flooded with tears, I sobbed unrestrainedly. I sank to my knees, thrust my arms into the air, and raised my face to the sky. The tears turned to laughter, singing, and dancing. My ordeal was over on November 8, 1782.

Time in Captivity: 4 years 274 days

CHAPTER EIGHTEEN

AN ENTHUSIASTIC GREETING FROM AN OLD FRIEND

NOVEMBER 1782

"Welcome to the United States Ship *Hague* and welcome to the United States of America," Captain Samuel Nicholson began his speech to the men who had come aboard. "Your captivity is over. Thank you for your service to our new country. America owes you a great debt. The *Hague* will carry you to ports in the states of Pennsylvania and Virginia. From those ports you'll make your way back to your homes and families, where you can resume your lives in this new free country. As soon as we replenish some supplies, we'll be underway to carry you home. The lieutenant will show you to your quarters below deck."

Once I got settled below deck, I returned to the top deck to get one last view of Canada, which represented five dark years of captivity, pain, and suffering. Within a couple of hours, the crew untied the dock lines, stored them in their place, and raised the sails. The cold November air filled the canvases and pushed us out to sea. I stood at the stern and watched the British town of Quebec, and that British flag, dwindle in size until it vanished. I moved to the bow and gazed at the bowsprit as it pointed to the middle of the wide St. Lawrence River toward the horizon and the Atlantic Ocean.

On the third day at sea, a Sunday, the *Hague* sliced through the peaceful ocean swells under a blue sky, propelled by a moderate breeze. The air was cool but warm enough to enjoy. That evening, four musicians—a fiddler, a cellist, a flutist, and a guitarist—sat on barrels and stools on the main deck. All the crew and soldiers chose seats on the quarter deck, upper deck, and main deck. The band delivered brilliant music, which prompted many to sing along. They finished to a standing ovation that demanded an encore. I think that even the stars enjoyed the music, for they were out in abundance declaring their approval. As I clapped, a puff of wind from behind lifted the hat off my head. I extended my right hand and caught it. The applause was shortened by a gust of wind that caused the ship to heel toward the port side. The fiddler declared, "The show's over."

How things can change in an instant at sea. For the gentle breeze turned into a vigorous wind that cut through our coats, brought clouds that hid the stars, and stirred up large ocean swells that tossed the ship between crests and troughs. We clutched for anything sturdy as the ship rocked.

"Everyone but the crew below deck," screamed Captain Nicholson, amidst the noise of the wind, the crash of waves against the hull of the ship, and the confusion of the moment.

We all scrambled. Everyone headed for the hatch and descended below deck. As the waves and the wind hurled the ship, I pushed with my legs against a bulkhead and held onto a support post. Then, a loud crash on the hatch door demanded our attention. One of my fellow passengers raced to the hatch to determine what had happened. He could not move the door. Two others helped him open it. As they did, a large section of a mast fell through. Cold seawater poured in around us. Two passengers hurled their supper, spraying many of us.

The power of Niagara Falls that I had admired from a safe distance was now on top of me and all around me. The fury of it overwhelmed me and our vessel. I wanted to run away, to escape the threat of death, but the bowels of the ship were like the iron bars of the British prison. The violent tosses, first up, then down, then over, were like the iron chains that restrained my ankles. The vast and violent seas were like the relentless prison guards mocking me, "You shall never be free. You will die here." I wrapped my arms around that support post. The person beside me clung to the post also. His eyes bulged, and his nostrils flared as he screamed. As frequent as these perils had become for me, this was an unexpected terror, from an unexpected source. I made it through the death threats of the Shawnee, Miami, and the British. After all I had endured, would I die on my way home?

Four crew members grabbed the mast section that had fallen through the hatch and hauled it out, then shut the hatch door. But the ship still bobbed on the waves, turned on its side, then turned to the other side. Below deck, we were powerless to help save the ship. The storm raged for hours, but we remained upright.

Finally, the roar of the wind, the assault of the rain, and the roll of the ship subsided. One of the crew opened the hatch door. The morning light disclosed many trembling hands and somber faces. We still held on to the support beams and to one another. I climbed on deck to behold a serene sea. In the center of the ship was a splintered post where the main mast had been, the rest of the mast lost to sea. Two masts remained and still held their sails; they powered the *Hague* toward Philadelphia. No sailors were lost to sea, but one had a large knot and bruise on the forehead when the broken mast knocked him in the head. The crippled *Hague* grappled with contrary winds and currents but sailed into Philadelphia harbor on December 16, 1782.

"You soldiers from Pennsylvania are free to leave and go back to your homes," Captain Nicholson said. "We have many rifles collected from the British soldiers. Each of you can take one as you leave. For those from Virginia, we'll take you there after the ship's repaired. Our departure date's January 20. You're free to stay with the ship or leave. If you leave, be back here on January 17. We may need you to help load supplies, or we may leave a day or two early."

After we dispersed, I approached the captain. "I plan to visit a family in Philadelphia. I'll be back in a day or so."

"Very well, son," the captain replied. "You'll have a bunk on this ship when you return,"

The next morning, I departed in search of the family of Benjamin Jones. Shops and taverns lined the street facing the harbor. I entered a tavern and found the owner.

"Excuse me, sir. I'm lookin' for the family of a tailor named Benjamin Jones. Do you know where they live?"

"Aye, lad. Mr. Jones made these here trousers I'm wearin'. He went off to war several years ago. I expect him to be comin' back soon, now that the fightin's over. His family lives on a small farm on the other side of town. Just follow High Street clear out of town."

As I walked along High Street the memories of the Detroit dungeon and Benjamin Jones flooded my thoughts. I remembered the pain of hunger and the cold winter without proper clothes. I remembered Mr. Jones thoughtfulness to serve my needs, even as his own life slipped away. His clothes probably saved my life. I was not that selfless. Even this mission to speak with Mr. Jones' family was hard for me. How would his wife react? Would she be angry? Or cry uncontrollably? It would have been easier to stay on the ship.

I found the house. My heart pounded. I took a deep breath, slowly exhaled, then knocked on the door. A middle-aged woman, wearing a blue shawl and white bonnet, came to the door.

"I'm lookin' for the family of Benjamin Jones. Do they live here?" I asked.

"Yes. I'm his wife. Do you know him?"

"Yes, ma'am. My name's Daniel Asbury. I was imprisoned in Detroit with your husband. He asked me to bring you a message. May I come in?"

"Yes. Please do. I haven't heard from him since he left to fight in the war, more than four years ago."

I followed her inside. "Thank you, ma'am. I mean no disrespect, but if it is alright with you, I'd prefer to keep my hat on. I was scalped by Indians some years ago, and its left a ghastly scar."

"Certainly, you may keep your hat on."

She directed me to a chair inside the house. "Can I get you a cup of tea?"

"Yes, please. I'd be grateful for a cup of tea," I answered.

She soon returned with two cups of tea and took a seat.

I began, "In the prison, the British treated us poorly and didn't provide us with the necessities to live. They hardly fed us, and when they did, it was spoiled. They also beat us, and some they hanged. Many became sick, but we weren't allowed a doctor's care. Mr. Jones was one of 'em that got sick. I tried to help him and shared some of my food, but his condition got worse. On his last night alive, he asked me to give you a message. That message is: He loved you. And he wanted me to tell his daughters that he loved them also. So, I'm here to deliver that message."

Mrs. Jones sat in silence. A stream of tears rolled down her cheeks. I fought back my own tears. I did not know what to say next. She looked down, closed her eyes, then looked back at me, trying to find words.

"Thank you, young man, for bringin' this news to me. It was kind of you to go out of your way to come here. I feared something like this had happened but held out hope that he'd come back. I want you to share this news with our three daughters. Can you stay the night?"

"Yes. I can stay," I replied.

That evening, Mrs. Jones invited her two older daughters and their husbands for supper (their third daughter still lived at home). Mrs. Jones prepared a scrumptious chicken pie made with potatoes, vegetables, and a layer of cornbread on top. Afterward, we sat around the table and sipped hot tea.

"Tell us about Father," The oldest daughter said to me. "Mother said you were with him when he died. What were his last words?"

"The last thing he was thinkin' before he died was how much he loved you. He asked me to tell you that if I had the chance," I replied. "That's why I've come." I told them how the clothes he gave me as he died saved my life.

That night, they gave me a bear rug and blankets to sleep on by the fireplace. I had Mr. Justice's coat that I put on top of me. The Jones were an amiable family, and I was pleased that I could deliver Mr. Jones's message to them. The next morning, I set off to return to my home on the *Hague*.

Captain Nicholson greeted me as I stepped on board, "Welcome back, Daniel. Did you see the folks you wanted to see?"

"Aye, sir. It was a successful mission."

"You can return to your bunk. I'm sure the galley could use a cook or the first mate can find some other work for you to do."

The cold wind blew through the ship's rigging, whistled through the lines, clanged the tackle against the masts, and flapped the American flag. That racket awoke me early on December 25. Christmas day spurred memories of my family gathered around our fireplace as Ma roasted a chicken over the fire. Again, I wondered if George was among them. I arose from the bowels of *USS Hague* and clung to Mr. Justice's coat to stay warm. By midday the Christmas songs of men and women on shore drew us to the ship's railing. Ten people faced our ship from the dock and sang "O Come all Ye Faithful."

When they finished, one of the singers shouted to us, "Come to our church in one hour for a Christmas service to celebrate our Savior's birth. We're from Christ Church, just down 2nd street."

One of the sailors responded, "We enjoyed your singin', but we ain't churchgoin' sailors."

A part of me wanted to go with the choir to the church service. I felt more open to it than I had in the past. I remembered my prayer the night before my hanging: "Bring my soul out of prison, that I may praise Thy Name." Had God answered my prayer? There was another part of me that wanted to stay on the ship with the other sailors. That was more comfortable and felt safe.

The men tipped their hats toward us, and they all turned toward the next ship on the dock, as one of them started "Joy to the World," followed by the whole choir on the second word,

Joy to the world! the Lord is come;
Let earth receive her King;
Let every heart prepare Him room,

By early January 1783, the new mast was in place, with its new sails. Ten of us passengers, former British prisoners, all Virginians, waited with great anticipation for the *Hague* to cast off and head toward home. On January 18, the crew retrieved the dock lines and raised the foresails. The mild southwest breeze filled the sails and pushed the ship away from the dock as the helmsman steered the Hague toward the center of the Delaware River. For ten pleasant days we sailed along the coasts of Delaware, Maryland, and Virginia. Then, the helmsman steered the ship toward land and the Chesapeake Bay. We anchored at Yorktown as the sun set, too late to go ashore, but we were home.

The next morning, we gathered on deck, all of us with broad smiles. Captain Nicholson addressed us, "I point out to you that we're now anchored at Yorktown, Virginia, the site where General Cornwallis surrendered to General George Washington, effectively ending the war. On behalf of the United States Navy, I thank you for your service to our new country and for the many hardships you've endured during the war. The country can never repay you, or even pay you a decent wage. However, each of you can take a rifle, for all men need a rifle. Also, take one of those powder horns, filled with powder, and some lead balls for your labor on this ship. There is a pile of hatchets and knives, and you are free to take one of each. You're now free from the tyranny of England. Go live your lives, return to your families, raise children, and build farms."

We all searched through the rifles that the captain displayed. I found a Pennsylvania rifle, like the one I purchased before joining the militia. I seized it before anyone else saw it. We each grabbed a hatchet and knife.

Rowed by the sailors, the long boats carried us to shore. As we set foot on Virginia dirt, we ten Virginians smiled, for we were that much closer to home. From there, eight of us headed up the road to Williamsburg, about twelve miles away, while two took the road to Hampton and Norfolk.

Arriving in Williamsburg late that afternoon, we walked into the Raleigh Tavern and bargained with the owner. "We're Virginia soldiers comin' home from the war. Might you have any work for us in exchange for a meal and a room?"

"Aye," replied the owner. "Follow me out back."

We followed him to the back of the establishment. He pointed and said, "See all those logs. They need to be cut and split for firewood. Do that and you can all have a meal and bed tonight. There're some saws and hatchets over yonder."

"Yes, sir. We'll get right to it, thank you, sir," we all responded.

"You're welcome. And thank you for your service to our country."

The next morning, I asked the owner, "Where is the road to Richmond?"

"You take that road yonder, to the James River," nodding in the direction of the street. "There, you will find a road along the north side of the river. You take that road to Charles City and then Richmond."

"Many thanks."

Two in our group traveled to the Brunswick community across the James River and six of us reached Charles City by sundown on our first day. At the tavern, in exchange for some work, we had a substantial supper and a sound sleep. The next night we stopped by a creek for the night and roasted a wild turkey one of us shot. By mid-afternoon of the following day, we arrived at Coutts Ferry in Richmond. From there, two took the Three-Notched Road to Charlottesville, and four of us journeyed by ferry across the James River to Richmond.

After we crossed the river in heavy snowfall, I parted from my three remaining companions, each eager to see his family. I entered the Hanover Tavern and approached the owner. "Could I trouble you to allow me to sleep by your hearth this snowy evening? I'll do some work for you to earn a meal."

"If you're willin' to feed the horses and clean out the stalls, I'll feed you supper. There's a bed over in the corner you can lie on for the night," he replied.

"I'm most appreciative. Just point me to the stalls, and I'll get right to it."

I trudged through the snow to the horse stalls, once again thankful for Mr. Justice's coat. The lantern displayed why the manager was pleased to give me the job. Twelve horses, hungry and weary from a day's travel, were anxious for their supper. The barn floor had not been cleaned for about a week. I hauled hay and feed and shoveled manure for a couple of hours, then reported back for my supper. They fed me what was left of the beef and vegetable stew. By the time I finished my supper, I was ready to lie down for the night, for it was midnight. As I lay there, I was thankful. Despite the hard work, I was now free. No longer confined by chains under the threat of whips, starvation, and death, I could make my own decisions and go where I wanted to go. Sleep overpowered the noise in the tavern before I could think another thought.

The next morning, I remembered my mission in Richmond to contact the family of Martin Overstreet, to inform Mary Humphries that William would be returning from the war, hopefully soon. After some food and tea, I inquired of the owner, "Do you know where the family of Martin Overstreet lives?"

"Don't know the fellow or the family," he replied. Then he yelled out to all in the tavern, "Does anyone know Martin Overstreet? Can anyone help this young lad out?"

"I think they live 'bout two miles from here," one man said. "On the outskirts of town. They have a family farm."

"How do I find 'em'," I replied.

"Just take this road, right here in front of the Hanover, and ask someone after you go a couple of miles," he added.

"I thank you for your kindness," I replied.

I traveled through town and came to the outskirts, where there were several small farms. Due to the snowfall, no one was outside their houses. I knocked on a cabin door.

An elderly man responded to my knock, "Yes sir, can I help you?"

"I'm lookin' for the family of Martin Overstreet," I said. "Do they live near here?"

"They live in the next house down the road, just around the bend," the man said.

"Much obliged," I said.

At the next house, a middle-aged man came to the door. "I'm lookin' for Martin Overstreet," I said.

"I'm he."

"I have a message for Mary Humphries, your sister. Is she here?"

"Yes, she is. Please come in out of the snow."

I followed him inside, where ten people, three adults and seven children, sat by the fireplace.

"Mary, someone is here to see you," Overstreet said. "Says he has a message for you."

Mary moved from the fireplace to where I stood. She held out her hand. "I'm Mary Humphries."

"My name is Daniel Asbury," I said, as I shook her hand. "I have a message from your husband, William Humphries. We were in prison together."

Mary gasped. She lifted her trembling hand to her mouth. "Is he still alive?"

"Yes, he is alive!"

"Let's everyone take a seat." Overstreet said. "Daniel, please have a seat."

"Daniel, you look like you could use some hot tea and a biscuit," Mrs. Overstreet said.

"I'd be grateful," I replied.

As we sat by the fire, I took a sip of tea. "William and I were in prison in Montreal. His message to you, Mary, is this: he is still alive, he loves you very much, and he is coming home soon."

Mary closed her eyes and lifted her head, as if mouthing a

silent prayer. "Boys, did you hear that? Your dad is alive and he's coming home!"

Two boys rushed to her side. They held their embrace for minutes, tears flowing.

"What happened that William was gone so long?" Overstreet asked finally.

I told them about being captured by the Indians, sold to the British, and transferred to Fort Chambly. I told them about the escape in the leaky canoe and how William and I were sentenced to hang. "While we were standin' on the gallows, about to be hung, a British soldier ran into the courtyard, and halted the execution. He carried the official letter announcin' Cornwallis' surrender. The fightin' had stopped and all executions must stop. That letter saved our lives."

Mary closed her eyes again while clasping her boys' hands. More tears rolled down her cheeks.

"Daniel, thank you so, so much for bringing us this news," Mary said.

We talked on into the afternoon. They had many questions about Indian and prison life. When I figured I had stayed long enough, I thanked them for their time, and made to leave.

"Daniel, you can't leave now, it's snowing," Overstreet said. "You must stay the night."

"I'd be much obliged. I wouldn't get far in this weather."

As we sat around the table eating supper, Martin Overstreet cleared his throat. "Daniel, I've been thinking about your story of how that British soldier ran out with letter sayin' the war was over. No more executions. Daniel, it wasn't that letter, or the commander, that spared your life. It was the Almighty! He has work for you to do."

"Well, Mr. Overstreet, I don't know 'bout that," I said. "I'm not a prayin' man and don't know much about that matter. My Ma prays every day. But my Pa and I, we're not religious."

"Well God's been answerin' your mother's prayers, bringing you back alive," Mrs. Overstreet said.

That night, I lay by the fireplace covered with a blanket and Mr. Justice's coat, but could not sleep. Mr. Overstreet's words, "It was the Almighty that spared your life. He has work for you to do." Memories raced through my mind of all the times I could have died: rifle shots, knives, panthers, and bears. *Why am I still alive?*

Mrs. Overstreet sent me on my way after a biscuit and tea. I made good progress with mild weather, as I camped and hunted for food. Powhatan was the next town, and I once again offered my services for a meal and bed at the Mosby Tavern. The third day out of Powhatan, a frosty north wind blew in sinister dark clouds and more snow. I suspended my journey to make a shelter for protection, like the one Daniel Boone made when we camped near Blue Licks, Kentucky. When the storm waned, I resumed my journey. After rounding a bend, a house appeared. A house represented hope for a meal and shelter for the night. A dog with a fierce bark greeted me. I slowed my approach.

A middle-aged woman opened the cabin door, stepped outside, and attached a leash. "Birdie, hush. Let's see what this young man wants."

I advanced a few steps but maintained a considerable distance. "I'm on my way home after bein' held a prisoner by the British durin' the war. Might I trouble you for a meal and a bed on your back porch? I'll be on my way tomorrow mornin'."

"Certainly," she said. "How long's it been since you had a meal?"

"'bout three days since I had a decent meal. I had a piece of turkey two days ago."

"My name's Sara Foster. My husband Henry's out back takin'

care of our pigs. I'll fetch him. He can draw you some water so you can wash up."

Around the table, Henry asked me, "Where does your family live, son?

"They live near New London, on the road to Big Lick."

"Well, it shouldn't take you but two or three days to get to New London. I know they'll be mighty glad to see ya."

"I'll be mighty glad to see them. I've been away more than five years."

'I'm so glad you survived the war and that you'll soon be home," she said. "That'll be a blessed day for them."

"Yes. I suppose so, and a joyful day for me."

The next day, Sara and Henry sent me off with a full stomach and a bag full of food that would last me about two days. On the third day I struck out on what would be the day I would see my family again. The road was muddy and slippery. The rain had become just a light cold sprinkle. Despite my hunger, the goal of seeing my family again propelled me onward. I began to see familiar trees, rocks, and farmhouses that whispered to me that I was close to home. A stream offered an invitation for a drink. I knelt on some rocks over a quiet pool and lowered my face to the water. I stopped in alarm. I did not believe what I saw. I did not recognize my reflection. My beard was long. My face was dirty and sagging. I took off my cap and was horrified at the scars. Would Ma and Pa recognize me?

I crested a hill, spurred by a sympathetic breeze at my back and the anticipation that I would soon see our cabin. Just before it came into view, a familiar sound entered my ears. It was the sound of dog barks. What a marvelous sound. My beloved Rex ran toward me. I dropped my gun and pack and waited for him. He jumped into my arms and we rolled on the ground. At least one family member recognized me.

CHAPTER NINETEEN

MY CHAINS FELL OFF

FEBRUARY 1783

I continued my journey toward our cabin, with Rex by my side. Pa came out and waited for me.

"Hi there. Sorry about Rex. He doesn't normally jump on people, especially strangers. He just barks at strangers, wantin' to chase 'em away," Pa said.

I had expected my family not to recognize me, but still my heart ached at the word "stranger." "Dogs just love me, and I love them," I replied.

"What brings you this way so late on a Sunday afternoon?" Pa asked.

"I'm on my way home. Been held prisoner by the British in Montreal durin' the war. Might I trouble you for a meal and a bed, even if it's on your back porch? I'll be on my way tomorrow mornin'," I answered. I am not sure why I said this. I had not planned to. The fact was, I felt like a stranger. Not that Pa was one—no, Pa was just as I remembered—but that I was not the boy he had known.

"You'd be welcome at our table this evenin'. And you can sleep by the fireplace where it's warm," Pa said. "Come on in and meet the family."

I followed Pa inside, and the pleasurable aroma of Ma's chicken stew welcomed me: it smelled like home. Ma stood at the fireplace and tended to supper preparations. Seated nearby were my five younger siblings. I longed to throw my arms around each one of them, but they looked at me blankly. How they had changed: they were all much bigger now. A torrent of tears demanded to erupt, but I mustered self-control to hold them back.

"This here's a traveler from the war," Pa said, introducing me. He was just released from prison in Montreal, and he's on his way home. What's your name, son?"

"My name's Daniel."

Pa hesitated and stumbled on his first word. "Welcome, Daniel. I've invited Daniel to share our table this evening and sleep by the fire tonight." He turned to me again. "We're the Asburys. You've already met Rex, our dog, and he's given you a hearty welcome." Pa pointed to each person in turn, telling me their names. "The other four have already moved out of the house." A small bit of tension in my stomach relaxed: George was alive.

"Pleased to make your acquaintances," I said. "Thank you for your kind hospitality."

"Now you make yourself right at home," Pa said. "You can take your hat off and get comfortable."

"If it's all right with you, I would like to leave my hat on. I received a terrible head wound during the war. And it is not pleasant to look at."

"You can keep your hat on, then," Ma said. "I hope you like chicken stew. We're ready to sit down at the table."

"Oh yes, ma'am, chicken stew sounds mighty tasty," I said.

Pa motioned for me to take a seat beside him and James. Then Pa led us in a blessing. "Lord, we thank Thee for Thou bountiful supply of our needs. We also thank Thee that Thou has brought young Daniel here to share this meal, and we ask Thy blessings on him as he journeys home. Amen."

I was stunned. I had never heard Pa pray before. I sat silent as others began to eat.

"Daniel, where's your family?" Ma asked.

"I'm almost home. They live on the road to Big Lick," I replied.

"Well, now," Pa said. "How did a soldier from Virginia get put in prison in Montreal?"

"I was in Kentucky and then some Indians captured me and then sold me to the British in Detroit."

"Maybe you know or heard of our son," Ma said. "His name was Daniel also." My heart raced and a drop of sweat ran down my arm. I gazed down at the table. "He went to Kentucky five years ago. And we haven't heard from him since. Do you know our son?"

I took a breath. "Yes, I know him. We were both in prison in Detroit. He is still alive, but Daniel has changed so much you might not recognize him."

"Did he talk about us?" Patsy asked.

My heart raced. My stomach churned. "Yes, he talked about all of you, and he missed . . . "

Genny asked something, but I did not hear it. They waited for me to answer Genny's question. I dropped my fork as tears escaped my eyes. "I can't let this conversation go any further like this. I can't hide the truth from you any longer. If you take a moment and examine me and ask me any question, you will see that I am Daniel Asbury. Ma, Pa, it's me." I inspected the faces of my siblings and said their names as I looked them in the eyes.

Ma rose from her chair and stared at me. She walked over to me, bent down to get a close look, and examined my face. "Turn your seat."

I turned and faced her waiting for her conclusion.

Slowly tears streamed down her cheeks. She screamed and

threw her arms in the air. "Daniel! It is you! How could I not recognize my own son? Stand up so I can properly hug you."

I stood. The dam that held back my tears broke loose and flooded my face. I threw my arms around Ma. Then, the whole family wrapped their arms around me.

"We believed you were dead," James cried.

"Or lost to the Indians," Patsy added.

"I've prayed for you every day," Ma said between sobs. "God is so good. He has answered my prayers."

"I feared this day would never come," I said. "I have yearned for this day for so long."

I do not know how long we stood in that embrace, but I could have stayed there forever. Eventually, we returned to our places at the table and wiped our tears with napkins.

"I should've known from Rex's greetin' that you weren't a stranger," Pa said. "He greeted you just like he greets us. He recognized you from a hundred yards away."

"Let me see your head and that wound you got," Ma requested.

I took off my hat.

Ma gently placed her hand on my head. Her breath warmed my crown as she examined my wound. She laid her cheek over it and wrapped both arms around my head. "Oh, my poor boy." Ma held me tight as more tears flowed down her cheeks. "Gracious. What happened?"

I told them the story of my capture by the Miami and how they sold me and my scalp.

"Scalped head or not, I am so glad you're alive and back home," Ma said.

I reached up and placed my right hand on my bald head. "It is a constant reminder that my life was spared."

"You were spared for a reason. God has something He wants you to do," Ma said.

Unsure how to respond, I changed the subject. "How are Elizabeth, George, and Molly?"

"Elizabeth and Molly are married. Elizabeth and Charles got married a couple of months after you left and they have two children. Molly got married last summer. George came home and then moved out to start his own farm. You'll see them all tomorrow."

"How did you get captured the first time?" James asked.

We moved in front of the fire, and I began my tale. I answered their many questions and requests for further details. We talked on into the night, but when Nancy fell asleep in Ma's lap, we figured it was time to go to bed.

I started to bed down next to the fire, but Genny called out from the rafters, "Come sleep with us up here. You belong with us."

Genny's invitation was like sweet music. Tears flowed down my cheeks again. I closed my eyes; thankful this day had finally come. I ascended the spiral stairs and found a place next to my brother and sisters.

The next morning, Ma sent James to tell the others that I had returned home. I had bathed and shaved my beard when Rex's bark announced the arrival of Elizabeth and her family. I wiped the lather off my face, grabbed my hat, and dashed outside into Elizabeth's outstretched arms. Charles wrapped his arms around both of us.

"Daniel, I thought I'd never see you again," Elizabeth said when we parted.

"I feared the same," I said.

"I'd like you to meet my two boys," Elizabeth continued as she held out her arm for the two young boys to come to her. "This is Daniel, and this is John."

A tear came to my eye. I stooped down and offered my hand. "I'm pleased to meet both of you. My name is also Daniel." Little Daniel's eyes lit up and gave me a big grin.

"I feared the worst," Elizabeth said. "I wanted to always remember you."

"I am honored that you named your first son Daniel."

Ma called us all inside while we waited for the others to come.

"Take off that hat and let me see that beautiful head of hair," Elizabeth said.

I looked down. "That hat is there for a purpose. I was scalped. I no longer have a head of hair,"

"Oh, Daniel, I'm so sorry. May I see it?"

"It's rather gruesome."

"I don't care. You're my brother."

I hesitated. Then I removed my hat and bowed my head for her to see. Elizabeth gasped. I wanted to cover my head again. She hugged me once more, even tighter.

"It's healed a great amount and looks much better than it did at first. I'm just thankful to be alive and back home."

George and Molly soon arrived, and the whole family gathered around the fire where I once again told my tales. George told me a bit about his time in the war, but mostly had questions about my experience.

I resumed my duties on the farm that week, assisting James who had inherited my old tasks. To my surprise, Pa opened every meal with prayer.

"Winter weather permittin', we still hunt on Saturdays," Pa said on Friday. "I expect tomorrow will be a suitable day for it."

"I'd love to go huntin'," I said. "Many times, the pleasant memories of our huntin' trips helped me through the anguish of prison."

On Saturday morning, Pa, James, and I mounted our horses and set out. We rode to the ravine where Pa had killed the bear. We spread out and waited, but nothing came. At midday, we came together for a small lunch.

"Pa, I was surprised to hear you pray over our meals this

week," I said. "That staggered me. I had never heard you pray before."

"Well, when your Ma started goin' to preachin' meetin's, and prayin' so much at home, I couldn't see what she saw in it. It wasn't for me. Then, when we didn't hear from you, we didn't know if you were dead or captured by Indians. I didn't know what to do. Your Ma and I talked about it, and she said, 'Let's pray and ask God to return you home.' There was nothing else I could do, so I agreed. We started prayin' together for you, and then I started goin' to the church meetings. Then I began to see how ornery I was, how I had run away from God. But the thing that got me was this—God suffered an incredible pain to save me. God lost His own Son to an unjust execution. That was the same thing I feared for you. I learned that He had provided my forgiveness through Jesus Christ dyin' on the cross. One night, I took a walk out back under the moonlight and gazed up at the stars. I told God that I had done corrupt and regretful things and asked Him to forgive me. I told Him I wanted to follow Him, not my selfish desires, for the rest of my life. Since then, I have experienced a peace and a joy and a confidence that He loves me. I found that His unlikely fondness for me, as ornery as I am, is like my fondness for you—only much, much deeper."

I sat there silent for a minute. "Thank you for explainin' that. I'll be thinkin' about it."

"I hope you will go with us to the meetin' tomorrow."

"Yes, I will go with you tomorrow," I replied. "I reckon that'd be the proper place to thank God for keepin' me alive and returnin' me home."

After our break, we returned to our positions. I made my deer calls, which amused Pa and James. After about an hour, I heard footsteps. I located Pa and James to make sure they were not moving in the forest. I moved my rifle into position to fire. The sound of the footsteps grew louder. Then, through the tree limbs, a nice eight-point buck emerged. I shot at his head, and he dropped to the ground.

"Good shot, Daniel," James declared.

"My, Daniel, your shot's improved," Pa said. "You hit him right between the eyes."

"Thank you. I got a lot of practice in the militia and when I lived with the Indians."

That night, around the dinner table, Pa said, "Daniel, your travels've changed you. You never refer to the Indians as 'savages,' like the people around here do. It is either the Shawnee, Miamis, or Indians."

"Well, Pa, I learned that they aren't savages. Not any more than any of us. They're less savage than the British, who say we all deserve to die for rebellin' against the king. The Indians treated me kindly, like family. We're invadin' their land and takin' away their huntin' grounds. They're fightin' for their rights, just like we're fightin' for our rights against the British."

"People have dreams of ownin' land, gainin' wealth, and improvin' their situation for their families," Pa said.

Then Ma said, "The distressin' thing is, those dreams and ambitions are at the expense of the Indians."

"Well, nothin's goin' to stop folks from movin' west now that the war is over," Pa said. "I'm afraid the Indians'll suffer greatly."

I lay down to bed in the rafters with the other kids and my mind raced. I expected life on the farm to be the same when I returned. However, so much had changed. Pa changing his beliefs unsettled me, but below that feeling of confusion, was a sense that it was right.

The morning of the first Sunday of March 1783 was bright with a clear sky. A strong breeze rattled the trees. Millie pulled our wagon to the Miller's farmyard where nearly one hundred people gathered for the meeting.

While we waited for the meeting to start, the preacher, a

large man wearing a shad-belly coat, a vest, and boots strolled up to us. A gold watch chain hung out of his pocket. "Tom and Martha, it's delightful to see you this mornin'."

"Preacher Gatch, nice to see you," Pa said. "I believe you know our children, but we have another one this mornin'. This is our son Daniel. He's just returned from the war, after bein' held prisoner in Montreal."

I reached over and shook his hand. "Pleased to meet you, sir."

"The pleasure's mine," Mr. Gatch said. "I've heard some horrid tales from American prisoners held by the British. I'm glad you made it out alive and are back home."

"Thank you, sir," I said.

The meeting began with a hymn, accompanied by a young man playing the fiddle. Henry Miller stood and made announcements. While he spoke, I bowed my head and prayed, "God, thank You for sparin' my life and bringin' me home. Amen."

Following his announcements, Miller said, "Now Reverend Gatch is with us today to speak from God's Holy Word. Reverend Gatch, please come forward. We wait expectantly."

Philip Gatch, with brisk, long strides, emerged from the back of the group. He still wore his long coat and wide-brimmed hat and carried a Bible. He opened the Bible and began, "The text I'll read from is Isaiah 53:3-6:

> He is despised and rejected of men; a man of sorrows, and acquainted with grief: and we hid as it were our faces from him; he was despised, and we esteemed him not.
>
> Surely he hath borne our griefs, and carried our sorrows: yet we did esteem him stricken, smitten of God, and afflicted.

> But he was wounded for our transgressions, he was bruised for our iniquities: the chastisement of our peace was upon him; and with his stripes we are healed.
>
> All we like sheep have gone astray; we have turned every one to his own way; and the LORD hath laid on him the iniquity of us all."

Gatch put the Bible down and looked over the people. He spread out his arms as he talked and walked from one side of the group to the other. "Who's this text in Isaiah talking about?" he asked in a booming voice. "'He is despised and rejected by men; a man of sorrows and acquainted with grief'. No one has experienced pain like this man. He not only experienced profound physical pain but emotional and social pain. He was despised and rejected by the people. But . . . " Gatch paused and took a deep breath. "His pain had a purpose. His pain was for us, that we might be healed. He has borne our griefs and carried our sorrows. The Lord has laid on Him the iniquity of us all, and with His stripes, we are healed. Who is 'He'? Who is He that was afflicted, like a lamb to the slaughter? I'll tell you who He is. He's the One who suffered for us, for me, for you. He's the One who died for us. He's the One who is God, who became man. He's the One who hung on the cross, bled, and died for me, and for you. His name is Jesus Christ. Who put Jesus on the cross to die? I'll tell you who nailed Jesus up there: you and me. It was our lies, our hatred, our cheatin', our betrayals of one another, our rejection of God. And we break His heart every time we seek glory for ourselves and ignore the only One who deserves glory—Jesus Christ.

"Do you think you have felt pain in your life? Jesus has suffered more. He has suffered our pain in our place. Look, there ain't no way to love someone without layin' your heart bare to their breakin' it. When God set out to lovin' us, He accepted all the heartbreak we'd send His way. And we all do break His heart and it's only on the cross that we can see God's heart broken and bleedin' right in front of us."

Gatch's words of Jesus on the cross and how I had put Him there, summoned memories of Chillicothe. I remembered Joshua burning at the stake and how I put him there by my deception and my self-serving efforts. It hit me like a shot to the heart and assaulted my soul.

"My friends, yes, we are guilty, but the thing that makes His heart vulnerable provides our forgiveness. Jesus carries the consequences of our sins on the cross. His death on the cross pays the debt we owe for our sins. 1 Peter 2:24 says, 'Who his own self bore our sins in his own body on the tree, that we, being dead to sins, should live unto righteousness: by whose stripes ye were healed.' Jesus bore our sins on the cross. He paid our penalty Himself. His wounds have healed us. Are you burdened by your own betrayals? Then, come to Jesus, and receive His forgiveness."

As Gatch spoke, I wrestled with the overwhelming weight of my guilt, like the prison chains that I was powerless to remove. Jesus offered forgiveness, but I sensed a powerful opposition to receiving it. I could not receive what Jesus offered. To admit to myself that I needed Jesus was daunting.

After Mr. Gatch finished his sermon, Henry Miller stood up and announced: "We'll now sing that favorite hymn of ours written by brother Charles Wesley, 'And Can it Be that I Should Gain?'" Ma let me look at her hymnal as we sang.

Died He for me, who caused His pain—
For me, who Him to death pursued?
Amazing love! How can it be,
That Thou, my God, shouldst die for me?

Jesus died for me even though I caused His suffering. The

fourth verse reminded me of the tussle with my self-centered purposes and how, in that British prison, I longed to be free from the chains that bound me. Now I could feel the chains of my misdeeds constraining me. We sang:

Long my imprisoned spirit lay,
Fast bound in sin and nature's night;
Thin eye diffused a quickening ray—
I woke, the dungeon flamed with light;
My chains fell off, my heart was free;
I rose, went forth, and followed Thee.

I longed for the chains of my guilt to fall off. I had to speak with Rev. Gatch.

As the crowd dispersed, I pushed my way past people standing and talking. I found Rev. Gatch and said, "Sir, I need help. I want Jesus as my Savior."

"Step over here, Daniel." He extended his arm toward a tree, away from other people.

He opened his Bible and read John 3:16. "'For God so loved the world, that he gave his only begotten Son, that whosoever believeth in him should not perish, but have everlasting life.' Daniel, what does that verse say you must do to have everlasting life?"

"Believe in God's only Son."

"And Who is that?"

"Jesus Christ."

"Yes. Now let's read Revelation 3:20. 'Behold, I stand at the door, and knock: if any man hear my voice, and open the door, I will come in to him, and will sup with him, and he with me.' Jesus is knocking at the door of your life. He wants to come in and have a relationship with you. But you must open the door and invite Him in. Can you confess your sins to God, and receive God's forgiveness through your faith in Jesus Christ? And can you invite Jesus to come into your life?"

"Yes," I replied, no longer able to hold back the tears.

"Let's bow our heads and pray. You pray after me. 'God, I know I am a sinner, and I ask for your forgiveness.'" I repeated his prayer.

"I believe that Jesus Christ is Your Son, and that He died for my sins, and that You raised Him from the dead."

I repeated.

"Lord Jesus, I trust You as my Savior and invite You to come into my life. I want to follow You as Lord, from this day forward. Amen."

I repeated.

Gatch put his hand on my shoulder. "Daniel, the first thing you need to do is tell your Ma and Pa what you have done."

"Thank you, sir. I will do that, but first, I'd like to pray alone. Will you excuse me?"

"Yes, Daniel. You go find a place to pray."

I turned away, told Ma I needed to be alone for a while, and found the back of the barn, out of view from the others. I sat on the ground against the barn, put my head between my knees, and wept, unrestrained. I asked God for forgiveness and invited Jesus Christ to come in as my Lord and Savior. My chains fell off.

Long my imprisoned spirit lay,
Fast bound in sin and nature's night;
Thin eye diffused a quickening ray,
I woke, the dungeon flamed with light;
My chains fell off, my heart was free;
I rose, went forth, and followed Thee.

—Charles Wesley

EPILOGUE

MARCH 1783 - APRIL 1825

In the years that followed my return home from the war, and my blessed encounter with my Savior, I helped Ma and Pa on the farm. We planted and harvested the fields, milked the cows, and tended the pigs and chickens. I resumed my schoolwork, along with my brother and sisters, for I had gotten behind on my grammar and numbers. My friend Ben Kelly returned home about a month before me. We went on many hunting trips together, just as we had promised before we parted in Chillicothe four years earlier.

I engaged my time with what became my first love as I prepared for my life's work—studying the Bible and learning all I could about Jesus. One Sunday, at one of the meetings, the preacher called upon me to stand up and share how I met the Savior. This reminded me of the village meetings in Chillicothe, where a warrior would share a story of bravery or a funny experience. I stood up in the meeting and recounted my captivity during the war and how, upon returning home, I met Jesus. Many people shouted "Amen" when I finished, and others came up to me after the meeting and told me how much my story meant to them. Sometime later, when the traveling preacher was not at our meeting, Henry Miller asked me to preach. I did the best I could and stumbled only a few times. Afterward, two people prayed to receive Jesus as their Lord and Savior. After that, I had many opportunities to preach. It was a great joy to preach from the Scriptures. An even greater joy was witnessing a skeptic place their faith in Jesus. I began to see this work was a high endeavor and of immense worth. I dedicated my life to pursue preaching to lost souls and nurturing churches to become lights on a hill to glorify God.

My years in captivity taught me that God is my sovereign Protector and Provider. He protected me when my life was in danger and provided for my necessities when my provisions were scarce. When I and my horse traveled trails in the western wilderness I encountered many dangers from fierce animals, rugged terrain, and violent people. God has always protected me and provided for my needs. I have also experienced the joy of meeting someone else's need, just as my needs were met by the Justices when I was in prison in Detroit, or when William Humphries carried my heavy load on the trek to Fort Niagara.

On February 1, 1786, I joined the traveling preachers of the Methodist Episcopal Church, on trial. My first circuits were the Amelia Circuit in Virginia and Halifax Circuit in North Carolina, working under the direction of the great preacher Francis Poythress. In 1788, the Methodist Episcopal Church admitted me as a full traveling preacher, assigned to the French Broad circuit in the mountains of North Carolina.

Many people presumed I was a cousin to Francis Asbury, the first bishop of the Methodist Episcopal Church in the American colonies. However, we are of no relation, though we were great friends and co-laborers in bringing souls to the Lord. We met on many occasions, and he came and preached in my circuit and at our camp meetings. When he passed on to glory, Francis bequeathed me his large chest, which I have treasured.

In 1789, the Methodists assigned me to the Yadkin Circuit in

North Carolina, but after two months assigned me to the Lincoln Circuit, which included areas west of the Catawba River, extended into the mountains, and into South Carolina. In Lincoln County, I discovered a group of Methodists who had moved from Brunswick, Virginia. This community of believers became the Grassy Creek Methodist Episcopal Church, later renamed Rehobeth Methodist Episcopal Church, the first Methodist Episcopal Church west of the Catawba River.

It was in that Lincoln County community by the Catawba River that I met and married Nancy Morris. I left the traveling circuit so that we could establish our family and farm, but still preached locally. The Lord blessed Nancy and me with many children. The first was a boy we named Francis, after our bishop. The second was a girl, whom we named Elizabeth, after my eldest sister. In all, we have raised twelve children. After ten years of preaching locally, I returned to the traveling circuit and continued preaching in various circuits in North and South Carolina until 1825.

I am now in the last years of my life. My children and grandchildren have pleaded with me for years to write down the story of my adventures as a young man. They call it adventure, but it was a gauntlet of hardship and pain. However, as I ponder these events, I have come to see that they are much more than adventure, suffering, or hardship. When I consider the contrast of my earlier suffering and pain with my current state of freedom, health, and the provision of my earthly needs, my heart is always drawn to praise and thanksgiving to the One who is the Shepherd and Protector of my soul. Of utmost importance, He has redeemed my life, a life that was aimless and self-centered, and made me useful for His holy purposes. No, this is not a story of adventure or suffering, but my story of deliverance and redemption. I often remember my days in prison in Detroit and hearing Charles Woodhull sing his song and prayer from Psalm 142:7.

Bring my soul out of prison, that I may praise Thy name.

Also, every time I sing Charles Wesley's hymn, I remember His deliverance.

Long my imprisoned spirit lay,
Fast bound in sin and nature's night;
Thin eye diffused a quickening ray—
I woke, the dungeon flamed with light;
My chains fell off, my heart was free;
I rose, went forth, and followed Thee.

In the years that have followed, these have become my song and praise for His deliverance.

As I look back on my life, I see signs of Providence directing my steps from the day I was born. For I was born on Sunday, captured by the Indians on Sunday, returned home on Sunday, and was converted on Sunday. And, I believe, if the Lord wills, I will die on Sunday.

AUTHOR'S NOTE

Daniel Asbury's death occurred on Sunday morning, May 15, 1825, and is described by R. N. Price as follows: " . . . he arose, apparently more cheerful and vigorous than usual, conversed on various subjects, and noted down a text from which he intended to preach a funeral sermon. In a few moments afterwards he was walking through his yard when suddenly he stopped, looked up to heaven, and with an unearthly smile, uttered a few indistinct words, and then fell lifeless on the ground."[1]

Rev. M. H. Moore describes Daniel Asbury as "an earnest, bold preacher; ever ready for the work; never dismayed by hardships to be endured in the way of success; a man of strong native intellect, but limited education, and yet a clear, forcible, successful expounder of the word of God. Like most of his contemporaries in the traveling connection, he was a 'man of one book'; and, unlike some who have succeeded him, he preached not poetry nor philosophy, but Christ crucified as revealed in that book. With a deep and rich religious experience; by a constant study of the revealed will of God, aided by the

1. RN Price, *Holston Methodism, From its Origin to the present Time.*

enlightening agency of the Holy Spirit; by a close walk with God and constant communion with him —he became a man of power, and was owned of his Master in becoming the agent in leading to Christ hundreds of souls who in the last day will rise up and call him blessed."[2]

Nancy Morris Asbury, an only child, became an orphan at the age of eighteen, just after marrying Daniel. She was the mother of twelve children and lived to see a multitude of grand-children and great-grandchildren. Nancy died in 1862 at the age of 91.[3]

Daniel Asbury was my great, great, great, great- grandfather. Daniel was the father of Henry Asbury, who was the father of John Asbury, who was the father of Laura Asbury Finger, who was the mother of Lela Finger Canipe, who was the mother of Laura Ellen Canipe Hackney, who was my mother.

The documented facts about Daniel Asbury's life are as follows: He was born in Fairfax, Virginia, on Sunday, February 18, 1762. His family moved to Bedford County, Virginia, around 1767. Daniel joined the Bedford County Militia on September 1, 1777, at the age of fifteen. He traveled to Boonesborough, Kentucky, with the militia. Shawnee Native Americans captured Daniel with twenty-six other soldiers, including Daniel Boone, while on a salt-making mission in Blue Licks, Kentucky, on Sunday, February 8, 1778. They arrived in Chillicothe on February 18, 1778, Daniel Asbury's sixteenth birthday. An old Indian chief and his wife adopted Daniel Asbury, and he lived among the Shawnees for more than a year. He escaped while on a hunting trip. He hid from his captors in a hollow log. His pursuers sat on this log and discussed what they would do to him when they caught him. After crossing the Ohio River in a previously hidden canoe, another band of Indians recaptured

---

2. MH Moore, *Sketches of the Pioneers of Methodism in North Carolina and Virginia.*
3. "Reverend Daniel Asbury and Nancy Jane Morris." From Ancestary.com

Daniel and scalped him. They sold him to the British, who imprisoned him in Detroit. The British chained Daniel and inflicted harsh treatment. They later shipped him to Canada. Daniel Asbury is listed on a prisoner exchange in Quebec, Canada, on November 8, 1782. Placed on a ship bound for Philadelphia and Virginia, he traveled back to Bedford County. Daniel called on his family home on Sunday, February 23, 1783, without identifying himself. They did not recognize him at first, but his dog recognized him. When he finally revealed his identity, a family celebration erupted, for they had assumed he had died during his extended absence. His oldest sister, Elizabeth, named her first child "Daniel" during his absence.[4] Shortly after returning home, on a Sunday, Daniel Asbury came under the influence of Methodist preachers and surrendered his life to Jesus Christ as his Lord and Savior. He joined the Methodist Church as a traveling preacher in the Amelia Circuit, Virginia, in 1786. In 1789, Daniel was appointed to the Lincoln Circuit in North Carolina, where he met and married Nancy Morris. Daniel and Nancy Asbury had twelve children. They named their first child Francis after the Methodist Bishop Francis Asbury. They named their second child Elizabeth, presumably after Daniel's sister. Daniel and Nancy Asbury are buried at Rehobeth United Methodist Church in Terrell, North Carolina, in Catawba County. [5]

The opening scene of *A Plea for Freedom* was inspired by true events that occurred in Bedford County, Virginia, in 1780. Charles Lynch was a wealthy landowner, planter, patriot, and

---

4. Ancestry.com
5. Belue, "Terror in the Canelands: The Fate of Daniel Boone's Salt Boilers,"; Bridges, Reverand Daniel Asbury's Amazing life; "List of Salt Makers captured with Daniel Boone at The Blue Licks." Ancestry. Com; Price, Holston Methodism, From it Origin to the Present Time; "Reverend Daniel Asbury and Nancy Jane Morris." From Ancestary.com; "Revolutionary War Record of Daniel Asbury (1762-1825)." From Ancestry.com

Bedford County Justice of the Peace. He also served in the Virginia House of Burgesses and became a militia Colonel during the war. Lynch and several other justices of the peace rounded up several Tories plotting violence against the patriot cause. They held informal trials and subjected the guilty parties to whipping, hanging by the thumbs, and forced duty in the Virginia militia. These activities were outside Virginia law and the direction of Governor Thomas Jefferson. However, these illegal actions of Lynch were decriminalized by the Virginia General Assembly in 1782.[6] Charles Lynch did not live in New London, Virginia, but about fifteen miles away. I do not know where the Asbury farm was located in Bedford County. I arbitrarily placed their house on the road to the Big Lick, salt springs on a branch of the Roanoke River, where the city of Roanoke, Virginia is located.

Daniel Asbury was fifteen when he joined the Virginia Militia in Bedford County. The minimum age limit for serving in the Virginia military was sixteen years old. In 1777, Congress established the number of companies that states had to provide for the army. The states passed this requirement on to the towns in their states to provide soldiers. Towns had to resort to drafting their citizens, who were given the choice of either joining the army, paying a large fine, or sending someone in their place. Draftees often sent their teenage sons, or apprentices, in their place, many of whom were less than sixteen. The age limit of sixteen often was not enforced—they just wanted soldiers to fight.[7] The draft notice presented to Daniel's father in this story was adapted from a similar notice provided in Rafhael's *A People's History of the American Revolution* and the Oath of Allegiance was adapted from the example provided in John D.

6. Raphael, *A People's History of the American Revolution, How Common People Shaped the Fight for Independence.*
7. See note 6 above

Sinks article, "Oaths of Allegiance During the American Revolution."[8]

For the shooting demonstration for the Kentucky Expedition militia in *A Plea for Freedom,* a man shot a loaf of bread propped between his brother's knees multiple times, not a common practice for today's military training. Danske Dandridge, in her book American Prisoners of the Revolution, Chapter Two, "The Riflemen of the Revolution," describes such feats to illustrate the marksmanship and prowess of the riflemen recruited for the Revolutionary militias. When the British first encountered these riflemen, they mocked them, saying, "a rabble in calico petticoats." Later, after these riflemen proved their merit and exceptional marksmanship, British soldiers dreaded and loathed them more than any other foe they encountered.[9]

I have attempted to tell Daniel Asbury's story to be consistent with the history associated with Daniel Boone, as described in Boone's biographies and other historical accounts.[10] In this novel Asbury has several conversations with Boone, but these are not known to have occurred. The account of Daniel Boone's capture by the Shawnee is documented in Daniel Boone biographies. The details of the capture, their journey to Chillicothe in the snow and under starving conditions, eating tree bark, eating the Indian dogs, and forced eating of deer entrails after a deer is finally shot are documented in Daniel Boone's biographies. Joseph Jackson, one of the captured salt-makers, recalled many years later, the speech Boone delivered to the Shawnee warriors to save the captives, and is recorded in Boone biographies.

---

8. Sinks, "Oaths of Allegiance During the American Revolution."

9. Dandridge, *American Prisoners of the Revolution*

10. Belue, "Terror in the Canelands: The Fate of Daniel Boone's Salt Boilers"; Brown, Frontiersman, *Daniel Boone and the Making of America;* Draper, *The life of Daniel Boone;* Kincaid, *The wilderness Road;* Morgan, *Boone, A Biography;* Ranck, *Boonesborough, KY, Its Founding, Pioneer Struggles, Indian Experiences, Transylvania Days, and Revolutionary Annals;*

Boone's speech in *A Plea for Freedom* is a paraphrase of that speech.

Ted Franklin Belue's article, *Terror in the Canelands: The Fate of Daniel Boone's Salt Boilers,* lists the twenty-seven men that were captured. Those mentioned in the telling of Daniel's story were: Daniel Asbury, Daniel Boone, Arabia Brown, John Brown, Ansel Goodman, William Humphries, Andrew Johnson, Benjamin Kelly, John Morton, and Richard Wade.[11]

Belue's article discusses the destinies of each of those men after capture. The article says that Daniel Asbury was shipped to Quebec from the British prison in Detroit and escaped from an island in the St. Lawrence River in a leaky canoe with five other prisoners in 1781.[12] However, as mentioned earlier, Daniel Asbury is on the Quebec prisoner exchange list dated November 8, 1782.[13] In my telling of Daniel's story, I place him on the island with the others who escaped in the leaky canoe, but he does not go with them. He was exchanged for British prisoners in Quebec a year later. The story of the escape in the leaky canoe is told on a website for Richard Wade.[14] The six prisoners who escaped were Richard Wade, John Brown, and John Morton of Virginia, and three men from Pennsylvania. For this story, I changed the name of John Morton to James Morton, so as not to be confused with John Brown. The six were successful in their escape, traveling back to the US after nine days, but almost starved, having no provisions for their trek. After they arrived in the US, they met with Governor John Hancock in Boston who helped them obtain the necessities for the journey to Kentucky and Virginia.[15]

---

11. Belue, "Terror in the Canelands: The Fate of Daniel Boone's Salt Boilers"
12. Belue, "Terror in the Canelands: The Fate of Daniel Boone's Salt Boilers"
13. "Revolutionary War Record of Daniel Asbury (1762-1825)."Ancestry.com
14. "Southern Campaigns American Revolution Pension Statements and Rosters." Pension Application of Richard Wade S3443.
15. Belue, "Terror in the Canelands: The Fate of Daniel Boone's Salt Boilers";

The names of all twenty-seven captured salt-makers are not included in *A Plea for Freedom* because most of the names were not pertinent to the story. In some instances, the events that occurred to salt-makers not named in the story are attributed to other characters. In *A Plea for Freedom,* Ansel Goodman offered his neck to the warrior wanting him to carry a heavy pot. According to Boone biographies, James Callaway was the salt-maker that offered his neck. Andrew Johnson did pretend to be a simpleton to fool the Indians. Johnson was the first captive to escape while Boone was in Detroit with Blackfish. Boone was the second to escape when he jumped on a horse while the others were chasing a flock of turkeys.[16] *A Plea for Freedom* includes an account of a river boat attack. These were not uncommon attacks. Belue states that Benjamin Kelly and James Girty were present during a river boat attack in 1779, near the time it occurred in *A Plea for Freedom.*[17] Charles Johnston provides an account of his capture when whites on the shore of the Ohio pleaded for help. The river boat travelers succumbed to their pleas. Indians came from the trees and killed two and captured three of their party. The whites begging for help were captives forced by the Indians to lure the travelers.[18]

Following his captivity, Daniel Asbury became a Methodist preacher.[19] Three others from among the twenty-seven salt-maker captives also became protestant preachers in the years

---

"Southern Campaigns American Revolution Pension Statements and Rosters." Pension Application of Richard Wade S3443.

16. Belue, "Terror in the Canelands: The Fate of Daniel Boone's Salt Boilers"; Brown, Frontiersman, Daniel Boone and the Making of America; Draper, The life of Daniel Boone; Boone, A Biography; Morgan, *Boone, A Biography*

17. Belue, Ted Franklin. "Terror in the Canelands: The Fate of Daniel Boone's Salt Boilers,"

18. Drimmer, Frederick, ed, *Captured by the Indians, 15 Firsthand Accounts, 1750-1870.*

19. Bridges, Mary Ellen Asbury (compiled by). "Reverend Daniel Asbury's Amazing life"; Moore, *Sketches of the Pioneers of Methodism in North Carolina and Virginia;* Price, *Holston Methodism, From its Origin to the Present Time.*

that followed their captivity: Benjamin Kelly, Richard Wade, and Ansel Goodman.[20] I wrote Daniel Asbury's story as though he and Ben Kelly were good friends, since they were the same age and their later lives took similar paths. I do not know that they were close friends.

Following an unsuccessful attempt by the Shawnee to attack Boonesborough in September 1778, Daniel Boone was court-martialed, in part because he surrendered himself and twenty-six men at Blue Licks, Kentucky. In his defense, Boone stated that the Shawnee were on their way to attack Boonesborough, which was defenseless at that time. Had they not surrendered, they would have all been killed and Boonesborough attacked, where many more would have been killed and captured. After a short deliberation, the presiding officers announced that Daniel Boone was innocent of all charges, and he was promoted to the rank of Major. Many of the captured salt-makers agreed with Boone's innocence. Benjamin Kelly wrote, "thought it very hard, but it was doubtless a wise thing in Boone, for by it he saved the lives of defenseless women and children." Following the capture, John Brown and Richard Wade, who became life-long friends and whose lives were in danger multiple times after their capture, said, "Colonel Boone was not to be blamed but lauded for his good management. It was conceded by all conversant with the circumstances that the course he pursued was the only wise, safe, and prudent course he could pursue . . . this treaty was the means of saving the host." [21]

References describing the Shawnee culture aided the telling of Daniel Asbury's story of life among the Shawnee. [22] In

20. Belue, Ted Franklin. "Terror in the Canelands: The Fate of Daniel Boone's Salt Boilers,"
21. Belue, Ted Franklin. "Terror in the Canelands: The Fate of Daniel Boone's Salt Boilers,"
22. Clark, *The Shawnee*; Howard, *Shawnee! The Ceremonialism of a Native American Tribe and its Cultural Background.*

addition, firsthand accounts of white captives living among the Shawnee in Ohio inspired story elements in *A Plea for Freedom*. In *A History of Jonathan Alder His Captivity and Life with the Indians*, Jonathon Alder tells his story of captivity as a nine-year-old boy living in Virginia in 1782.[23] Shawnee warriors took him to Ohio, to Chillicothe, where he lived for many years. Coincidently, Alder was adopted by an old Indian chief and his wife, the same description given in accounts of Daniel Asbury's captivity for his adoptive parents, just three years after Daniel's escape from the same Shawnee village. Jonathan Alder's account inspired several elements of how I told Daniel Asbury's story: the terrifying shadow, the scaring of the panther lured in by deer calls, the adoption ceremony, and the encounter with wolves. The scaring of a panther lured in by deer calls was apparently not an uncommon experience, as it is mentioned by James H. Howard when he cites the same experience, "A Shawnee is said to have been seized by a panther which he attracted by his calls, but that animal was as frightened as he when it found out its mistake, and fled in continently." [24]

Frederick Drimmer's *Captured by the Indians* includes several accounts of Shawnee captives taken to Ohio.[25] In this publication, "Prisoner of the Caughnawagas," describes many details of James Smith's adoption experience and of their war dance before battle. Another chapter, "Three Came Back (Charles Johnson)," described the contrasting characters of two Shawnee guards, one "humane and generous," the other "ferocious and brutal," that inspired the antagonist Crooked Eyes in *A Plea for Freedom*. The account of Dr. John Knight describes the burning of Colonel William Crawford at the stake in 1783, which provided an example of how the Shawnee performed the ritual

23. Nelson, *A History of Jonathan Alder, His Captivity and Life with the Indians.*

24. Howard, *Shawnee! The Ceremonialism of a Native American Tribe and its Cultural Background*

25. Drimmer, *Captured by the Indians*

for this story. The burning ritual is also described by Howard in his book of Shawnee culture.[26]

The recipe for chicken stew, described in Chapter 1 of *A Plea for Freedom,* was obtained from *Log Cabin Cooking* by Barbara Swell, under the recipe for Brunswick Stew.[27] The Shawnee meal of hominy, corn cakes, and boiled venison described in Chapter 6, when the salt-maker captives arrived after a 10-day trek with little food, was the same meal that O.M. Spencer enjoyed after his capture and march under conditions of limited nutrition in the book *Captivity of O.M. Spencer*.[28]

Shawnee words used in the story were taken from English-Shawnee dictionaries.[29] The limited number of Shawnee words provided in the dictionaries prevented accurate translations for the Shawnee names in the story. In some instances, I chose Shawnee words that were close to the English meaning in the story but were not exact translations. One article on Daniel Asbury's life gave his Shawnee name as *Tunimanhconicheice,* with no translation, and a second Shawnee name as *Nahashamo,* which means "White Chief."[30] I was not able to determine the meaning for *Tunimanhconicheice.* I wrote the story using both names, "White Chief," and arbitrarily assigned the meaning of *Tunimanhconicheice* as "Stalking Panther."

In *A Plea for Freedom,* Daniel Asbury's circumstances of having killed a Shawnee in Kentucky, then being adopted by the deceased Shawnee's family in Ohio is fictional. However, this

---

26. Howard, *Shawnee! The Ceremonialism of a Native American Tribe and its Cultural Background*, page 124
27. Swell, *Log Cabin Cooking*, page 25
28. Spencer, *Indian Captivity of O.M. Spencer*
29. Chrisley, Ronald L. *An Introduction to the Shawnee Language*; Ridout, *Ten Years of Upper Canada in Peace and War, 1805-1815." An Appendix of The Narrative of the Captivity among the Shawanese Indians, in 1788, of Thos. Ridout, Afterwards Surveyor-General of Upper Canada; and a Vocabulary, Compiled by Him, of the Shawanese Language*.
30. Bridges, "Reverend Daniel Asbury's Amazing life."

scenario may have been true for Daniel Boone. Shawnee warriors captured Daniel Boone's daughter, Jemima, and two other girls while canoeing on the Kentucky River near Boonesborough in July 1776. Daniel Boone led the rescue party that pursued the kidnappers. The rescuers caught the kidnappers and shot and killed Chief Blackfish's son. Chief Blackfish adopted Daniel Boone into his family after capturing the salt makers in 1778. Blackfish had two small daughters that Boone befriended. He gave them maple sugar he purchased with the trinkets he received from Henry Hamilton in Detroit.[31]

The number of American prisoners who died in British prisons exceeded the number who died on the battlefield. Edwin G. Burrows, in his excellent book *Forgotten Patriots, the Untold Story of American Prisoners During the Revolutionary War*, estimates that of 30,000 American soldiers that were held in British prisons, 18,000, or 60 percent, died of starvation, disease, and neglect.[32] This is 2.6 times higher than the estimate of 6,800 American soldiers who died on the battlefield. Burrows concludes that the unfortunate fate of so many American prisoners during the Revolutionary War was the result of "a lethal convergence, as it were, of obstinacy, condescension, corruption, mendacity, and indifference." Burrows conveys the story of Elias Baylis, a British prisoner in New York who sang Psalm 142 while in prison (Burrows, page 22). This story, along with the account of General Nathaniel Woodhull, were the inspiration of the story of Charles Woodhull in *A Plea for Freedom*.[33]

Another important contribution to the knowledge of the experience of American soldiers held in British Prisons during the Revolutionary War is *American Prisoners of the Revolution, by*

---

31. Brown, Meredith Mason. *Frontiersman, Daniel Boone and the Making of America.*

32. Burrows, *Forgotten Patriots, The Untold Story of American Prisoners during the Revolutionary War.*

33. See note 32 above

Danske Dandridge.[34] The book contains written personal accounts of eyewitnesses of the conditions the prisoners endured. Dandridge reports the same anecdotes of Elias Baylis and Nathaniel Woodhull as Burroughs. Nathaniel Woodhull died in his wife's arms shortly after she arrived. At Nathaniel's request, she distributed food from their farm to the other prisoners. ("The Trumbull Papers and Other Sources of Information," Dandridge). Dandridge's "The Case of John Blatchford" inspired Daniel Asbury's reprieve from the hanging at Fort Chambly.

The antagonist in *A Plea for Freedom,* Samuel English, was inspired by accounts of Provost Marshal Captain William Cunningham. Dansk Dandridge documents the actions of Cunningham, "whose cruelty and wickedness are almost inconceivable." Cunningham was born in Ireland in 1738 and came to America in 1774. He became closely associated with Tories. General Gage appointed Cunningham Provost Marshal in New York. Cunningham caused the death of thousands of prisoners by confiscating and selling their provisions, exchanging wholesome food for spoiled food. He kicked over buckets of food provided by the city's benevolent people for the prisoners and ordered the hanging of hundreds of prisoners.[35]

Church membership in the Methodist Episcopal Church in the United States grew from 13,740 in 1783 to 214,307 in 1813, primarily due to the circuit riders' unwavering devotion to the Lord and His ministry. They spent many hours in personal study of the Bible and in prayer, often while riding on horseback from one congregation to the next. The circuit rider's annual salary was $64 per year, but often only received half that. Because of the low pay, it was difficult to support a family, and many had to

34. Dandridge, *American Prisoners of the Revolution*
35. See note 34 above

leave their circuit of churches and settle down in one area to provide for the needs of their families.[36]

Circuit Rider Philip Gatch, a traveling preacher throughout New Jersey, Pennsylvania, and Maryland, ended his traveling preaching due to poor health. He married Elizabeth Smith in 1778, to live in Powhatan County, Virginia. However, Gatch continued to preach and travel occasionally. John McLean, in his *Sketch of Rev. Philip Gatch*, cited from Gatch's journal, "Six young men, the fruits of this revival in our neighborhood, became preachers; five of them, namely, D. Asbury, Chastain, Pope, Maxey, and Locket, became traveling preachers." Only one of the five had a first initial, "D. Asbury." I assume Gatch does so to distinguish Daniel Asbury from Francis Asbury, the Bishop of the Methodist Episcopal Church in the United States. Philip Gatch may have been the preacher that God used to bring Daniel Asbury to faith in Jesus Christ. Philip Gatch spoke out against the practice of slavery. When he married Elizabeth Smith, he inherited several enslaved individuals. He set them all free, saying, "I, Philip Gatch, of Powhatan County, Va., do believe that all men are by nature equally free; and from a clear conviction of the injustice of depriving my fellow-creatures of their natural rights, do hereby emancipate and set free all the following persons . . . " Gatch moved to Ohio in 1798 because of his disgust for slavery. He did not wish to die and leave his children in a state that practiced slavery.[37]

---

36. Powell, *Methodist Circuit-Riders in America, 1766-1844*

37. McLean, *Sketch of Rev. Philip Gatch.*

BIBLIOGRAPHY

Belue, Ted Franklin. "Terror in the Canelands: The Fate of Daniel Boone's Salt Boilers," *The Filson Club History Quarterly*, Volume 68, No.1, January 1994, page 3-34.

Bridges, Mary Ellen Asbury (compiled by). "Reverend Daniel Asbury's Amazing life." 1910. Ancestry.com.https://www.ancestry.com/mediaui-viewer/collection/1030/tree/17339934/person/501362489/media/8e52608f-dd60-448b-baa9-677b1a952f6f?queryId=12b60d8b-6a78-4033-9d5c-ced49659867a&_phsrc=pLz20& phstart=successSource . Accessed on February 21, 2024.

Brown, Meredith Mason. *Frontiersman, Daniel Boone and the Making of America*. Louisiana State University Press, Baton Rouge, LA. 2008.

Burrows, Edwin G. *Forgotten Patriots, The Untold Story of American Prisoners during the Revolutionary War*. Basic Books, a member of the Perseus Books Group. New York, NY. 2008.

Chrisley, Ronald L. *An Introduction to the Shawnee Language*. Printed in the United States of America, 1992.

Clark, Jerry E. *The Shawnee*. University Press of Kentucky, Lexington, KY. 2007.

Dandridge, Danske. *American Prisoners of the Revolution*. Michie Co., Charlottesville, VA. 1911.

Draper, Lyman Copeland. *The Life of Daniel Boone*. Edited by Ted Franklin Belue. Mechanicsburg, PA: Stackpole Books, 1998.

Drimmer, Frederick, ed, *Captured by the Indians, 15 Firsthand Accounts, 1750-1870*. Dover Publications, Inc. Mineola, N.Y. 1985.

Howard, James H. *Shawnee! The Ceremonialism of a Native American Tribe and its Cultural Background*. Ohio University Press, Athens, OH. 1981.

Kincaid, Robert. *The Wilderness Road*. Lincoln Memorial University, Harrogate, Tennessee. 1990

"List of Salt Makers captured with Daniel Boone at The Blue Licks." Ancestry.com. https://www.ancestry.com/mediaui-viewer/tree/40478992/person/302202673297/media/89c82ec0-717e-4876-a04e-ec1322f39f64?_phsrc=wzY124&_phstart=successSource. Accessed on June 2, 2022.

McLean, John. *Sketch of Rev. Philip Gatch*. Swormstedt & Poe, Cincinnati, OH. 1854.

Moore, M. H. *Sketches of the Pioneers of Methodism in North Carolina and Virginia*. Southern Methodist Publishing House, Nashville, TN. 1884.

Morgan, Robert. *Boone, A Biography*. Algonquin Books of Chapel Hill, Chapel Hill, NC. 2007.

Nelson, Larry L., ed. *A History of Jonathan Alder, His Captivity and Life with the Indians*. The University of Akron Press, Akron, OH. 2002.

Powell, Jr., William A., *Methodist Circuit-Riders in America, 1766-1844*. A Thesis summitted to the Graduate Faculty of the University of Richmond, in Candidacy for the Degree of Master of Arts in History. August 1977.

Price, R. N. *Holston Methodism, From its Origin to the Present Time*. Publishing House of the M.E. Church, South, Nashville, TN; Dallas, TX. 1904. page 235-239.

Raphael, Ray, *A People's History of the American Revolution, How Common People Shaped the Fight for Independence*. HarperCollins Publishers, Inc., New York, NY. 2001.

Ranck, George W., *Boonesborough, KY, Its Founding, Pioneer Struggles, Indian Experiences, Transylvania Days, and Revolutionary Annals*. John P. Morton & Co., Louisville, KY. 1901.

"Revolutionary War Record of Daniel Asbury (1762-1825)." From Ancestry.com, https://www.ancestry.com/mediaui-viewer/tree/17339934/person/501362489/media/3b84b03f-f21f-4c47-a1a6-0d288b4f5915?_phsrc=wzY137&_phstart=successSource. Accessed on June 1, 2022.

Ridout, Thomas, *Ten Years of Upper Canada in Peace and War, 1805-1815." An Appendix of The Narrative of the Captivity among the Shawanese Indians, in 1788, of Thos. Ridout, Afterwards Surveyor-General of Upper Canada; and a Vocabulary, Compiled By Him, of the Shawanese Language*. Toronto William Briggs, 1890. pp 339-375.

Sinks, John D. "Oaths of Allegiance During the American Revolution." https://www.sar.org/wp-content/uploads/2022/11/Oaths-of-Allegiance-During-the-American-Revolution-8-May-2021.pdf. District of Columbia Society, Sons of the American Revolution, 8 May 2021. Accessed on December 20, 2024

"Southern Campaigns American Revolution Pension Statements and Rosters." Pension Application of Richard Wade S3443. https://revwarapps.org/s3443.pdf. Accessed March 23, 2023.

Spencer, O.M. *Indian Captivity of O.M. Spencer*. Edited by Milo M. Quaife. Lakeside Press, Chicago, 1917.

Swell, Barbara. *Log Cabin Cooking*. Native Ground Music, Inc.1996.

ACKNOWLEDGMENTS

I thank my wife, Heidi, for her enthusiasm and excitement for this book, even before I wrote my first word. Years earlier, when the book was only an idea, she purchased reference materials on Indian captivity and the Revolutionary War in anticipation of the book. Heidi was my advocate and encourager during our travels to Virginia, Kentucky, and Ohio while researching Daniel Asbury's story. Her suggestions and insights have made the book better. She has been my cheerleader, adviser, and helper throughout the journey.

I thank my daughter, Rebecca, for her continual encouragement and suggestions throughout the writing of this book.

I thank the following people for their review and comments on early drafts of the book: Gail Hackney Hardin, Bill Hardin, Spencer Hackney, Scott Hardin, Analise Hardin, Craig Hardin, Miles Honeycutt, Jackson Honeycutt, Keith Blomberg, Billie Blomberg, Paul Tshihamba, Andria Tshihamba, Dan Struble, and Karen Struble.

I thank Patricia Sullivan and Margaret Diehl for their expert advice and suggestions to improve the book. I thank Kippen Miller for his skillful and insightful editing, and hard work to make the book better. Thank you for caring about Daniel's story.

I thank Teri Rider and Jori Hanna for believing in the story, seeing its potential, and using their expertise to ensure it shines and reaches as many people as possible.

I thank the following people for their encouragement and

prayers during the writing of this book: Dave Conner, Dan Kronstad, Mike Sholtz, Mark Barger, Kathy Barger, Paul Gramann, Tom Kemble, Stephen Immordino and Scott Cornelius.

ABOUT THE AUTHOR

Raymond Hackney grew up in Gastonia, North Carolina and currently lives near Chapel Hill, North Carolina with his wife Heidi, daughter Rebecca, and two cats (Chester and Huey). Raymond earned his Bachelor of Arts in Chemistry, Master of Science in Public Health, and Doctor of Public Health all from the University of North Carolina at Chapel Hill. He worked in public health for the University of North Carolina and Duke University. Raymond has enjoyed hobbies involving the outdoors including camping, sailing, white water canoeing, and hiking. His international travels have taken him to South America, the Middle East, China, Europe, and sailing in the Caribbean.

Connect with him online at raymondhackneyauthor.com, or through social media:

facebook.com/ray.hackney.12

THANK YOU!

Thank you for reading! If you enjoyed this book, please leave a review on Amazon, Goodreads, BookBub, The Story Graph, or anywhere else you like to track your recent reads. Alternatively, you could post online or tell a friend about it. This helps our authors more than you may know.

- The Team at Torchflame Books

Follow Torchflame Books for news about our authors and upcoming new releases @TorchflameBooks.

Find your next great read at www.torchflamebooks.com.

www.ingramcontent.com/pod-product-compliance
Lightning Source LLC
LaVergne TN
LVHW091118080826
845145LV00008B/1958

* 9 7 8 1 6 1 1 5 3 7 0 5 5 *